Hard to HOLD

NEW YORK TIMES BESTSELLING AUTHOR

K. BROMBERG

PRAISE FOR K. BROMBERG

"K. Bromberg always delivers intelligently written, emotionally intense, sensual romance . . ."

—*USA Today*

"K. Bromberg makes you believe in the power of true love."

—#1 *New York Times* bestselling author Audrey Carlan

"A poignant and hauntingly beautiful story of survival, second chances, and the healing power of love. An absolute must-read."

—*New York Times* bestselling author Helena Hunting

"A home run! *The Player* is riveting, sexy, and pulsing with energy. And I can't wait for *The Catch!*"

—#1 *New York Times* bestselling author Lauren Blakely

"An irresistibly hot romance that stays with you long after you finish the book."

—#1 *New York Times* bestselling author Jennifer L. Armentrout

"Bromberg is a master at turning up the heat!"

—*New York Times* bestselling author Katy Evans

"Supercharged heat and full of heart. Bromberg aces it from the first page to the last."

—*New York Times* bestselling author Kylie Scott

"Captivating, emotional, and sizzling hot!"

—*New York Times* bestselling author S. C. Stephens

ALSO BY K. BROMBERG

Published by JKB Publishing, LLC

ISBN: 978-1942832300

Cover design by Helen Williams
Cover Image by Wander Aguiar
Cover Model: Lucas Loyola
Editing by Marion Making Manuscripts
Formatting by Champagne Book Design

Printed in the United States of America

Prologue

Rush

I take a deep breath and close my eyes.

Their fists pound against the blacked-out windows of the SUV with my name a constant repeat on their lips.

"Is it true?"

"Are you really a homewrecker?"

"Rush, how could you?"

The paparazzi. The press. The media.

On any normal day, their presence means I'm doing my job properly. It means I'm playing great and the team is kicking arse and all is right with the world.

Today though . . . *fuck*, today, I just need to get the hell out of here for a while.

If I could look past their flashing lights and demanding voices, I'd see the gate to my house. The house I never in a million years dreamed I'd own in Formby. My pipe dreams from back then are currently a reality, and how bloody crazy is it that the connection between then and now still remains? Still binds?

Every part of me begs to drive back to Anfield Stadium and get lost in the green of the pitch and the ability to block the outside noise that I'm known for. My salvation then and my serenity now, but still the one constant in my life.

And now? Now that's all been jeopardized by IOUs being cashed in, for a situation that's blown too far out of control for me to rein it back in.

"That's some shitstorm out there, isn't it?"

I meet the eyes of my driver in the rearview mirror and hesitate before I nod. There's something in the way he looks at me, as if he's begging me to tell him the reason the reporters are surrounding his car is a lie and that I'm not really guilty of what they're accusing me of doing.

But why would they think any differently? Isn't that what everyone expects from me?

I nod in response, even though I'm dying inside to tell someone, anyone, that he's right—that I'm *not guilty* of this.

Unclasping my seatbelt as his eyes are still on me, the denial so damn ready on my tongue doesn't come. "Yeah, mate. Fun times." My words sound like an exasperated sigh.

But I don't say anything else.

Not an admission.

Not a word.

I can't.

"I don't know how to thank you—"

"No need to," I say and look to my left at the other passenger in the car, needing to cut Archibald off before he says anything else that can be overheard by the driver.

I've known the man all of my adult life. The profound sadness that weighs heavily in his eyes and the defeat in the set of his posture eats at me. There's also a calculation to him too. A hard glint I catch every now and again, and I've known him long enough to feel like this has been preordained for years.

He's simply cashing in at the perfect time.

And here I thought that all along he'd been acting out of the goodness of his heart and conscience.

I should have known better. I should have seen through the scripted speeches and knowing glances. The teenager in me is still trying to hold on to what I thought was sincerity, but now realizes was far from it.

Yet he sits there staring at me with a muted smile that says he knows I'm doing this at a great personal and professional cost. He knows I'll say yes because of the debt I owe to him and his family. Lifelines have a funny way of coming full circle, and mine just did.

Too bad I have to do this for it to be complete.

Fuck.

"Does Helen know?" I ask cryptically.

Archibald gives a quick shake of his head, his eyes telling me of course she doesn't. How could he ever explain that he's trading one son for what he's always claimed was another?

The smile I give him is forced at best, but what the fuck does he expect? I'm about to be thrown to the wolves.

Wolves who are after blood and being led to the wrong scent.

"We could go around the block again if need be," the driver says.

"It's my home." My chuckle lacks amusement. "They'll still be here regardless."

"How about I ease the car forward until they get out of the way? Then we'll be able to get through the gate so you don't have to get out and deal with them," he offers.

"There's no parting that crowd," I murmur as another knock on the window sounds beside my ear. "Besides, I won't be here for long. I have to pack and then get going."

"You could stay with us, you know," Archibald murmurs. "No one would question it."

"No thanks." But they might question it. Right now, he's just a man beside me escorting me home, trying to help keep the peace. Anything more than that and people might take a second look.

"Just until this all dies down," he says.

"Do you really think that's the best idea?" I ask with more bite than intended before turning to face him. It's the first time I've let him see the exhaustion in my eyes, and the first hint of the worry wearing me down that I've kept hidden from everyone else. "If people look too closely, they might see something different than you want them to." I take a deep breath and prepare myself. "Here goes nothing."

Without another word, I grab my bag and push open the door.

The sound is deafening.

The flashes are blinding.

Sure, I'm used to them, but not like this. Not with this intensity. Not after being accused of screwing my teammate's wife.

"Rush, is it true?"

Click. Click. Click.

"How long have you been seeing Esme?"

Click. Click. Click.

"Are you going to be transferred because of this . . ."

Click. Click. Click.

"A comment please, Rush."

Their cameras bump my shoulders as I fight my way through them, my name a symphony of strident sounds on their lips. One question after another, "No comment," a repeat on mine, as I obey the gagging order the management team put into effect. All the sounds—their questions, my name, the clicks—fade to white noise around me.

They push and prod and belittle.

They make me feel like I did when I was a kid.

They make me remember the childhood I escaped from.

They bring back the shame I thought I'd left behind.

I reach the pedestrian gate to my yard, but there is one reporter standing in front of it. She's the first whose gaze I meet and actually acknowledge.

I've seen her before. She's pale—skin, hair, eyes—but her smile has always been kind and her questions always polite.

But there's an accusatory lift of her eyebrows when our gazes meet, and when I glance down to what is in her hand, I know why.

It's a copy of *The Sun* with the grainy black and white photo on its cover.

I don't have to stare to know what it is. I've studied that image repeatedly in the past three days and have every detail memorized. It's the unmistakable image of the British princess of pop, Esme, on a hotel balcony with a man's arms wrapped around her. Trees from where the photographer hid obstruct some of their bodies, but there's no denying the man looks like me. The clothes, the haircut and style, down to the same bloody shoes—everything—looks exactly like me.

Premier Footballer Cheats with Team Captain's Wife, Pop Star - Esme.

It's the title I've seen splashed fucking everywhere, and the look in the reporter's eyes tells me she believes it. That she's disappointed in me.

That she believes I could do that.

Why shouldn't she though, when my manager and my own teammates don't even question the validity of the bloody photo? The shiner I have beneath my left eye from where Seth punched me reinforces it.

They simply assume it's true. They *simply* believe that I would do that. That I have no moral fiber. No belief in the sanctity of marriage.

And that's what angers me the most.

I reach past her and pull on the gate, pass through, and leave the press shouting even louder as I walk across my lawn to the front door.

I want to tell them that if they looked closer, they'd see the truth.

But why the hell should I?

Why is it their expectation that I have to prove my innocence, as they chant my name while wearing it on a jersey across their shoulders?

For the hundredth time tonight, *why the fuck should I?*

Chapter ONE

Lennox

CHEAP ALCOHOL DISGUISED IN FANCY GLASSES IS PASSED AROUND BY the trayful. Attendees clothed in either beaded gowns or black tuxedos mill about, each one acting more in the know than the person they're talking to. The soft and slow drawl of jazz being piped in through the speakers allows for easy conversation.

"He has to be the greatest of all time. How can you refute that?"

"No way. How can you think they'll even be close to clinching the title this year?"

"Did you hear all the shit he got himself into? Thank God, I'm not his agent. Talk about a fucking headache."

I take the last sip of champagne and set the flute down on the empty cocktail table behind me—along with the binder of information we received in our earlier conference—as I stifle a yawn.

"By that yawn you're fighting, Kincade, I'm going to assume you were one of the ones out late last night riding the mechanical bull."

I freeze at the smooth voice of Finn Sanderson—fellow agent extraordinaire, smooth-talking asshole, and the reason Kincade Sports Management is currently struggling.

"What is it they say? What happens in Vegas, stays in Vegas? It's not every year the Sports Summit is held in a good location such as this." I shrug, completely ignoring my aching muscles from riding said bull, and add a sarcastic smile to my lips as I turn to face him. "And the yawn was simply because I knew you were headed my way, so I was preparing myself for our conversation. I didn't want to be rude and do it in front of you."

"Such a pleasure as always," he murmurs and leans in to kiss my cheek, his own sarcasm not far from the tip of his tongue.

Self-control has me not flinching at his touch so I grit my teeth instead. "Can't say the same."

"I get you like this cute banter-y thing you do, but honestly, Lennox, it makes you seem a little more beast and a lot less beauty." He purses his lips as he stares at me over the rim of his glass, eyes taunting just like his words. "It's quite unbecoming."

A million things come to mind about what he's done that's unbecoming—stealing our clients by taking cheap shots at us, being a complete ass to my sister before they broke up, the fact that he *breathes*—but I don't say a thing.

"And you're enjoying Vegas, Finn?"

He stutters in his response as he tries to figure my change of tactics, from rude to pleasant, but I just keep smiling at him. I'm fully aware that after my sister, Dekker, stole his client, hockey god, Hunter Maddox, out from under him, other agents are probably watching this exchange and waiting for the fireworks to ignite.

"Who doesn't?" He lifts his chin in acknowledgment to a passerby. "So, you're off to Chicago after this?"

"For what?"

His expression falters momentarily as if caught off guard before he rights it. "Nothing. Never mind. I got things mixed up. Too many agents at this convention to keep shit straight." He chuckles.

"If you're mixing me up with the rest of the guys in here, you're definitely losing your touch, Sanderson."

"Losing my touch?" He coughs the word out. "Aren't you the one who let Austin Yeakle slip through your fingers last week?" he asks, referring to my failed attempt to recruit the top college football draft pick. I thought I'd closed the deal only to be told an hour after I'd left his house that he'd chosen a different agent and firm to represent him.

To say it was a blow to my ego is an understatement.

"He's one athlete amid a field of many."

"Yes, but none of those *many* are going to make half of what he'll make."

"Do you have a point, Finn?"

He smiles. "Seems to me like you're losing more than you're winning these days."

"I have a full client list and plenty of hustle left in me," I say, taking another flute of champagne off a passing tray, thinking of the several potential clients from the Golden Knights and the Raiders I have meetings with later this week, both hometown Las Vegas teams.

"Is that why you turned down the offer from the MLS?" he asks, referring to the Major League Soccer organization, and throwing me completely off guard. My face must reflect it too. A smug smile crawls onto his lips. "Yeah, I know about the offer. Question is, why didn't you take it?"

A myriad of reasons flicker through my head but the biggest one—the reason both my father and I decided it was best to reject the offer—still burns the brightest: why would the MLS contract me, a sports agent, to help be an ambassador to promote their upcoming season?

I'm not a celebrity or a star athlete, and I'm definitely not a marketing guru. Getting fans to engage with the sport like they do, say American football, has been an ongoing task since the league started, and I'm not exactly sure how I'm qualified to be the one to do just that.

"I have my reasons," I say with a definitiveness I don't feel.

"Huh." His eyes hold mine and that mocking smile comes back. "They must want you bad considering Cannon told me they were holding the position open for you should you change your mind."

They are? That's news to me.

"What can I say? When you're good, you're good." I shrug arrogantly.

"You're holding out on me, Kincade. What exact skill set do you have that I can't give him, huh? It must be something for him to hold open a position for you and only you."

I roll my eyes at the innuendo and its implications because in typical Finn Sanderson fashion, he wants what he can't have and hates everything about it. So much so that he'll diminish me so he can feel better about himself and his shortcomings.

"Ask him yourself if you're so curious."

"Something new and different seems so exciting, though."

"I've got enough excitement," I say even though his words tug at me. "And am more than busy with my own workload."

"Right, I forgot." He winks at me. "You and your hustle. Dare I ask who you're hustling after right now?"

"Wouldn't you like to know." This time I let my laugh float freely and notice heads turn our way without them hiding it. "Why? Are you in need of some clients? Has your charm run out and now you need to steal from my playbook?"

"Steal?" He laughs. "I do believe that's from the Kincade playbook. The name Hunter Maddox ring a bell?"

"Considering he's engaged to my sister, I don't think you can blame the man for wanting to be represented by our agency . . . since he's soon to be family and all."

"So is that the KSM master plan? Have the four of you reel men in with love then sign them to the agency? Steal them away from another agent?"

Prick.

I take a step closer to him and lower my voice. "First, if their agent was doing his job properly, they wouldn't go looking. Second, KSM is a sports agency, not a prostitution ring. Third, the fact that you even said any of this tells me you're worried about us. Good. *You should be.* Clients aren't just paychecks, Finn. And from what I hear these days, that's all you think they are. No wonder you're losing athletes left and right," I say a little louder than necessary.

"You're projecting again." He gives a shake of his head but I can tell I wormed my way under his skin. "KSM is the one scrambling. I'm the one sitting back and enjoying life."

"Keep thinking that." I glance over his shoulder into the crowd and lie. "You're the one who played dirty first, stealing our clients by dangling imaginary carrots in front of them that magically disappeared the minute they signed with you."

"Whatever works, right?"

Smug bastard.

"We've made it our mission to get our clients back and then some. Hunter was the first of many to make the switch to KSM from Sanderson Sports."

"Are you telling me I should be scared of four women and their aging father?"

It's my turn to chuckle loud and mocking. "Underestimate us. I dare you. While there's room for both of our agencies in this world, I'd love nothing more than to have your clients see you for who you really are."

"What? *Incredible?*"

"Hubris has been the downfall of every empire, Finn. I'm going to enjoy watching yours crumble. Now if you'll excuse me, I see someone I need to speak to."

"I was expecting more from you than running and tucking your tail between your legs, but"—he shrugs as I walk past him—"isn't that par for the course when it comes to you?"

"Excuse me?" *What in the hell is he talking about?*

"You always were jealous, you know."

"Of what?" I ask.

"That I picked Chase over you." His smile is lightning quick, and even though I want to throttle him for being such an ass, the comment is just so typically Finn Sanderson that I can't help but shake my head and sigh. "But then again, it seems you miss a lot of things. It's been real, Kincade."

And there's something in the dismissive way he says it and the unyielding stare that again, makes me feel like I'm not understanding an underlying meaning.

Shrugging it off, I tell myself that's his plan, and make my way to the ladies' room, needing a break from Finn and everything that comes with him—insecurity, anger, frustration, dislike.

The good thing about a sports management conference? There's rarely a line in the women's bathroom since we're a minority in the field.

I check my makeup and hair in the mirror just to waste time. Five days is five too many to listen to arrogant, male sports agents brag with puffed chests to other overinflated chests about things that don't really matter.

Did I acquire new knowledge from the conference? Nothing more than I usually do, but it did reaffirm my resolve never to date another sports agent—their egos are worse than a professional athlete's.

It's when I put the cap back on my lipstick that I realize I left my binder on the table when I was doing my banter-y thing with Finn.

Shit. Shit. Shit.

The binder isn't the big deal. It's the scrap of paper on the inside with names of five of Las Vegas' most prominent professional athletes and the times I'm meeting with them over the coming days that's the big deal.

And big deal as in I'm going to try and court them away from their current representation and over to KSM.

Unethical? *Possibly.*

Something that is done every damn day in this business? Definitely.

But the last thing I need is another agent discovering my binder, opening it to see whose it is, and then finding my name written in big, black sharpie on the inside pocket, right below where that scrap of paper is stuffed.

Without trying to look like a worried woman on a mission, I hurriedly head back into the crowded room.

When I spot my binder right where I left it on the table, I slow my stride and acknowledge a few colleagues with smiles as I pass them on my way to get it.

With my binder now in hand and too many days under my belt swimming in these testosterone-laden conferences, I decide it's the perfect moment to make my stealthy exit. The quiet of my hotel room, the room service menu, and the need to kick off these heels sound like the perfect way to spend the rest of my evening.

Sure, I love the hustle and networking of these conferences, but I'm exhausted.

As if the universe is against me and doesn't think gorging myself on room service is a good idea, I get stuck behind a group of ten or so conference attendees crowding the path to the exit. They're watching something on one of their phones and so my "Excuse me's" fall on deaf ears.

Just when I'm about to find my way around the men, I'm stopped in my tracks.

"She didn't know shit about Chicago. Not a goddamn thing. Do you think Papa Kincade realizes she's the weak link of their organization and isn't letting her go?" *That* voice and then *that* chuckle following the words, belong to the prick himself, Finn. "Seems to me like he's coddling her and her precious ego. Being pretty only gets you so far."

I'm frozen in shock, indecision, hurt—you name it—as laughter rings out around him. Do I stay where I am, hidden by the crowd before me, or let my presence be known?

And what in the hell is going on in Chicago?

"Rumor is all the Kincades coddle her. Ever notice how when they're going after an athlete who might be tough to recruit and sign, they send one of the other three sisters?" another male voice says followed by a whistle.

"They can send Lennox my way any day to negotiate," a third man says. "Like we can negotiate how she should leave those heels of hers on when she takes everything else off."

"I've heard there's plenty of that. Hell, maybe I should pretend to be an athlete, because that's the lengths she'll go to convince someone to sign with her," the whistler says.

My stomach churns and I can all but see the elbow nudging in that boys will be boys manner. I'm dumbfounded by the comment but know exactly where it comes from. It's a misrepresentation of the truth, but how stupid was I to think the perception would be any different?

"You talking about Bradly?" guy number two asks.

"Of course, I am," the whistler says. "Last thing I need to be reminded of is how I lost one of my top clients because I don't have a pussy."

My jaw falls lax and I swear I blink rapidly as if either of the two actions will make me unhear what I just heard.

Is that what the rumor is? That I'm sleeping with clients to entice them away from their current agent?

Anger inflames and emboldens my disbelief. I knew there were rumors—hell, I'm a female agent dealing with male athletes, so I expect rumors—but not this.

Call me naïve, but holy shit.

I'm jostled from behind and brought back from my shock to listen again.

"So is that what happened with Chicago? The organizers realized they were getting all boobs and no brains and rescinded the offer?" the second man asks.

"Don't be an asshole," another man says, but the chuckle he emits after it sounds more like encouragement than anything.

"Or was she too stupid to realize this might be a good thing for her?" the second man continues.

"Who knows," Finn answers. "She was on the list and then the next thing I know she was off it. Best guess? The Kincades fear she'll embarrass the family name and agency."

"Once a beauty queen, always a beauty queen," another guy says.

Another ring of laughter sounds off as if the prick is demonstrating a pageant wave. I'm gripping the binder so hard I'm not sure how it hasn't broken.

"Who's stupider? Chicago for asking her to speak, the MLS for thinking she can bring value to their league, or her for not taking the job when it might give her some credibility?"

"Credibility?" another voice says. "As in how short her skirt and how big her bra size, spank bank, type of credibility?"

I don't have time to process the words or the insults or anything other than the fact that I'm hurt beyond belief. Sure, it's Finn and he's a prick but we have a strained history given he dated my sister, Chase, for some time. And being that we are on the same playing field in competing for clients, we're allowed to hate each other. But I don't have history with these other guys—fellow colleagues—and now he's poisoned their opinions of me.

Or maybe they already had those opinions.

Maybe everyone in here does.

And just as that thought hits me, the crowd parts, and Finn and his merry gang of pricks come into view on the other side of them.

My hands may be trembling and tears may be burning in my throat, but I lift my chin, square my shoulders, and stalk right over to them.

I have one rule I've learned in my years negotiating with athletes: when it comes to men, never let them know they've gotten to you. The minute they do, you're immediately at a disadvantage.

And there's nothing I hate more than that.

"Gentlemen," I say in the sweetest voice I can muster. At least one of them has the courtesy to choke on the sip of beer he just took when he sees me. "I couldn't help but overhear your scintillating conversation concerning my merits—or lack thereof. I get Finn is insecure over how my agency is slowly kicking his ass in the high-profile client department and feels the need to denigrate me because of it, but the rest of you"—I take my time and meet the pairs of eyes who are ballsy enough to find mine— "should be ashamed of yourselves for talking shit about a woman the way you just did. But then again, I guess us bimbo beauty queens should be used to it." I nudge the man to my left like I'm one of the guys, and he stiffens in discomfort. "Am I right?"

"That's not what we were—"

"Yes, it was." I smile and wave a hand at them as if it's no big deal. "I'm sure your wives and daughters are thrilled to have such forward-thinking husbands and fathers." I smile again to let my sarcasm sink in. "And for the record, Finn. The balcony in New York? Your fumbling hands?" I look to one of the men and wink. "It's more than clear why my sister threw him to the curb."

I reach out, take Finn's glass of whiskey from his hand, and take a sip without asking. I give a shake of my head as the liquid burns on the way down. These jerks do not deserve any more time from me. They're morons. And their opinions will never go beyond the maturity of a thirteen-year-old.

"For the record, I don't need to use sex to lure clients. One man's incompetency is another person's gain."

"But *after* you sign them as a client? That's when you sleep with them?" Jason asks, his smug smile widening. "I mean since we're setting the record straight and all."

"Look at you trying to be Finn's wingman." I shake my head and tsk. "How cute. Don't ever expect him to return the favor, though. He loves himself too much to be a wingman." I look around the circle. "Well then, you gentlemen enjoy the rest of your night. I'm going to head up to my room and practice my pageant wave and counting to ten." I nod and then stride out of the room with my head held high, silently fist-pumping in a cheer for myself.

God, yes, it feels good to tell them to politely fuck off, but it doesn't take away the sting of their words and the questions they evoke within me.

More than the crass shit these assholes have said is the unsettling feeling that this is how everyone else in this industry sees me. Is that what they think of me? As the window dressing for Kincade Sports Management? The pretty sister with more boobs and less brains who's called in to woo the simple-minded male athletes over but not the tough, demanding ones?

God only knows what they probably say about the tough-minded ones I have won over. Or rather . . . how I won them over.

Gross.

My sisters are all gorgeous in their own right, but just because I participated in beauty pageants as a means for scholarship money for college—and the one last connection I had with my mother after she died—doesn't mean I'm not a graduate of one of the best sports management programs in the country.

But the minute the elevator doors close and the adrenaline of the moment is gone, other thoughts start tumbling out of control in my mind.

Little things here and there from the past few months. Texts from my sisters where they'll take a potential new client because I'm too busy, despite my insistence that I'm not. The sudden shift in schedules our father sometimes makes that doesn't sit right with me.

Chicago.

What the hell is going on in Chicago?

They're wrong.

Those guys have to be wrong.

But with each step I take, tears threaten, and my feet feel heavier.

My heart even more so.

Benign decisions about who takes on what client or engagement at the office with my sisters and father in regards to clients or negotiations, begin to cloud my thoughts.

The discussion over the MLS offer replays, and right behind it is my father's adamant instruction that there was more than meets the eye to the offer and that I shouldn't take it.

What was the real story behind it?

Before I even have my heels kicked off and the door of my hotel room shut behind me, I'm calling my little sister.

"Aren't you supposed to be in some boring dinner surrounded by equally boring men where the one who is actually hot is so obsessed with himself that he's no longer good-looking?" Chase asks instead of answering with a hello. But when fury eats at the emotion and confusion I suddenly feel, I struggle to get any words out. "Lenn? You okay?" Her voice is softer this time, more loaded with concern as she uses our family nickname for me.

"What's going on in Chicago?" I demand.

"Chicago?" she stutters, and it only makes me more curious, because Chase doesn't stutter. She's always surefooted and knows what to say.

"Yes. Chicago. There were some guys here talking about it and how I was invited there for something, but turned it down."

"It's not a big deal. It was nothing."

"Chase." Her name is a warning.

"It's a small conference happening next month. They asked one of us to speak at it about being a female sports agent in a male-dominated industry and—"

"They asked for one of us or they asked for *me* specifically?"

Her silence speaks volumes, and the tears that burned earlier now well in my eyes.

"It's not what you think," she says. "It's nothing to worry that pretty, little head of yours over."

I grit my teeth at the words and at a phrase I wouldn't have thought twice about coming from my sister yesterday but hear complete condescension today.

Was Finn right? Am I being pushed aside because my dad and sisters don't think I can hack it? Am I just Sports Agent Barbie to be brought out and played with when no one's really being serious?

"We talked, and Dad made a snap decision to send Brexton to it. He thought she was better suited to speak on—"

"On what? Being a female in this industry who understands what sexism feels like?" I shake my head in disbelief even though she can't see it. "Any one of us could have stepped up and spoken with content and then some to spare."

"And Dad sent Brex."

"So basically, none of you have confidence that I can represent KSM and what we do properly?"

"That's not what I said."

"You don't have to say it for me to know you mean it. So what else, are you on *the Lennox isn't qualified bandwagon* now? Or is it the *she's unethical and sleeps with clients* one?"

"What?"

"Oh, I know," I say, now on an emotional roll. "It's *the only thing that Lennox is good for is to stand there and look pretty* group."

"What is your problem? Jesus, Lennox. Chill out."

"Chill out?" I say in angered disbelief.

"Yeah, chill, you're getting all worked up over shit that's not making any sense. You knew the Bradly thing was going to cause a stir and obviously it did or else you wouldn't have brought it up. And of course, you're gorgeous, and that does you a million favors but what does that have to do with your job? When it comes down to it, KSM is Dad's company. What he says goes. End of story."

Her words are like mental whiplash meant to distract and distort, and I feel more confused than ever. But the one thing I know for sure is we've never called it our father's company. It's always been ours.

"Since when?" I laugh mockingly. "When was the last time no one spoke up against something they disagreed with in our office? We're always speaking our minds and asserting opinions." I sink down onto the bed, hating the sudden churning in my stomach. "Besides, what is this it's his company bullshit? When was the last time any one of us referred to it like that?"

"That's not what I meant and you know it."

But it is what she meant. It is what I heard. It is how I feel.

"What about the MLS offer, huh? Did you all discuss that too? Did you all worry that I'd sleep with Cannon Garner and, by doing so, would sully the Kincade name? Is that why Dad made up some lame excuse that there was more to the offer than meets the eye?"

"We didn't discuss it at all. Dad's been around a lot longer than us. Has more insight. When he says there's something shady going on, there typically is."

"So now you all think I can't handle myself."

"You're plate's pretty full. All of ours are. If Cannon wanted you for the right reasons, then he would have persisted. One phone call asking isn't enough to prove otherwise."

"So, what? Everyone's looking at Little Lenn and thinking she isn't capable of handling more than one thing at a time?" I snort. "Is this when you pat me on the head, hand me a lollipop, and tell me to sit in the corner like a good, quiet little girl would?"

"You're kind of being a bitch, Lenn."

"And you're *kind* of not being honest with me," I snap as her sigh fills the line. "Does this have to do with me losing Austin Yeakle?"

"Of course not."

That hesitation before she says the three words tells me, it does. I close my eyes and pinch the bridge of my nose. It was a screwup on my part—definitely—so now I've been relegated to window-dressing duty?

"Because if I'm being punished for him then you should all be punished for the last client you lost too."

"This isn't a you thing or a me thing, Lenn. This is a decision by Dad. Maybe he thinks you've been running full bore for so long you need to step back and not be stretched so thin." She mutters a curse word. "God forbid Dad assumed you could use a little time off to . . ." But when her voice drifts off and she struggles finding the right words to say, I can't help but super-impose their words with her silence and know what they said holds merit.

But there are two things that bug me about the conversation more than anything.

My family knows I like to roam. To be in new places, new towns, and when I'm not, I get restless. Being somewhere new calms my restlessness. I'm sure a therapist would have a field day with the reasons why—she still searches for her mom in every crowd, being in New York reminds her what she's lost—and while they might have a point, I'll never admit it.

But for my dad to say I might want to stay home for a bit and use that as an excuse, doesn't sit right with me. He knows me. He knows this is what I thrive on.

The second thing that eats at me?

Chase is my sister, the one I've typically always been the closest with out of the three, so doesn't she realize that I know her?

And I know more than anything that she's lying right now.

Chapter TWO

Lennox

I STARE AT THE DEPARTURES BOARD, HANDS IN MY POCKETS, AND AN unsettled feeling owns me more than I'd like to admit.

The closing lecture of the conference was the last thing I wanted to attend this morning.

So I didn't. Instead, I had a few meetings with the potential clients I had noted in my binder and now, here I stand, way too tired after too many sleepless hours. Hours where I overthought what Finn and his gang of pricks said, about my conversation with Chase, and recalling the things that have happened here and there over the past months that now I look at with a different perspective.

Feeling hurt isn't anything new to me, but when it stems from those I love, it stings more.

Self-reflection doesn't exactly ease what I'm feeling either, but maybe it's called for here. I can't trust Chase to be frank with me, and Finn is an asshole. But is there some truth to what he said? Do I pass up opportunities if I feel one of my sisters could do a better job? Yes, but some of that is because it's one of our strengths as a family business to do that. *But is that the only reason?*

Do I doubt myself and hide behind my looks? Maybe it's time to test that out.

So with my cell phone in my back pocket burning from too many unanswered texts from Chase, I stare at the departures board and long to be somewhere else than where I need to be.

Eeny, meeny, miny, moe.

I play a random game of it, visually moving from city to city with each word of the nursery rhyme like I always do, but for some reason, this time around when I land on Los Angeles, I smile.

Sunshine, sand, palm trees, and *Johnny*.

Johnny.

My smile widens at the thought of one of my oldest friends.

But Johnny makes me think of soccer and how he used to play in college, and soccer makes me think of the MLS offer, and the MLS offer makes me think of all the crap that was said last night.

I glance at the departures board, my teeth worrying my bottom lip between them for a few seconds, while I ponder my colliding thoughts.

Los Angeles.

Johnny.

A change.

A little avoidance in not going back to New York for a while to deal with my family.

I slide my phone out of my pocket, scroll through my contacts, and have it ringing within seconds.

"Cannon Garner," the head of MLS league development says on the other end of the line when he answers. For some reason, I fumble over the words on my tongue. "Hello? Lennox?"

Shit. Damn caller ID.

"Yes, hi. Sorry. I had a bad connection," I lie. "I know we talked previously about the offer—"

"You mean the offer you turned down?" He chuckles.

"Yes. That one, but it was strictly because of my schedule, and it's since opened up."

"So something happened between now and when I spoke to your father two days ago? I guess miracles do exist," he says sarcastically and knocks the ground out from underneath my feet.

He called my father again?

Chase lied to me. Either she lied to me or didn't know about the call. Either way, my spine stiffens and my defiance fortifies.

"They do indeed," I murmur.

"So what exactly do you want to know about the offer?" he asks with a smugness in his tone that has me shaking my head.

Yes, I'm asking for the job, Cannon.

"I was curious. We never went into specifics. What exactly do you believe I can bring to the organization to help promote it?"

He emits another low chuckle that makes me feel like I'm a mouse being toyed with by a cat. "Interesting you should call. I was sitting here pondering what my plan B was going to be considering you were leaving me high and dry by not taking my offer to work with me."

"Plan B's never pan out," I argue playfully.

"Lucky for you, then, I hadn't figured it out yet." There's silence for a beat before he continues. "I'd love to meet you face to face to discuss what value I think you can add."

My eyes find the departure board again and scroll down to the flights headed to the City of Angels.

I hate feeling like a pawn in my dad's mastered game of chess and know without question I'm going to take this offer just to prove a point— no one makes decisions for me.

"When would you like to meet?" I ask.

"What works for you?"

I rock back on my heels, knowing what I want and what I should do are two different things.

"I can be there by three today. Does that work?"

"It does. I'll send over the address and information."

"Sounds good."

The call ends and all I can do is shake my head and laugh as I walk toward the ticket counter, well aware that he never answered my question: what he wants from me.

Los Angeles.

Sunshine, sand, palm trees, friends . . . and now possibly an additional responsibility.

The sunshine, sand, and palm trees are a given.

The best part about Los Angeles is my friend of eight years. Someone who knows everything about me so I don't have to pretend I have it all together. I'm already in a better mood thinking of him, his goofy smile, and everything his presence seems to bring me.

Even better is the last one. A new professional role. One that will have me juggling my everyday KSM duties with who knows what Cannon will require of me. In his initial pitch, he told me the role would be small, influential, and for a limited period of time. All things I can more than handle with my current workload.

I might have to jet off here or there for a day to deal with a client, but the best thing about my job is I can do it anywhere. Negotiations are rarely done face to face these days and most athletes can be soothed via text, phone, or Zoom. My home base can be a Starbucks, my bed, or while pacing on a sidewalk somewhere.

So this MLS deal is perfect. It'll let me escape from my everyday scenery for a bit, while the new challenge might be just what I need to get my head back in the game.

Besides, it's a good excuse not to return home and face my family when I'm not one hundred percent ready to.

I should call people—my family to let them know I'm not coming home, Johnny to let him know I'm headed his way—but I don't want to.

All I know is that this feels good—*right*—and I'm not sure why.

As I approach the counter, the attendant looks up with a bright smile and asks in a too cheerful tone, "May I help you?"

"Yes. I need to change my flight."

"Where to?"

"Los Angeles, please," I say, then hate when I look to the counter beside me and see one of the men from Sanderson's circle last night. I don't acknowledge him but rather skim over him as if I never saw him before turning my attention back to the lady in front of me.

"And a return date?" she asks.

"No. One way, please."

Chapter
THREE

Lennox

I TAKE A DEEP BREATH AND PREPARE MYSELF FOR WHATEVER THE next few moments will bring. I've been rushing nonstop since my plane landed.

A text to Johnny while sitting for endless minutes on the tarmac letting him know he has a visitor for the next couple of weeks.

A frantic scramble for a rental car so I could get here on time.

Then there's the traffic. Christ, if I thought New York was bad, it has nothing on Los Angeles and its myriad of complex, congested freeways where you have to merge and change roads more than I ever have before.

But I'm here with a few minutes to spare, and the powder I just dusted over my nose is still fresh on my fingers.

I glance around the conference room at its rich colors and dark wood tones. Its walls are lined with the logos of each soccer team participating in the league. The glass wall on the other side of the room looks out over a warehouse space with cubicles upon cubicles, but with hoverboards and dog beds littered throughout resembling a Silicon Valley tech start-up.

Soccer.

Ugh.

Not exactly my most favorite sport to say the least, and I'm not immune to the irony of the moment. That I'm here, seated in the MLS's offices, waiting to hear what skill sets I have that will grow the love of soccer country-wide for MLS.

"Lennox Kincade." Cannon's deep baritone fills the room and by the time I turn to face him, my eyes are bright and my smile is welcoming.

"Cannon." I rise from my seat and shake the hand of the man in front of me. Tall and broad-chested with dark features and from what I remember, assertive with a touch of that authoritative arrogance that is both attractive and annoying. "So good to see you again."

"Can I get you anything to drink or eat?" He motions for me to sit. "I'm assuming you just came from the conference in Vegas."

"I did, but I'm good, thanks." I take a seat and grab the pen on top of my notepad.

Cannon takes a seat and folds his tall body into the chair. I study him as he takes his time preparing what he's going to say. He's handsome, in a too polished type of way, which makes me think his hands never get dirty and that if I held his handshake long enough, there wouldn't be a callous anywhere to be found.

Not that that's bad . . . but just not my type.

His eyes meet mine again, followed by a smile before he starts. "As you know, it's been a struggle for soccer to find mainstream success in the US like other sports per se, such as football or baseball."

"It's definitely been a challenge," I muse with a nod. "We don't have the foundation in America like there is overseas in the Premier League or La Liga. On the other hand, with the rise of youth club soccer here in the US, and with those kids growing up loving the sport, you might be able to take advantage in the coming years of the building blocks that are happening."

"Exactly." His smile grows wider. "Funny you should mention the other leagues, but we'll get back to that in a moment. Part of my promise in taking the helm here is to get the public excited about the league and what we have in store for them. I'm to encourage more players to come on board and play here versus venturing to teams overseas. I'm trying to attract the right star power for lack of a better word."

"Makes sense."

"And that's where I'm hoping your expertise will come in."

"You have my attention," I say.

"I heard about how the Women's National Basketball Association asked you to join their board a few years ago for the sole purpose of being a players' advocate," he says.

"They did and I was. My goal was to let the team owners know what players wanted, what was fair practice, and how to entice players to be part of a league trying to grow its fan base and appeal in the sport's market."

"And how did you feel about the role?" He angles his head to the side and waits for an answer.

"I loved it. I was making the league a better place for the athletes."

"What did that entail?"

"Meaning?"

"Meaning, did you go to events or functions, or were you strictly a board meeting attendee?"

"More board meeting than not. I had my regular work at KSM and luckily that allows me the flexibility to work from any hotel room. If they needed me to be at meetings in Chicago for a week, I could go. I'm lucky that in most instances, I can meet my clients' needs with a simple phone call."

"And that wasn't too much for you?"

"No. Actually, it was a nice break from my day-to-day," I say, thinking of the satisfaction I got from knowing I was making the league and its parameters—contractual and otherwise—better for the players.

Cannon runs a finger over his chin as he stares at me, as if his thoughts were elsewhere momentarily. "So, what if I told you that I wanted you to do the same for the MLS but with a stronger focus on winning over players."

"Meaning?"

"Meaning still sitting in various meetings to tell us where we fall short, but also being an advocate for us. Educating and enticing players as to why they should play here for us instead of venturing overseas to play."

I nod slowly, mulling over his words. "I thought you originally said you were looking for an MLS ambassador to create a buzz in the hopes of widening the fan base and soccer's stature in American culture. Expanding the fan base beyond high school and college level to become a lucrative career option."

"You would be an ambassador of sorts. Titles don't change what the job is."

"Wouldn't you be better off having someone who can stand in front of a crowd and create a draw? If that's what you're looking for, I can't provide that."

"I know how to do my job, Lennox. But thank you. I appreciate the advice." He chuckles and gives a shake of his head. "I already have an ambassador like that. He'll be announced to the public in the coming days."

"Okay, so this is like a one-two punch? He's working the public side of it and I'm working behind the scenes? Are there any more positions like this?"

"I love a woman who likes details," he says with a smile.

I let the comment go, uncertain if it's a dig or not.

"But yes, you're correct. He's the public persona while you're the cog behind him trying to make sure everything looks appealing so that the incredible MLS he's speaking about becomes a reality."

"So what? I need to show up to events to schmooze and convince investors that we're making the league stronger, work behind the scenes . . . what else are my duties?"

"Nothing more than make the players happy and want to play here."

I tap my pen against my pad as I try to look at what the cons in taking this job could be other than strapping my time . . . and even that isn't a bad thing.

"Happiness is a fickle thing to measure," I say.

"I have no doubt you can achieve it." His smile lights up his eyes.

"Okay. Say I agree, what commitment are you looking for from me since I do have my own clients to take care of?"

"Three months. That's the term of the deal. Of course, you're free to represent your KSM clients during the time. We have no problem with that. But three months and then you're free and clear from us."

But why? I mean, I get my history with the WNBA, but something feels too good to be true here.

"And what's in it for me, Cannon?"

"A break in the monotony of stroking arrogant athletes' egos." He chuckles because he's right; at times it does get old. "And a way to carve out more of a niche for yourself. Sure, you're part of a very successful sports agency, but don't you want to stand out for something? Don't you want to be the sister athletes request by name? Or teams or leagues, because you're known as being a miracle worker who advocates for athletes?"

I twist my lips as I stare at him, his words hitting so very close to home after the knock my confidence has taken over the past twenty-four hours.

Isn't this what I need? A bit of a boost. Something I can call my own? Maybe Cannon is right. Maybe I need to carve out a niche for myself.

Better yet, be introduced to more athletes who might not know the agency and perhaps pull a few onboard with us? I'd be lying if the thought didn't have me nodding ever-so-subtly.

"And the compensation?" I ask as if I already haven't decided that I'm taking the job.

His smile pulls up at one corner of his mouth and he slides a folder across the table. "It's all in here, including compensation as well as bonus potential. I'm sure it'll be to your liking."

I glance down at the folder as he removes his hands from it and then back up at him.

I think of my mantra at the airport earlier today. Sunshine, sand, palm trees, Johnny, and now, a *new opportunity*.

Sounds perfect to me.

There are a million more questions I should ask, but I don't.

This is something different for sure. A change of pace I never knew I was looking for, and a challenge I didn't realize I'd been needing.

Take the job, maybe add some new clients to the KSM portfolio, and maybe increase the market's awareness of me as an agent.

Don't take the job and go right back to what I left—misnomers about what I can bring to the table and accomplish for our family business.

Prove to whom though? My fellow agents who were mocking me? My family who, by their actions, seem to agree with them? Or is it merely to myself so I believe without question that I'm just as good as I thought I was?

Cannon clears his throat as he taps a finger on the folder he's left in the space between us. "Compensation, job requirements, a non-disclosure, and the like. Take this evening to look it over and then we can talk here tomorrow at ten. Does that work for you?"

"Yes. Sure." I say the words with indecision in my tone but my mind is already made up.

A change of scenery, pace, and duties . . . that might be just what this girl needs to get her groove back.

Chapter
FOUR

Lennox

JOHNNY'S VOICEMAIL COMES THROUGH THE SPEAKERS OF MY RENTAL car loud and clear as I navigate my way through the Hollywood Hills.

"I like how you don't even ask me if you can stay but rather just drop a text saying I'm going to have a house guest for the next few weeks. That's so very Lennox of you, it's ridiculous." His laughter rings throughout the car and makes my smile grow even wider. "The door code is one-three-one-three to get in. You can take the bedroom on the third floor with the spa tub you loved last time you were here. Make yourself at home but just a warning—" The message continues but it's a pixelated garble that I can't understand. He must have called me when he had poor cell service. "—So deal with it. You'll be fine. Try not to get into any of that trouble I know you're fond of. I'll be home with dinner around five. I'm assuming you want that crappy Chinese food you always want when you visit. And I'll oblige this once, but so help me, Lenn, if this is the shit you expect me to eat the whole time you're here, I'll kick your ass out."

I laugh at the empty threat as the call ends. He secretly complains about the crappy food but it's a tradition, and he knows how I like my traditions.

With a glance at the GPS, I take a right down a street that doesn't feel familiar, even though I've driven it before, just as my phone rings.

I've been avoiding this call all day long so I might as well confront it head-on.

"Hello?"

"Where the hell are you?" Dekker asks without preamble.

"Los Angeles."

Her next words come out in a screech. "You're where?"

"LA. City of Angels. California." *The opposite coast of where you are.*

"What for?" There's judgment in my sister's tone that I hate.

"I had a meeting with Cannon Garner with the MLS."

"Why would you do that? I thought we talked about his offer and decided it was a bad call for the company."

"We didn't talk about anything, Dekk," I say and uncover another lie that Chase told. "You guys must have talked and then you guys must have decided. I don't believe my opinion ever factored into anything."

"It's not that, Lenn . . . it's—"

"It is that. I don't need to be coddled. I don't need—"

"Sit back for two seconds and think about his offer. Why would the MLS call for a sports agent to work in and promote its organization? You represent athletes, not leagues. Why out of all the agents in our field did he only offer the position to you and no one else even after you said no?"

"After Dad said no," I correct.

"Does it matter? The same question still applies." Her frustrated sigh fills the line. "He's singling you out for a reason. Cannon's known for needing everyone who works for him to fit a certain mold. Add to that he has quite the reputation for not being respectful to women who work for him."

"So now the only reason Cannon asked me to work for him is because I'm pretty? Not because I'm knowledgeable? Jesus, Dekk, if Dad told you to call and give me a pep talk, you're definitely doing a shitty job of it."

"C'mon. It's talked about quietly in circles that he's a womanizer who uses his influence and position to get what he wants out of the women he hires. Hell, ever since he met you a few years back, he's been trying to get you to work with him in any capacity, even when it doesn't have anything to do with your area of expertise. He obviously has a thing for you."

I feel like I've been hit with whiplash. I didn't know anything about Cannon's reputation, but who am I to believe it after I heard the rumors being spread about me?

And while I should really step back and take the time to listen to what my sister is saying, all I hear is what she's not saying. "So God forbid you think he's really hiring me to do a real job, right? It's more than obvious no one in this family thinks I'm capable of shit."

"Quit making assumptions. Knock the chip off your shoulder and listen to what I'm saying to you."

"The chip on my shoulder?" My voice is ice-cold as events I'm sure she has no idea about collide in my mind and piss me off.

"Lennox." My name is a frustrated sigh on her lips. "I'm only looking out for you. The last thing I want is this prick to think he's going to get more from you than just your professional input."

"Right." I roll my eyes, but then make the final turn down Johnny's street and want to cry as his house comes into view. Thank God.

There's something about him that always makes me feel whole again. Something that's been there since we first met in college all those years ago.

"All I'm saying is that there's more than meets the eye with his offer."

"An offer you don't know the first thing about," I accuse.

"I don't have to. I know Cannon is either going to try to get in your pants or he's setting you up somehow. Like ask you to do something unethical so you take the fall and he doesn't."

"Wow. That's a huge stretch you just made."

Her silence reigns as I pull up to the sleek, modern house in front of me. It's all straight lines and hard edges with a minimalist exterior. It's such a contrast to the green foliage it's hidden behind, but I know the truth. The back of the house opens up to unhindered views of the city below with not a single neighbor in sight.

"Listen, Dekk. I'm a big girl who makes the decision about who I allow in my pants. I can more than handle myself. Also, have a little faith in me. I'm not going to do anything stupid that will risk the agency's or my reputation.

And if she mentions Bradly, I might scream. That once fun fling has now become an albatross. "Look, I need a change of scenery, a different perspective for a bit, and this MLS gig might provide just that."

"You've already made up your mind, haven't you?" she murmurs.

"I have."

She laughs, as do I, because in that moment, I know she's not angry but simply wary. *For me.* At least, I hope so. "And this is why I love you, Lenn, and wouldn't expect anything less. My stubborn, independent, free-spirited sister."

"Exactly."

And it's about time I felt that way again.

Within minutes, I'm out of my rental and inside the house. I'm greeted with the wood accents and neutral tones of Johnny's house that no doubt Mommy and Daddy's money helped to pay for, but a cool ten million for a house in the Hollywood Hills is a mere drop in the bucket.

I run my hand over the gorgeous marble island and take a piece of candy from the dish on top of it. He still has his sweet tooth, I see. But I startle when I see the stash of supplements and protein powders at the opposite end of the counter.

Who took Johnny and what did they do to him? Because he is the unhealthiest person I know in the fittest of bodies.

Huh.

Maybe that's why he bitched about getting Chinese food tonight. Too much sugar and GMO or who the hell knows what? I can eat it without worrying about how it affects my waistline.

A fast metabolism is a blessing of mammoth proportions.

Once upstairs, I open my suitcase and am hit with the scent of stale cigarette smoke on my clothes that can only be reminiscent of a long week in Las Vegas.

"Ugh," I mutter, hating the smell, but knowing the perfect solution: throw what I can in the wash while I jump in the pool and soak up the California sunshine.

With the washing machine humming and my bikini on, I all but sprint from the back door to the pool and jump in, in full cannon-ball mode.

When I resurface, the laughter that's on my lips dies a shocked death when I look up and see the man standing at the edge of the grass.

Standing there with sweat glistening off his tattoo-decorated skin and corded muscles, a cocky smirk pulling up one corner of his lips, expressive eyes laden with amusement, and a body that's . . . completely naked.

"Well, I've had a lot of women go to a lot of lengths to get to me, but this is most definitely a first," he says in a British lilt. "Fancy a swim now, did you?"

My heart stutters the minute our eyes meet—his pale green to my dark blue.

I know who he is immediately.

Who wouldn't?

Soccer—er football star extraordinaire, aloof bad boy, and the untamable phenomenon, Rush McKenzie.

The one who's naked in all his well-endowed glory at the edge of the pool while I'm standing inside it wondering what in the hell is going on.

The same Rush McKenzie who was embroiled in a scandal in the UK last month. The one that my sisters and I took one look at in *The Sun* newspaper and thanked our lucky stars he wasn't our client, because God knows what bullshit, fallout, and consequences would follow in the wake of that shitshow.

Apparently, this is the bullshit that follows. McKenzie heading to America for some rest and relaxation, unaffected and arrogant without a care in the world of the devastation he left in his wake.

To the teammate whose marriage he allegedly destroyed.

To his own team, which was so tangled up in taking sides, they played like crap and all but handed their opponent the win in the Champions League finals.

To his career. In a year where he's up for a contract renewal, this wasn't the best time to pull this stunt.

To his reputation . . . but then again, I'm not really sure that he cares one bit. While the man can do no wrong when he touches the ball on the pitch, his penchant for causing trouble isn't anything new to him.

Why am I not surprised that he's here in Johnny's house? I ran away here too, didn't I?

Our eyes meet—hold—his smile widening with each passing second, the charm turned on and then some.

I've heard the term magnetism before. I thought I understood it. But I didn't have a clue what it meant, what it felt like, until this very moment.

Until him.

I immediately hate him for it.

But it's more than his incredible body, crooked smile, and undeniable presence—so much more—that has me standing here fumbling for words when words are typically my strong suit. Every single thing about him captivates every single thing within me.

And that's even after knowing what he's rumored to be capable of.

Something's definitely wrong with you, Lenn.

And to think I swore off men.

"Don't flatter yourself," I say with a shake of my head as if I'm trying to break the spell he seems to have on me. My eyes dart down to where they shouldn't, curious about the tattoos, among *other* things, that highlight his body, before meeting his eyes again. "I was hot. I thought I was alone. I wanted to take a swim. All three are well within my rights."

"What a coincidence. I was sore from my workout. I wanted to use the sauna. I thought I was alone. Funny how that works."

"Hence you being naked."

"Yes. *Hence.*" He takes a few steps forward, completely unabashed over his nudity, and why should he be when he looks like that—a Greek god plus tattoos. He reaches down and scratches his lower abdomen, drawing my eyes to track where that wicked V trims at the waist before coming to the thickness of his cock resting against the defined muscles of his quads.

"Don't you want to put some clothes on?" I ask and motion to the chair where I can now see his towel is, pretending like the sight before me doesn't affect me, when how can it not?

"Why, darling? It seems you're quite enjoying the view. Why would I want to deprive you of it?"

"Seriously?" I ask with a partial chuckle that in no way reflects the fact that what he says is true.

Rush McKenzie is definitely easy on the eyes in more ways than one. He's sparking my libido to life without even trying.

But I refuse to give him the satisfaction of looking again—especially after the last comment he made. So instead we stand under the gorgeous California sun staring at each other.

There's wicked lechery in his expression, while mine has a heavy dose of disbelief.

And desire.

Because I'd be lying if I said my mind didn't wander off and have a dirty little fantasy beginning with all the lines my tongue would like to trace over those defined abs and beyond.

Just when I swore off men, one worth breaking the promise to myself comes waltzing right in—and naked at that.

I can't make this shit up.

And after one long, glorious look at Rush, I don't think I want to.

Chapter FIVE

Rush

Interesting.

Devastatingly gorgeous when I've only seen her from the shoulders up and yet, she's so very *interesting,* staring at me from where she stands in the pool.

From where she hasn't backed down when most women would have given that annoying giggle and jiggle of tits so I could see what's being offered up.

But not her.

Not this woman, with her sapphire-blue eyes that have no shame in staring.

"So you broke into a house that isn't even mine and won my attention. Now what do you plan on doing with me in the short time between me ringing the police and them showing up?" I ask, knowing a lot can be done in that short amount of time. From past experience.

But her coughed-out laugh and raised eyebrows tell me this isn't the usual fangirl encounter. She's too calm, too unfazed.

All hints of the person who moments ago ran out of the house to do a cannonball without a care is gone, and has been replaced with the curious, calculated woman standing before me.

Problem is, I saw that side of her—the reckless, the carefree—and it's tempting to find it again when I shouldn't give a toss.

"Let's see," she says as she moves toward the steps of the pool. "I know the code to get in the door so I'm not breaking in." She moves up a step revealing perfectly shaped tits—not too big, not too small—nestled perfectly beneath the two red triangles of fabric. "I've known Johnny for about eight years so I'm more than welcome here." Another step up, and now I'm treated with the narrowing of her waist where the glitter of a jewel is in her navel. "And last, I don't have an ounce of interest in you whatsoever, which I'm sure comes as quite the shock to your ego."

Liar.

It's in the set of her chin and flicker of her eyes back down to my cock that tells me otherwise.

But when she steps out of the pool, and I'm greeted with the entirety of this woman, I'm knocked off my stride. She's a good five foot eight, fit but not too muscular, with curves that highlight every damn inch of what holds any normal man's attention. She's soft and supple in that perfect way that we men like—to hold on to and sink into—but not feel like we're going to break her.

Bloody hell.

I take a step forward. "That makes two of us then."

"At least that's settled now." Her lips twitch, because she knows I'm lying just as sure as I know she is. "I'd ask if you're staying here, but I'll make the assumption the answer is yes."

I nod. "I might be lying low for a while."

Her laugh tugs at the corners of her mouth. "Lying low? In Los Angeles? I think someone may have lied to you about what this city is all about. It's seen or be seen. If you want to lie low, you go somewhere like Montana and play with horses."

"There's only one thing I have in common with horses," I tease and earn a roll of her eyes and a shake of her head.

"I don't think Los Angeles is far enough away from the attention you're escaping."

"It doesn't seem anywhere is far enough these days."

She walks toward me, still sizing me up, and right when I think she's brazen enough, about to lean in for a kiss I'm more than willing to give, she reaches down for my towel beside me.

She quirks an eyebrow when her eyes meet mine, knowing what I thought she was doing, and I laugh.

I like this woman. Plain and simple.

We stand a foot apart, the towel in her hand, water still beaded on her skin, and for the first time I notice the dusting of freckles across the tops of her cheeks. Cute on a woman who defines the word sexy.

"Lennox Kincade," she says, and now I'm even more intrigued than I was seconds before. I know the name, I've met one or two of her sisters, but never Lennox.

The question is why the hell not?

"Rush McKenzie."

"So I assumed," she says as she bends over and runs the towel down each long leg making a production of it as she goes.

Yeah, I'm looking, love. A man would be stupid not to watch.

"I wasn't aware that you and Johnny knew each other," she says.

"Johnny knows everyone."

"True."

"I met him at the Super Bowl years ago. I was in Stance's stadium suite during the game," I say mentioning Johnny's parents' company, Stance Sports, "and we hit it off. Since then we meet up every now and again. He extended the offer to get away from the chaos. I took it."

She twists her lips and puts a hand over her forehead to block the sun as she looks at me once again. "You're flying at half-mast there, mate," she says mocking my accent and highlighting it with a smirk.

"We don't like to show all of our talents right off the bat."

"So much for first impressions then."

"Jesus," I bark.

But just as she goes past me, I grab her wrist so we're face to face. This time, I can make out that there is a ring of light blue around her pupils before it turns dark. Unique.

"Seems you're already in enough trouble, McKenzie. I think the last thing you need to do is start some with me."

"Is that a warning or a threat?"

"Maybe it's an invitation." She smirks. "'Cause God knows I could use a little of all three right now."

Without another word, Lennox Kincade strolls into the house leaving me to watch the devastating swing of her hips, the curve of her ass, and the slope of her shoulders from behind.

And here I thought I was going to dread my time in the States.

Seems to me I may have found something to help me pass the time.

Hell, if I'm going to be blamed for causing trouble, I might as well enjoy a little of it in the meantime.

Chapter
SIX

Lennox

"So that's it? You're here for secret meetings you can't talk about?" Johnny asks over the rim of his glass. He's sprawled over the outdoor sofa with the flames of the fire between us, playing off the blond in his hair.

"Not secret, per se." And I wonder why I'm not telling Johnny about Cannon's offer when obviously Finn knew about it, so it's not exactly a secret. "Just . . . pending." I flick my gaze toward the inside of the house where Rush is moving about the kitchen making a smoothie with a dedication I can't say I have when it comes to putting green things into a blender.

The protein powder and supplements on the counter make perfect sense now.

"Yes?" Johnny asks, the lone word drawn out until I look back toward him and his raised eyebrows.

"Yes, what?"

"Yes, as in stop looking over there. He's already in a shitstorm of trouble."

"You're the one who neglected to warn me he was here."

"Blame it on crappy cell service, but I did tell you. You just didn't hear it."

"Maybe you should have told him too. I mean, who trounces around someone else's house buck-ass naked?"

"Apparently a man who doesn't give a fuck what others think of him," he says and glances toward Rush.

But why should he? As a soccer player, Rush has a phenomenal physique. His lean, toned body is a testimony to years of hard work and self-discipline.

I study that body right now and then remember exactly how incredible it looked earlier standing a foot away from me . . . and naked.

"Don't you dare get that look in your eyes, Lenn. The last thing he needs is to add you to his mix."

"Me?" I mutter. "What's wrong with *me?*"

"The man has been accused of sleeping with his teammate's wife, a famous singer, for Christ's sake, so of course the image spreads like wildfire. Who does that kind of shit?"

"Not that I'm okay with cheating, but from the tabloids, it seems shit like that happens all the time here in Hollywood. Why are you batting an eye at him if you don't think ill of everyone else who's doing it?"

"I bat my eyes all the time at what I see and hear in LA, but as it pertains to Rush, it's not exactly the best timing when his contract is up for renegotiation and his entire club is up in arms over whether he stays or goes. What do you think management is going to do? Trade him to keep the peace or keep him on and have every other teammate freaked he's going to fuck their wives too?"

"I call bullshit. They won't trade their star player."

"Seth is their captain though."

"He's nearing the end of his career and is nowhere near as popular or dependable as Rush. Greed for another championship comes before all else."

"Talk about adding insult to injury though. Rumor was that Rush would slide into the captain's role next season. Steal Seth's wife *and* his status on the team." Johnny glances Rush's way and blows out a telling whistle. "I hear it's a clusterfuck over there. The guys are fighting over who's taking what sides and management's in constant talks on how to smooth this over, when it's really not their job to manage their players' personal lives in the first place."

"Sounds like chaos," I murmur but recall overhearing comments here and there about Seth. Rumor is he's not the nicest of guys. "Rush is here to lie low until shit cools off?"

"Or another scandal overshadows his."

"Hmm," I murmur, realizing my gaze has gravitated back to Rush again.

"After all that, you're still going to sit here and stare at him?"

"You're just jealous that I'm not staring at you." I toss my coaster at him. "And *eww*. That would be gross if I did since you're the brother I never had."

"True." He chuckles but levels a look at me. "Doesn't any of what I just said, what Rush has done, give you pause in making those googly eyes at him?"

"I'm not making googly eyes at him." It's called smoldering. I smolder when I look at him because even across the distance, his pull is undeniable. "Did he do it?" I ask.

"What do you mean, *did he do it?*" Johnny looks at me like I'm crazy for asking, but in my quick search on my phone earlier before he came home, I didn't see a single article or post where Rush said anything other than, "no comment."

Why did I search for it? Why did I want there to be something that could redeem his actions? Why do I care?

Because, I don't think Rush McKenzie is that man. The man who doesn't give a flying fuck about the enormous ripple effect caused by cheating with a teammate's other half. I've known a lot of shitty people in my life, have seen infidelity after infidelity with other athletes I've represented. And even though Rush is cocky and arrogant, I don't sense the same . . . sleaziness I've seen many times before.

And honestly? I'd be surprised if Johnny would allow him such easy access to his place if he thought it was true as well. That's one of the reasons we're such great friends.

"Well, has anyone asked him if he did it?" I ask. "I mean . . . sure he has that cocky swagger and crooked smile that could charm the panties off any woman—even pop stars apparently, but—"

"Sorry, that isn't something I take notice of," he says and rolls his eyes.

"And that's why you're jealous, because you can't buy it with any of that money you have laying in stacks around here," I tease.

"You're a pain in my ass." His smile widens.

"You wouldn't want me any other way."

"You're right, though a little dose of you goes a long way." He winks. "Question is, why do I let you visit when clearly your intentions are to abuse me relentlessly?"

"Because you love me." I give my oldest friend the biggest, cheesiest grin I can muster.

"You're right. I do. It's an illness." He pours more merlot into his empty glass. "To answer your question, I've asked, but he won't talk about it. When I bring up anything about it, he stays tight-lipped. The club put a gag order in effect to keep club business in house."

"Smart on the club, but I think it's a little too late for that considering there's a photo of the two of them on every tabloid out there." I laugh.

"I guess it was issued after the team got into somewhat of a brawl over it." He shrugs. "I'm going to respect his wishes and leave him the fuck alone about it since everyone else in the world won't."

I purse my lips and know what it feels like to be accused of something out of misperception. "I still think someone needs to just come out and ask him."

"How about that not be you, huh? I need to keep the peace between my housemates for the time being." He lifts a glass my way. "Speaking of coming out and asking things, you want to tell me why you're here? We've known each other long enough to know you only show up out of the blue when you're running from something."

Shit. That's the problem when you run to the one person who knows you better than most.

Our gazes hold across the firepit, and then I tell him everything about my last twenty-four hours—the conference, Finn, my conversation with Chase then Dekker. All of it.

"You know your family loves you like mad, right?" he finally says after a long silence and a quiet, thoughtful stare.

"They can love me all they want, but that doesn't make any of this better. What they think of me or what others think of me, for that matter."

"There's more to the story, isn't there?" he prods.

I swear under my breath as a ghost of a smile tints my lips. How is it that he knows? How is it that he's going to make me admit to the one thing I don't even want to admit to myself?

My long exhale stretches across the silence as I think of the two major clients I've lost over the past two months. Clients who I thought I had everything covered, but obviously dropped the ball somehow by not giving them what they needed. Clients I didn't tell my sisters and Dad the whole story behind because it just painted me in a worse light than them leaving already did.

"So in a state of rebellion, you flew here to take whatever job it is you've been offered to prove it to yourself that you're not that person."

"Basically." I shrug. "And to prove it to them too."

"Have you ever thought maybe that's what you're hearing—that they don't think you're doing a good job—but it's not what they actually think?"

And this is why I came here. Johnny always gets me on a level like no one else. He won't push, but he'll tell me straight every time and right now, I need that.

"Too many coincidences for me to think otherwise."

"Says the woman who reads into everything," he says while I glare at him. "Look, I hear what you're saying, I understand why you feel the need to do whatever clandestine thing you're apparently doing to prove your point, but know that so many of us love you because you're the perfect mix of brains and beauty. Screw assholes like Sanderson who cause you to doubt yourself. We wouldn't want you any other way."

"Easier said than done when you're the person escaping to your friend's house instead of heading home, wondering if maybe they have a point and if maybe, you have in fact been resting on your laurels more than not lately."

"The question is why are you resting on your laurels?"

I open my mouth and close it as I try to figure out the answer. Because I'm bored? Restless? Because, lately I've felt like there's something more and I'm not quite sure what that more is yet? Maybe I just want to feel more independence—a little bit of me—instead of always being part of the Kincade family.

Not that anything is wrong with being a part of my family. We love each other madly (when we're not bickering), but at the same time, my identity has never been anything but them. But the business.

But the beauty queen.

But the third daughter of four.

I lean my head onto the back of the chair and close my eyes for a moment. How do I put that into words for the person who'd love more than anything to be part of a family like mine?

Johnny Stance is the perfect example of parents throwing money at their son because they're too busy building an empire and enjoying its riches to parent him themselves.

"Where'd you escape to?" Johnny asks.

"Nowhere. I'm here. I appreciate you letting me be."

"You're welcome to stay as long as you want. You know that."

"Thanks," I murmur and turn my head to the side where I can look into the house again. Rush leans over the counter with his forearms resting on it as he does something on a laptop. A pair of dark gray sweats with the Liverpool Football Club logo emblazoned on them hang low from his hips, and the green smoothie he made moments ago is half empty beside him.

"You're looking again," Johnny murmurs.

"Can you blame me?" I laugh. "I mean, Jesus. Look at him. He's kind of perfect."

"If you're into broody assholes who every football player would kill to be and every woman would love to fuck."

"Basically," I say with a shrug and a laugh, as if it's common sense.

"Like I said, Lenn, he doesn't need you."

"And what the hell is that supposed to mean?" I ask, welcoming the change of topic and the playful tone that's back in his voice.

"It means right now it seems he needs to be grounded . . . anchored. You don't like to be attached, you like to have fun, and for him, fun is nothing but a media magnet. You like to rebel when you're in this mood, and it seems he already has or he wouldn't be here. Hell, it's his middle name." He ticks each point off on his fingers. "And you never shy away from what you shouldn't be doing."

"What I should be doing is *him*," I murmur as Rush stretches his arms over his head causing his sweatpants to slip some.

"Jesus, Lennox. Really?"

I shrug and offer him a *cat ate the canary* grin. "Can't fault me for being honest."

Chapter
SEVEN

Lennox

"WHAT DO YOU MEAN THIS IS YOUR *LOO*?" I ASK, FEELING RIDICULOUS using the term, when I look to where Rush stands in the doorway, one arm resting on the jamb with those same sweatpants riding low on his hips. He smells like soap and citrus and hell . . . does he really have to smell good too?

"No, I said I have to go to the loo. This is the bathroom, and it's mine. The one I've been using since I arrived. All of that shit you just slid into the drawer"—he motions with his free hand to the toiletries I just cleared into it—"is *my* shit."

And there's something about him standing here—or maybe it's because I want him to notice me when he's kept to himself all evening—that makes me push for banter, for an argument, for anything to ease that sexual tension snapping between us.

"And your point?" I smile sweetly in the mirror as I pull my robe tighter around my waist.

"God knows there are a million other bathrooms in this house," he says.

"Good, then you can find one that suits you better. This one has the best lighting to do my makeup in," I say and cross my arms over my chest as I turn to face him. Even now, I'm sucker-punched by the sight of him— the cut of his jaw, the fullness of his lips, and the thick lashes framing his crystalline green eyes. He's truly stunning in the most masculine way.

"Sucks then that you'll have to do without it since this is the one that suits me." He returns the same catty smile back at me. "I was here first."

If he wants to go there . . . "Finders, keepers."

"Really?" He laughs and runs a hand through his hair to get it out of his face. "You're something else."

"So I've been told." I angle my head and stare at him. The silence lengthens and begs me to ask the question that doesn't fit in the playfulness of the moment whatsoever. "Why did you come here?"

"To Johnny's?" He alters the question to suit him, and I don't expect anything less. "Probably for the same reason you're here. Because I needed a place to go where I knew there would be no judgment, and Johnny is that. Besides, the view and the pool don't hurt."

I'm both surprised and impressed by the honesty of his answer and give a nod in response. I recall my conversation with Johnny earlier. *"Doesn't any of what I just said, what Rush has done, give you pause in making those googly eyes at him?"*

No.

In fact, there's an allure to it. To wanting someone who everyone is warning you away from. It's enticing and thrilling—rebellion always is.

He lifts his eyebrows to elicit a response from me, but I think the tension between us is response enough. It's undeniable—I know he feels it too—and neither of us opt to break or dissipate it.

So we stand in the small space, inches apart, as so many more questions whirl in my head that I don't dare ask yet: *How long are you staying? What are your plans?*

Most of all the same one I asked Johnny: *did you do it?*

Rush owes me no answers. Hell, he barely knows me, and yet here we stand, in close quarters with my mind wandering and my body wanting.

I itch to reach out and touch him. His jaw. His hair. His arm. Anything to make a connection, and that's such a weird thought for me because I'm typically not a touchy-feely person.

But I refrain, because there's something in the very little I know about him that tells me to take a step back. That listening to my gut instinct, I know he'd be devastating—to my senses, to the status quo I'm used to, and to my heart, when I swear it doesn't like to feel.

"What are we doing here, Lennox?" he asks, his voice a whisper.

I part my lips to speak and watch as his eyes flicker down to look at them before coming back to my eyes.

"Negotiating with you," I murmur, deflecting just as he did.

The space is large by any guest bathroom standards, but the minute he moves into it, I feel as if all the oxygen has been sucked from it. All that's left to breathe in is him.

"Is that what you call this?" he asks as he takes a step closer. "*Negotiating?*"

Like I said, Lenn, he doesn't need you right now.

"Yes. We've negotiated. I won." I flash a victorious and over-the-top grin his way. "And now we're figuring out what bathroom you're going to use since this one is occupied by me."

"I don't think we were privy to the same conversation. There is no way I ceded this loo to you." A little-boy smile paints his lips as he makes fun of my misuse of British terms. The smile and its charm need to go far away. The last thing I need is to find another thing attractive about him.

"You did. I heard it."

"In my unspoken words?" He laughs.

"Yep." I nod. "I can read minds."

"Suit yourself." His chuckle is low and seductive and causes chills to chase up my spine as he steps closer.

"Your negotiating skills need some work, McKenzie," I tease.

"So do yours," he says, and I yelp when he pushes his sweats off his hips and steps out of them.

"What are you doing—"

"Seems to me we're sharing the bathroom now, so"—he meets my eyes in the mirror—"you shouldn't be shocked that I'm having a shower. Since you can read minds and all."

I throw my head back and laugh. It's all I can do, really. And it's way less polarizing than looking at his incredible body. "Good for you," I say with a definitive nod. "You go do that."

"I will."

"For future reference, shock value doesn't work well with me."

"Noted. I was going more for the fact that I needed a shower and you're in my bathroom." He fights a grin. "Impressed?"

"It takes a lot more than that to impress me."

"I know. Your loss of negotiation skills is a sure sign you're still in awe of what you saw earlier by the pool."

"Oh please," I say with a roll of my eyes as the shower turns on and he steps into it.

"Don't worry, love. I'm still recovering from that bikini of yours too."

My eyes flash up to meet his through the fogged-up glass, and I'm treated to a lightning-fast grin.

All I can do is shake my head and try not to be affected by his words as I walk out of the bathroom, cross the hall into my room, and lean against the door when I shut it behind me.

There's a smile on my face as I close my eyes and replay the whole exchange in my head over again. He's a tease and a flirt, and if these are my thoughts after only two exchanges with him, I know I'm in trouble.

The past couple of days have been a blow to my ego and sense of self. Is it such a bad thing that Rush makes me feel a little better about myself? Is it even worse that I've been working nonstop for months on end that I haven't taken care of me?

By taking care of me, I mean reaching out and taking what I want. And damn it to hell, I want him.

I have a feeling Rush isn't a man who hesitates either. He takes and demands, and if you can't keep up with his pace, he moves on.

There's a challenge in that, an attraction.

What is it about me being attracted to athletes? The strong hands, the powerful bodies, the air of arrogance of a man who knows he's good at something, the dedication . . . it's like they're my kryptonite.

"Christ," I mutter and tuck an errant strand of hair behind my ear.

Rush would be a terrible mistake. A terrible, gorgeous, satisfying mistake. I know it after only one day, but the funny thing is, it's one I know I'm already going to make.

And I don't feel sorry about it in the least.

I'm a woman who goes after what she wants—without shame or fear . . . and, I want Rush McKenzie.

Chapter EIGHT

Rush

11 years earlier

MY STOMACH GROWLS SO LOUDLY I CAN HEAR IT OVER THE thundering of my pulse in my ears.

Just act normal, Rush. Move slow, look around at the produce, and then thumb through the magazine as if you don't feel like your stomach is eating its way from your insides out. Don't think about the biscuits you've stashed in your pockets or the banana you've tucked in the back of your waistband beneath your jacket.

The lightheadedness hits me again. It's cruel and unrelenting as it blackens my vision, and I'm forced to grip the side of the shelving so I don't pass out.

It's been twenty-four hours—maybe, I can't remember—since I last ate a leftover bite of protein bar that my teammate offered me. Since then, I've had two, three-hour training sessions where it took everything I had to focus on putting on the performance they expect.

The same performance I'm praying will get me out of this bloody nightmare.

Because I'm so close, so very close to winning the only scholarship the Liverpool Academy gives out every year.

The scholarship—a chance—that might change everything for me. Not only would it take me a step further toward playing in the Premier League, but it would also provide me a place to live and an allowance for food. It wouldn't be much but it would be way more than I have now.

Then I'd be able to stop pretending one of those flats on Crestfall Lane is mine. People see me walk up to it, but they never notice the kid in his football kit continues into the alley behind it. No one questions the abandoned post box out front that sometimes has mail in it addressed to a Mr. McKenzie. No one realizes the lock on the little shed back there is mine. That I've found a place to keep me out of the rain, that has a sink in it so I can wash my clothes and myself.

So I can pretend that I'm like any other normal teenager in Kirkby—going to school, spending every spare moment on the pitch, drinking a pint on the sly.

But this is what I need to do. This is how I have to live so my dreams come true. So I have a chance.

It's playing professional football or . . . or nothing.

No one cared when cancer took Maude McKenzie's life.

Even fewer thought to wonder where her fifteen-year-old son was and what was to become of him.

"Excuse me, young man." I startle at the voice of a little old lady standing beside me and staring at me with her owl-like eyes. "Can I get in there?" She points to the bags of noodles in front of me.

I'm jolted back to the present. To the hunger pangs and the sore muscles from training. To the hope tinged with despair. To the drive to keep this all hidden. Because if I don't get the hell out of here, I'm going to faint and then someone will notice the food I'm about to steal.

Then it will all be over.

The dream.

My escape.

Everything.

There's a reason I'm in this shop. It's the only one I haven't been caught stealing from yet. The only one where the shop assistants at the front don't start following me around to check for any sleight of hand.

"Yes." I give a quick shake of my head. "Sorry. I was—"

"Thinking about the big game tonight, huh?" she asks and motions to the Liverpool Football Club hand-me-down training gear I have on. "Man U doesn't stand a chance."

"They sure don't," I murmur before offering a quick smile and hurrying from the shop with my head down, and my arms wrapped around me to ward off the chill of the coming evening.

As soon as I clear the edge of the building, I rip down the peel of the banana and can't eat it fast enough. My stomach aches and growls. With half the banana gone, I tear open the packet of biscuits with a frenzy only someone who is truly hungry can understand.

You want to slow down, to save some for later, but all you can think about is sating the hunger pangs now. All you know is that you need them to go away for a while, because there's no way you can go to another training on an empty stomach.

How can you be better than everyone else when you're hungry?

How much longer can you hold out?

With a biscuit in one hand and the half-eaten banana in the other, I rush around the corner and run smack into someone.

We both emit a strangled cry in surprise, but mine is also because the food in my hands falls to the ground. The banana has broken off and rolled across the dirt and the biscuits have spilled out of their package. I'm so busy silently crying over the food that it takes me a second to look up and see my teammate, Rory, and his dad beside him.

Or the policeman who just stepped up beside me with his intimidating glare and shiny handcuffs.

"Again?" the policeman asks, as tears of humiliation burn in the back of my throat. It's one thing to be caught stealing again, it's another to be caught doing it in front of Rory and his very affluent dad, Archibald Matheson.

"I—uh—uh," I stutter. "I did no such thing. It's on the ground. You can't prove it was me."

"What seems to be the problem, Officer?" Mr. Matheson asks. As nerves course through me, I forget what he does for a living, but I've heard Rory say shit about him here and there during training. What I do know is from what I've heard—he seems to have enough influence that one word from him to the academy and I can watch all my chances vanish.

Every single one.

"This boy here"—the policeman grabs my bicep and tugs my arm, "has been caught stealing several times from shops around here." He turns to me and starts to drag me with him. "Let's go down to the station. I can't look the other way since the owner is askin' me to press charges. He's ignored your sticky fingers before and now wants to teach you a lesson." He tugs on my arm again. "C'mon. You know the drill."

"No." The word is a strangled cry filled with panic. "I can't go. It's the last week of tryouts. If I go, I won't be able to train. I won't be able to—"

"He did nothing wrong, Constable," Mr. Matheson says in that baritone of his that has both the policeman and me whipping our heads to look at him. Mr. Matheson puts his hands on his son's shoulders and pushes him forward. "It was my son, Rory, who did it."

I think the look on Rory's face mirrors mine—shock, disbelief, confusion—but mine also holds something else, hesitation.

Why would Mr. Matheson do this? Why would he offer up his son to take my place? Why would a rich man step in for a nobody like me?

"Sir," the policeman says as he pulls me back to where the biscuits and banana litter the ground, "you and me both know your son didn't do this."

Mr. Matheson's chuckle is long and low. "But I do know." He takes a step forward as Rory stares at him, doe-eyed and confused. "I can see how it'd be easy to mistake the two of them for each other. Why, with the same training gear on, same hair and height, anyone could do it, but I assure you it was my Rory here. In fact, I was just lecturing him myself. I was telling him that actions have consequences and lo and behold, you came along to reinforce just that."

The policeman looks from Mr. Matheson to me and then back again as his grip loosens ever so slightly on my bicep.

"But, Dad—"

"Nonsense, Rory. You and I both know it's not fair for Rush to take the blame for your mistakes." He pushes him forward some more. "Now go on. Go deal with the consequences of your actions. Go with the constable."

"But what about the school trip I'm supposed to leave on? What about—"

"Nonsense. We Mathesons take responsibility for our mistakes."

I watch the exchange, feeling like I'm not a part of the situation, but rather a balloon floating around its edges. Nothing of this makes sense to me and yet, even at the age of fifteen, I know I'll never forget this moment as long as I live.

Partially because it feels like it's the first act of kindness shown my way in so long that I struggle with how to accept it. And if I do accept it, that means I have to remain quiet and let Rory take the fall for my crime.

A boy that will be on my team if I get the scholarship.

My eyes dart to the food on the ground again as my internal struggle rages over how I can casually pick it up and salvage it before the rest of it is ruined. With a sigh of resignation, the officer releases my arm, takes a step forward closer to Mr. Matheson, and lowers his voice. "It's quite all right. We can keep this between the four of us. Why don't you just go on about your way like this never happened and—"

"Why the difference, Constable? Shouldn't both boys be held to the same set of laws and standards?"

"But, sir."

"Constable, it's *Inspector* Matheson," he says and reaches his hand out as both the policeman's and my lips fall lax.

Inspector?

I stare at him again with eyes wide. Why is he doing this?

"Go on," he continued, giving them a shooing motion. "I'll be by the station shortly to sort everything out."

Rory gives his dad one last desperate, pleading look before turning and following the policeman, his shoulders slumped, his feet shuffling.

"So, Mr. Rush McKenzie," Inspector Matheson says, as I look over my shoulder to where Rory had been before moving back to his imposing dad. "You from around here?"

I shake my head. "We've moved around a lot." It's the half-truth, because when my mom was alive, we did move a lot. Promises to live with distant family members had them buying us train tickets, taking us from one side of England to another more than once. This just happened to be the place we took root in the few years before she became sick and died. The place she promised we'd live so I could be closer to my dream. "But I'm here for good now."

"I see." He studies me in the most intense way. "You've got quite the talent on the pitch, son. I've heard your name mentioned in the right circles. How come you've never formally played with a club before?"

Because food comes before club fees.

"Haven't had the opportunity," I lie.

"I'm sure you'll get one now. I've watched you play over the past few weeks, you know."

"Yes, sir." I eye the biscuits again as his feet move and smash another one into the ground. It takes everything I have not to protest aloud.

"You're trying out for the team? Your presence is causing quite the buzz as it should. I think you're the one to beat right now."

I swallow down the hope surging through me. "Thank you, sir."

"The coach is a good friend of mine." He starts to say something else but then stops himself. "Do I know your parents? I don't believe I've seen them around the pitch."

"No. Don't have any, sir."

"Everybody has parents," he says through a chuckle.

My smile is tight—to be polite—as I try to change the topic. "I need to be getting home, now."

"Where to? I can give you a lift. The sky's going to open up any minute now."

"I can walk," I say. He's the police. He'll kick me out or turn me in for certain.

"Nonsense. Let me take you."

"You've done more than enough already, sir." This time when I meet his eyes, I think he really sees me. The shame. The embarrassment. The fact that I feel "less than" in so many ways. The second-hand uniforms I scrounged together from the lost property. The boots with a hole in their side and with studs worn down to nothing.

The opening and then closing of his mouth tells me he understands more than I'll ever admit to and that maybe, just maybe, he gave me a lifeline he never knew he was giving just now. When he threw his son under the bus for whatever reason he had to protect me.

"Okay then." He blows out a breath and nods. "I'll leave you be, but I'm not going to allow you to walk home in the rain that's about to come down. The last thing we need is those talented feet of yours off the pitch because you've gotten sick." He reaches into his back pocket, pulls out his wallet, and stuffs some notes into my hand without looking at them. "For the cab ride, then."

"Sir. I can't—" I fumble with the words and the money. "*Why?*"

His dark brown eyes hold mine as lines etch the sternness in his face. There's enough in his sigh to tell me he's disappointed in Rory, and it makes me more uncomfortable than not. I don't have to explain any more for him to know what I'm asking.

"Do you know what it's like to have a son who thinks he can do what he wants because of my position? To do things and then get away with them because others are upholding some unspoken code? Humility is a good thing, Rush, and Rory needed some of it." He looks down to where the toe of his Oxfords crushes another biscuit before meeting my eyes again. "And because you never know when you might need a favor in return." He offers me a smile after saying words I don't understand. "See you on the pitch tomorrow, son."

Son.

It's a word I don't think any male has called me before and it stops me in my tracks. It makes me feel cared for. And before I can say something stupid, Inspector Matheson walks the opposite way without a backward glance to where I stand.

It's only then that I notice he gave me so much more than a cab ride home. He gave me enough money to have food for a few weeks.

I open my mouth to call after him, to say thank you, anything, but he's nowhere to be found. I stand on the street corner staring at the notes. Inspector Matheson just unknowingly gave me the single greatest gift anyone has ever given me.

Time.

I'm not the smartest kid in the world, but I know where I'd have ended up if the policeman had taken me in.

Foster care. Or with relatives who live on the other side of the country and away from the dreams I'm so close to achieving.

"*Your presence is causing quite the buzz as it should. I think you're the one to beat right now.*"

I gave up praying years ago, but I pray anyway.

God, help me get that scholarship. Help me use what Rory's dad gave me to make it. Please let those dreams come true.

Chapter
NINE

Rush

I'M ON EDGE.

My life is about to take a drastic turn, and I'm scared to fucking death that once it does, it'll take me one step further away from everything I know. And that I'll never be able to find my way back.

I exhale a loud sigh as my agent drones on in my damn ear. "I've got to be honest, mate. You lost me about two minutes ago. All I need to know is if you've heard anything from management yet." I stand at the edge of Johnny's backyard and take in the view below me. Once you look past overpriced houses stacked upon overpriced houses, the valley and its greenery-hiding glass and concrete falls away to the city beyond.

The rising sun at my back reflects off the skyscrapers in the distance and beyond that is a sparkling blue strip of the Pacific.

If it's so bloody gorgeous, then why am I missing the gloomy skies and dark pubs from home so much? It's only been two weeks.

Because you miss the pitch. The stadium rising around you as you train. The history that you're now a part of and afraid to lose.

Being here I feel disconnected . . . like it's all slipping through my fingers and I can't do anything about it.

But I'm trying to be patient, to listen to Finn, to do exactly what is being asked of me.

"Have you gone online? Looked at the papers from back home? I mean, I get you're ignoring your publicist right now—she's told me that much—but you know better than anyone that this is a total shitshow and shitshows take time to blow over," Finn says. "If it does blow over."

I roll my shoulders at the last comment and pinch the bridge of my nose.

Did I fuck up by doing this? Did I ruin everything I've worked for? Should I have said screw it to loyalty and paying things back and been the arsehole I'm known for?

Isn't that ironic?

"This shit takes time, Rush. It's not every day my client causes a riot within their own team."

"And I already told you the answer is there to find if people look close enough."

"What in the fuck does that mean? I'm your agent and you're giving me this cryptic bullshit when I'm the one who's supposed to be on your side, who's supposed to be fighting for you."

Then why am I here in the States?

I ask the question to myself over and over.

"I've been placed under a gagging order not to speak about anything else."

"This is fucking bullshit, Rush, and you know it. I can only do what I can do with the information I have," he says for what feels like the millionth time. However, I still remember how he came at me upon hearing the breaking news. How he shouted and yelled at why couldn't I keep my dick in my pants and just play the damn game.

He assumed the worst, just like everyone else. "I'm the one on your side, who's supposed to be fighting for you." Sanderson should be the one person I don't have to prove myself to, who believes in me as a man and a player . . . and yet . . .

"I'm here, aren't I? I'm doing what you asked of me."

That seems to soothe him, as he clears his throat and reins in his temper. "I know it sucks, but lying low for a bit is your best bet right now."

"You're in contact with the club though, right? Management? I'm in the best shape of my life, mate. At peak performance. I can't risk not playing this season."

"You'll play all right, just not for—"

"No. I belong with Liverpool. It's where I want to play," I say, my tone letting him know I'll accept nothing less.

"Then maybe you shouldn't have fucked a teammate's wife."

I sigh and scrub a hand over my face in frustration. "I told you I didn't—"

"Yeah, yeah. I know. You didn't do it." He chuckles and it grates on every one of my nerves. Its sound says *I don't believe you*. It says I hear what you're saying but it's total shit. "Besides, it doesn't matter if you did or didn't, it only matters what the public thinks and unless you can prove otherwise, then you're guilty as sin."

"This is so fucked."

"It is, but that's why you're in Los Angeles. That's why we're going to keep your face visible, show you're doing good for the sport, and then we'll get them back to the negotiating table and see what we can do. Trust me on this."

"I do . . . but this is *my* life."

"And it will continue to be, it'll just take time for the ashes to cool off."

"Okay."

"Call me later and tell me how everything goes today. I promise it won't be as miserable as you think it will be. It's a paycheck—"

"I have more bloody money than I could ever spend, Finn. I don't need a paycheck unless it's from Liverpool."

"*Or the like*," he adds again, then goes silent as his words settle on the line and hit me harder than expected.

I've played with LFC my entire career. Starting with that damn scholarship when I was fifteen, I worked my way through the ranks, until I got to where I am today—starting center forward for LFC and next year's captain.

If there is a next year.

"Playing elsewhere isn't an option."

"It might have to be." He sighs and I hate the sound of it, because I always know something more is coming. "You being here is a public but not public way to show that you're not hiding. It comes off like you're here in the US for a job rather than the truth—that you're trying to ignore everything till it dies down. It's passive-aggressive in a sense, but says you're not afraid to show your face and that you have nothing to be ashamed of."

"I'm just on edge."

"I know, but you can practice anywhere. You don't have to be back home to stay fit."

But I need to be back home to live my life.

We finish the conversation and when I hang up, I don't feel any better about the current situation. It doesn't help that when I go to close out the apps on my phone, the image sitting front and center on Instagram is his, the reason I'm in this current predicament.

It sours my mood even more.

I start to head back into the house when I see her—Lennox—the woman I haven't been able to shake from my mind since the pool yesterday and the bathroom last night. She's standing in the kitchen with a tea towel balled up in her hand, laughing at something Johnny said.

What's her story? What's *their* story? Obviously, they're close because one doesn't just pick up the phone and ask to stay somewhere if they're not.

Are they exes? Do they like each other but are dancing around the notion of it? Or are they just what they seem? Good friends.

But there's the flirting—like what I'm watching now and what I observed when they were on the patio last night—that muddies the water.

The pang of jealousy is quick but fleeting, because it doesn't matter what they are or what they aren't. I know the way she looked at me last night, and I know interest when I see it.

And she was interested.

It takes a lot more than that to impress me.

I call bullshit on her comment.

The attraction was mutual. The need was there and ready to be tested.

As I watch her slide her ass onto the kitchen counter and swing her legs over its edge as she listens to something Johnny says, I run a hand over my jaw, thinking of the look in her eyes last night—confidence and want. I think of her perfume—light and flowery. I remember the goosebumps that chased over her arms when we were inches apart.

Sure, she was sassy and sarcastic, but damn it to hell, all of that mixed together was a heady mixture that begged me to test the waters.

It took everything I had not to kiss her last night.

It was even harder not to knock on her bedroom door and ask if the lacy pair of barely-there knickers that she "accidentally" dropped in the bathroom are part of her normal attire, because if they are . . . damn.

But there was something that stopped me from doing it. And now that I stand here and watch her through the glass—her blonde hair falling down her back, her tan legs swinging, her full lips smiling wide—that something just became so much clearer.

I want her too.

I'm in a world that feels so out of control. My every movement is calculated, planned by someone else, and the consequences of every action determined before I even act.

Public perception managed.

Does anyone know how hard that is for someone like me who's fine at following the instructions every coach and manager football has thrown at me, but living my life outside of football? That's been mine and mine alone. Do they realize every part of me wants to rebel against this order?

But then there's her—Lennox. A rival agent to my own. A bad decision. A complication I shouldn't risk.

An itch I suddenly have.

Shit.

I chuckle. What is it they say about itches? They need to be scratched.

Since when do I care about perception or what's deemed right?

Isn't that partially what got me into this mess?

Isn't that why I know I shouldn't touch her?

Then again, she looks like a woman you can have uncomplicated sex with. Who can deal with two people crossing paths without ongoing expectations.

So maybe, good sex with a gorgeous woman won't hurt anyone at all.

Chapter TEN

Lennox

"So it's signed," I say as I push the employment contract across the desk toward Cannon and his slight smirk. "Now are you going to tell me what more I've just agreed to? I assure you I read the fine print and noticed its mention of two main goals, yet you seem to have only mentioned one."

"Don't sound so enthusiastic. This isn't a prison sentence, Lennox." He chuckles as he taps the papers on the table to square their edges before setting them to the side.

But his comment hits home. There are job duties with vague descriptions that he's simply explained away as legalese that's not pertinent to me specifically.

And yet, the longer he sits across from me with that *cat ate the canary* grin, the more I think I may have just made a mistake.

I force a swallow. "Cannon?" I prompt. "Details."

"A woman who's assertive. I like that."

I ignore the comment and the flirty wink he gives after it, covering it with a tight smile. "It's necessary in my line of work. The contract states I have to make players happy, win them over. I took the bait and signed, now you do your job and give me details. That's how this is going to work." I add on a saccharine-sweet smile to the end of my words.

He grunts crudely and I internally cringe, thinking of Dekker's warning about his reputation.

"Your job is to make players happy. The first part of that is what we talked about—contracts, benefits, determining what they're looking for.

The second part is that I want you to make one player in particular especially happy so he decides to leave his current club and come play for the MLS."

And the other shoe drops.

"I'm not following you." I huff out a sigh because clearly I am following him, but choose to play dumb so he's forced to spell it out for me. It's never wise to assume.

"That comment alone tells me you are."

I lift my eyebrows in response, my mind immediately homing in on the especially happy bit of his comment. Maybe after coming off Finn's bullshit the other night, I'm sensitive to any implication that I use sex or my looks to win over clients, but I swear to God, that's what Cannon is implying. "I'm afraid to ask what you're asking of me."

"I want you to recruit a player for us."

"Just one?" I ask as he nods.

"We'll get to that." He leans back in his chair and studies me for a beat. "I want you to use all of your skills, persuasion, and knowledge to convince said player that moving to our league is a decision worth considering."

"So I'm posing as an MLS ambassador under the guise of being a player advocate, but what you're telling me is that's all a ruse because this player and getting him to commit to the MLS is the real end goal."

His smile widens almost as if he's proud of me for reading between his unspoken lines. "Yes." Unabashed. Definitive.

"That's . . . shady. A fox in the hen house kind of shady."

He snorts in dismissal. "I like to think of it as being proactive and a tad aggressive. You'll still be carving your niche with the first task, but the second one, this player? He'll be your added bonus."

"Why not just go through his agent? Wouldn't that be simpler than paying me to negotiate with his agent?"

"I don't want you speaking to his agent at all. Any and all conversations will be strictly between you and the athlete."

"Does he know this is the endgame that you have in mind for him?" I ask.

"Not at this time . . . no."

"So is it my job to tell him outright or is it more, 'rah, rah, go MLS' all the time until he sees how great the league is and never wants to leave?"

His laughter echoes through the room. "The latter."

"Again, this would be easier if you just went straight to this agent. Cut out the middle man," I explain.

"His agent doesn't have the pull and influence that you do." He clasps his hands in front of him and leans forward. "I've done my research on you, Lennox. You're persuasive, firm when you need to be, but likable too. You don't take no for an answer."

I open my mouth and shut it, ignoring his praise as I run every scenario through my mind. There are so many ways this could go wrong.

"So, you're paying me to circumvent his agent and lure an athlete away from his existing team." That would piss me off if someone did that to me. But . . . at the end of the day, the agent still gets paid.

Unless of course, he wants me to steal the client as well.

"Don't get all ethical on me. You agents do it every day when you trade players, so don't get all high and mighty on me now." He gives a sharp nod. "Think of it more as I'm paying you to influence a player to play here."

"Smoke and mirrors."

"Your words, not mine," he says.

"For clarification's sake, when it comes down to it, obviously after the end of the "ambassador" deal, which clearly is a ruse to help sell him on the league, you make a contract offer to him. I'm the one wooing and selling him, so how is that fair that you'll then give the offer to his agent? That agent will present it to his client and then make a commission on it, when I'm the one who has done all the work. Don't you think that's convoluted—"

"Then steal him for yourself." He lifts a brow as I startle. "That solves everything, right? And wouldn't that be a nice, shiny feather in your cap? You took this job when I know for a fact your father told you not to take it."

"No, he didn't."

"I talked to him last week, Lennox," he says and it does nothing more than reinforce the puppet strings I felt controlled by yesterday. "I know he wasn't thrilled with the offer. Bright side? You went against his wishes, took the job, and when you steal this new client, look what you win in the process? A shiny, new star athlete any agency would kill to have on their client list."

I rise from my chair and walk toward the windows looking out to the offices beyond. He has a point. A huge point.

"You get a huge win for you and KSM"—why the shady sales pitch when I've already signed the contract?—"and then get a little victory in the process."

"What do you mean by that? A little victory in the process?"

"Finn Sanderson is his agent," he deadpans. "Do you know him?"

Son of a bitch.

And the hits just keep on coming.

I try to mask my surprise. There are so many pieces to this puzzle right now that I'm having a hard time lining some of them up, but damn, I should have known.

"Of course, I know him." I clear my throat. "In fact, he was at the conference in Vegas too," I say as my mind mulls over the notion that Finn teased me about taking this job. A job where it would put me shoulder to shoulder with his client.

I rack my brain, running through Finn's clients, but his list is longer than KSM's and there's no way in the midst of this conversation that I can concentrate to do it.

Something doesn't sit right with me.

"And?"

"We'll just say he's not my most favorite person."

"Good. Then it seems you won't be worried about the ethicality of stealing his client out from underneath him."

Does he know about the other night? About Finn and his bullshit? Why would he think I'd feel victorious?

Cannon smirks. I'm not sure if this is a pretend or real deal. "Finn Sanderson is an all-around prick. I've dealt with him, and everyone I know who's dealt with him hates him too for his shady tactics." *The irony.*

I twist my lips and stare at Cannon as I weigh the pros and cons of this. Score a big win for KSM. Redeem myself in my family's eyes. Screw over Finn.

Cons?

And just as I start to go over them, something catches in my mind.

"You said earlier, he—*the athlete*—would be my added bonus. What did you mean by that?"

"His signing a contract to stay is the only way you earn one hundred percent of that bonus you agreed to."

"Wait, what?" I chuckle to cover my surprise. Now he's playing hardball. "I can't control what someone does or doesn't do."

"Sure you can." He grins. "You do it every day."

Our gazes hold and challenge each other's almost as if he's daring me to back out now. And while this whole thing might seem underhanded, there's a challenge to it. An allure for me. If I win something hard-fought and well-earned all while redeeming myself in the eyes of my family . . . how could I say no?

"Who?" It's a single word, but it's enough to tell Cannon Garner that I'm not backing out.

His grin widens. "*Rush McKenzie.* You've heard of him?"

I stare at Cannon, blinking several times as I internally swear at myself.

My brain should have connected the dots.

It should have said: Rush Mackenzie is here in the United States, the MLS is wanting me to win over a star player, and therefore two plus two equals four.

I should have connected the dots.

But I didn't.

I was too goddamn busy being mesmerized by every damn thing Rush was when I should have been thinking like an agent instead of thinking like a woman who wanted him to kiss me.

Because I did.

I'd be stupid to say otherwise.

I even dreamt of his strong hands running up my torso and then over my arms to frame the sides of my face. Of his lips so full and freaking perfect pressing against mine where they were gentle at first before turning demanding.

As I lay in bed last night, I admitted to myself that I wanted him and had every intention of acting on it.

Funny how fate just stepped in the way and told me I couldn't. No way in hell could I after Finn's accusations.

Either that or she's testing to see just how much restraint I have.

"Surely you have, haven't you?" Cannon asks, and I give a quick shake of my head to pull myself back to the here and now.

"Have what?"

"Heard of Rush McKenzie."

I almost choke on my next breath of air.

Great. Perfect. Should I dare to mention how last night I'd vowed to have sex with the man? I mean, wouldn't that complicate things?

"Of course, I have." I swallow over the sudden disbelief. "Premier League. The star Liverpool is hanging their hat on to win future championships. Kicked that tremendous goal in the World Cup match last year between England and France. And is currently embroiled in a scandal in the UK."

"No press is bad press, right?"

"Are you telling me that Rush McKenzie is the man you've hired to be the face of the MLS? The one you're centering this campaign around? *The ambassador?*"

"He's charismatic and an incredible player. A man who guys want to be like and women want to be with. He's a marketing team's dream."

First of all, why would Rush ever agree to something like this? From an agent's perspective, it's a poor decision.

Second, landing him as a client would be a huge boost for Kincade Sports Management.

Third, seriously? I finally decide that I'm willing to break my sex drought with someone, have some fun, and he's now the someone I have to recruit? I can't accomplish my second point without forcing myself to abandon my third point.

But it's okay.

I can do this.

I can do my job and recruit Rush, because the long-term professional outcomes will outweigh the short-term satisfaction I'd most likely find with him.

At least that's what I tell myself as I attempt to abandon my overthinking and focus on Cannon and this clusterfuck.

"Why would Rush ever agree to this?" And of course, the comment comes out with a bit too much snark so I try to correct it. "I mean—"

"Look at it from my standpoint, Lennox. While many people in the US don't follow MLS, some do follow the Premier League. Rush is a well-known name. His presence spans from product endorsements to *People's* sexiest man candidate to future Hall of Famer. Add to that, his club is currently questioning renewing his contract. There's pressure for them not to, from what I understand."

I emit an unladylike snort. "Since when does a football club give up its strongest player due to pressure? The British love their controversy, so why give up the one thing that might attract more crowds . . . as if they need to worry about that at all?"

"Look, I'm in agreement. One hundred percent. But you can't fault a guy like me for seeing an opportunity and seizing it."

"So is this what you mean about knowing Finn?" I ask the one question I was trying to figure an answer to. "Obviously you brokered this deal with him to get Rush here for the short while."

"Yes. I'm not a fan," he says as I slowly nod. "Wouldn't it be great if I could swoop in and grab him to play for the MLS? Pay him more than he could ever dream of, secure him a place to play—when he'd most likely have to retire over there—all while having him stay stateside. He could promote the league at the same time he's dominating it. It would be a win-win for both of us."

And it would be the end of his illustrious career.

"The US pays nothing compared to what other leagues pay. I mean, surely you're aware that players play for the MLS with the hopes of someday getting picked up for the Premier League and not the other way around, right?" I ask.

The look he levels me with says I've insulted him and his knowledge. "I'm aware, but I'm also a manager who's trying to do his job." There's a sharp bite to his tone that reaffirms I'm now his employee, and I need to keep my opinions limited.

"Noted," I say with a definitive nod while silently shaking it in disbelief.

I get it. I really do. In fact, I don't even fault him for trying, but he's reaching for the stars when he should be reaching for something a little closer to earth.

"Look, I get what you're saying and appreciate the outside opinion. His contract is for the next three months. After that, we'll go from there."

What Cannon isn't saying is that he hopes Rush isn't picked back up again so he has no choice but to stay here and play.

What type of agent would ever recommend this to their client?

I walk to the window that overlooks a practice pitch that connects to the league offices. The turf is a vibrant green and the two rows of bleacher seats that surround it are a dark red. There are a few men down on the grass going through ladder drills before sprinting to the far end to try to head across into the undefended goal.

I stare for a few seconds wondering if Rush is down there, but I don't see him. And why would he be if he's here to be the face of the MLS? Regardless, I take the time searching for him so I can piece my thoughts together.

"He's the golden ticket, Lennox."

"Nothing is ever the golden ticket, Cannon." I turn to face him, my back now to the glass and my arms crossed over my chest.

"True." He nods, but doesn't continue until his eyes find mine. "But he's here. The opportunity presented itself so I took it. You know that anyone else in my shoes would have done the same. Besides, fingers crossed, he'll get a chance to get a feel for the league, to fall in love with America, and maybe stay."

"Maybe," I murmur while silently kissing that full bonus away. However, now I'm more determined than ever to steal Rush away from Finn for the sole purpose of telling him not to fall for any of this.

And isn't that the predicament Cannon never figured into the equation? That I would think he's crazy, trying to steal one of the best players of his era from the place where he shines the brightest?

"Rush is what this whole venture hinges on."

"And when you introduce me to him, he'll have no idea about your plan or why I'm really here?"

"Other than to make him happy by 'making the league a better place for all footballers,' no. Besides, I'm sure he can come to his own conclusion that we'd want him to stay here long-term."

"That's it?" I quirk an eyebrow and wonder if he sees how many million ways his plan can backfire.

Sleep with Rush and not only screw the integrity of this recruiting and job, but also prove every damn guy that was talking shit about me right.

Don't sleep with Rush, recruit him, sign him, and give Finn exactly what he deserves.

Fate doesn't give opportunities like this that you can take advantage of very often in life.

"Seems like I have my work cut out for me."

"Shall we get started then?" Cannon asks and I nod. "Let's bring him in and get the two of you acquainted. We have a lot of work to do."

Chapter
ELEVEN

Rush

BLOODY HELL.

Seriously?

This is my reward? Lennox as my babysitter while I'm in the States?

The thought has been on repeat in my mind since walking in here and seeing her. Since hearing Cannon explain that the two of us would be working side by side, despite the original solo arrangement I signed on for.

Shocked? Yes.

Complaining about it? Fuck no.

I definitely don't mind sharing the spotlight with her, but I can't say I understand why Cannon has a sports agent on board when promoting and being an agent have nothing to do with one another. If her role is being a player's advocate, then why will she accompany me to dinners, functions, and matches?

He'll hear no complaints from me though. Not a one. Because the introduction of her just made the next three months that much more manageable.

I say more manageable, but I'm still fucking pissed about even being here. About that hand fate fucking dealt.

"You'll be heading to Los Angeles in three days. I'll find you a house for rent—something—but we need you to lie low, Rush. Stay fit. Keep your nose clean. Smile pretty as you push the MLS, and then kick serious ass when you play the exhibition games. Word will get back to LFC about how good you look."

"Los Angeles? The MLS? C'mon, Finn. Are you kidding me? That's bollocks. That will be like going back to the Liverpool reserves. Fuck that. Surely you can see how stupid that—"

"You don't get choices, Rush."

Finn was right. I don't get choices at this stage. And now, glancing at Lennox again, I take in her hair piled on top of her head in some fancy bun, the length of her neck, the blue of her eyes behind a set of black frames, and willingly accept my torture/punishment.

I must have done something right in my past life to deserve this—or this is my reward for taking the blame for everything back home. Getting to stare at her in the pinstripe power suit she has on definitely isn't a hardship, especially when I know what that banging body beneath it looks like.

The funny thing? She doesn't look the least bit happy about this.

Not at all.

"So," Cannon says as he rises from his seat at the conference room table, "I think everything you need to know is right here in your portfolios. Schedules of events, press junkets, the like. Inside you'll also find the three exhibition games you'll be playing in, Rush. A little something to whet the appetites of American fans."

"We'll have a look," Lennox says, refusing to make eye contact with me still. "And make plans."

"Perfect. Anything you need, Rush, Lennox will make sure you get it."

I don't think he wants me to take him up on that offer. She has a lot of things I need and not a one of them has to do with football.

"Okay," I say.

"Great. Good. Then I'll leave you two to go over everything." He hooks a thumb over his shoulder beyond the closed blinds on the conference room windows to the cubicles beyond. "I have a meeting I'm late for, but as you'll find in the itinerary, we'll announce your position with the team tonight at the kick-off party, Rush. Then we'll set off on a two-week press junket to get the word out."

It's still hard to drum up excitement for this, but at least there's Lennox.

"Sounds good."

We both watch as Cannon grabs his stuff and leaves the conference room. When he shuts the door behind him, bathing the room in silence, I turn to look at Lennox sitting across from me.

"We meet again," I murmur.

"I can't seem to escape you," she says shortly, standing and walking to the window to stare out at the pitch beyond.

"Is that love I feel from you right now?" I ask. "I'm kind of feeling like it is."

But she doesn't turn my way, she doesn't look or break a smile, and I'm confused as fuck over what I've done to piss her off. The woman who stared at me in the bathroom last night, with eyes begging me to kiss her, and the woman obviously pissed off are not one and the same.

"This is a horrible decision on your part, Rush. You shouldn't be here." Her voice is flat and stern, and when she turns to face me, those eyes of hers say more than I could ever fathom.

"What's that supposed to mean?"

And where does she get off judging me when she doesn't know me or the reason why I'm here?

Then again it seems that's par for the course these days.

"Nothing. I'm sorry." She sighs. "I just wasn't expecting you or this, or anything really." She gives the explanation but it takes a few seconds for her shoulders to relax and her expression to soften. Yet, I still don't buy that she's happy.

"Neither was I," I say.

We stare at each other across the space with the game that I love at her back and a future of unknown for me in between us. It's shit. I can't explain anything to her.

"Rush." She says my name as if it's an olive branch she can't quite understand why she's extending. There are so many things I can read into her tone—confusion, disappointment, question—but she shakes her head just as quickly and offers a smile for the first time. "Are we really stuck together in this?"

There's something in her eyes. Something that tells me she's on shaky ground, when I've never seen her be anything but confident.

"Stuck together?" I ask with a laugh. "Wow, the flattery."

"That's not what I mean."

There goes that stiffening of her spine again.

"Then what *do* you mean? Is there something about this pairing that I should be worried about? It's not the bathroom situation, is it? You're worried that now you've seen me naked it's going to be too hard for you to concentrate on taking work seriously? Is that it?"

"Rush." My name is part-sigh, part-exasperation, but both confuse me.

"Or is it that I know your negotiating skills leave something to be desired." She doesn't crack a smile, so I move toward her. "What's the deal, Lennox? Something about this situation is bugging you and you're not telling me."

"It's nothing." She twists her lips as she stares at me—almost as if she's caught in indecision—and she's such a shit liar that I know something is off.

"You know," I murmur, thinking humor might bridge the gap and get that smile back on those full lips of hers. "We should stop beating around the bush and just admit to what's really going on here."

"What's that?" she asks in an equally soft voice, as if there's someone else in the room listening to us.

"That you concocted this whole scenario just to get me into bed with you. I mean, I get it. I do. It's not every day you're faced with a handsome, tattooed, talented, British bloke like me."

Her sigh fills the space as she turns to face me. "Yes. That's it. That's exactly right." She throws her hands up. "Let's go right now and get it over with."

"Get it over with?" I laugh. "Because that's not a blow to my ego or anything."

"I don't think anything affects your ego."

"Guilty," I say and raise my hand giving her a sheepish grin. "But since Cannon implied your job is to make sure I'm happy, the least you can do is keep a smile on those gorgeous lips of yours."

She gives me the smile I've been working for, and my balls don't draw up in a good way at the sight of it.

"I assure you that nowhere in my contract does it say ensuring your happiness is a requirement."

"It does. I saw it." I move closer to her, unable to resist tucking that errant strand of hair that's fallen from her bun behind her ear. I hear her quick intake of breath at my touch, and know this woman will be beneath me within no time at all. And I'm not quite sure what it is about her that causes such an urgency in me to want to do so. "So what do you say? Should we sit down and make a list of all the ways you could make me happy?"

She lifts a lone eyebrow and eyes me, a smile gracing her lips. "I'm flattered. I truly am," she says in that prim yet irritable tone as she takes a step away from me, "but nothing's going to happen between us."

My chuckle fills the room as I step back from her and take a seat at the conference room table.

Something's shifted in the way she looks at me. She wants me, but she's somehow pulled away.

What the hell happened in the last twenty-four hours? And how do I get it back?

Challenge her.

Lennox Kincade is a natural-born competitor. That will get that spark back.

I grab a pen and look up at her with a devilish smirk. "Shall we get started on that list?"

Chapter
TWELVE

Lennox

I'M IN A SHITTY MOOD.

I'm standing here with a smile plastered on my face and Rush is standing beside me as Cannon puts us through the paces of his dog and pony show-announcement, but I don't feel an ounce of excitement toward any part of it.

None.

Truth be told, I regret the decision to take this job with Cannon, but hell if I'd ever admit it, because that would make my sister right about him being shady—and she's always right.

But I am the one who signed the contract without getting the particulars answered . . . so that's on me.

And it makes me grumpy and surly and hating the entire day's events.

I despise when plans are changed and buck against anyone telling me I have to do something other than what my mind has made up to do.

Like Rush.

One hundred percent, but how do I prove everyone wrong? How do I say I don't sleep with clients to get them and then turn around and sleep with the one client I've been contracted to get?

Add to it? *Fucking Rush.* The devastating smile he flashes my way through the crowd of people clamoring for him. The way he leans over when he passes by me and whispers with that knee-melting accent into my ear something to make me smile.

He's not doing me any favors.

Especially to the promise I made myself the minute he walked into the conference room earlier when Cannon "introduced" us for the first time. After that initial sucker punch of seeing him again, I told myself that I'd put my career before my own physical needs and use this opportunity with the MLS to do just that.

In many respects, being away from the family makes that a little easier. I'm not someone's sister here or someone's daughter. And I will recruit Rush away from Sanderson to KSM, gaining a new star client without my father's intervention.

I stand offstage and behind the curtain as Cannon drones on and on to the crowd, waiting for his *SportsCenter* moment, which I'm sure Cannon has calculated with precision to get the most bang for his buck.

But if he keeps talking much longer, he's going to lose his audience's attention.

"Hey there." Rush's smooth whisper hits my ears the same time everything else about him does—his cologne in my nose, his hands on my waist, the heat of his breath on my cheek.

I stiffen immediately, when all I want to do is a cross between sinking into him and turning around and kissing him senseless.

Neither is an option.

"Are you avoiding me, Kincade?"

"No. Of course not."

"I'm thinking you are. I'm thinking you're still mad at the list I made in the conference room." There's a hint of amusement in his voice and I have to fight my own urge to be playful back.

Playful is only going to end up with me in trouble.

"Your list was ridiculous."

"I beg to differ," he says as he leaves his hand on one side of my waist but moves in front of me. "Taking me to a game so I can tailgate. Teaching me what the American fascination with ice cubes is all about. A muscle car—I need to drive one. A huge pancake breakfast."

"Ridiculous. I'm not your tour guide." I chuckle and take a step back to give myself some space from him and those lips I keep glancing at.

"I could make another list for you, you know." The step he takes eats up the space I just gained. "Of what else you could do to make me an even happier man . . . but that one doesn't need to be put on paper." He taps his temple. "That one is memorized right here."

There's arrogance in his voice and seduction in his eyes, and hell if this little alcove just didn't become ten times smaller.

I swear my swallow is so loud it's the only thing I can hear over the pounding of my pulse in my ears, but I hold tight to my resolve.

"Rush. I can't. We can't. It's not professional of me—"

He squeezes the side of my waist, and my body heats beneath his touch as he leans in and whispers so his breath tickles my ear. "I love the prim and proper thing you have going on right now. The pencil skirt, the high heels, and those square shoulders. I really do. In fact, I'm not sure if I love this look or the one from the other night where you were staring at me and all but begging me to kiss you more. But—"

"I was not." *I was too.* "Please. You think too much of yourself."

His low rumble of a chuckle is a temptation all in itself. "You keep telling yourself that, Lennox, but we both know the truth." He runs his hand down my body so it rests on my hip, a soft groan coming from the back of his throat that would sound crass from any other man but from him sounds like seduction. "Today, you're closed up tight, like you're so bloody afraid to give in to what you want. And what you want is me."

"You're—"

When Rush's lips meet mine, I tell myself this is crazy. He's kissing me when he has to be on stage any minute. If someone sees us, my professionalism would be shot to hell.

I mentally fight him off, while I part my lips to touch my tongue to his. My body reacts before my head can process otherwise.

There's always something in a first kiss. The first hint if you fit together. The initial inkling whether his style of kissing is one that makes your stomach flutter, your core ache, and causes your hands to fist in his shirt. That immediate knowledge that you want to do this again or that you need to walk away and never look back.

The problem is when the kiss—every soft and demanding moment of it—ends, I'm staring straight into those amused eyes of his and know this will be harder than I thought. There is undeniable chemistry here. But . . . I need to be strong. Resistant. In control.

I can try. Damn it to hell, I'm going to try, but he's like the most potent of drugs—addictive at the first hit.

"We can work together, Lennox," he says, his accent hitting the last syllable higher, "and still sleep together."

"No one said I was sleeping with you." The words sound hollow rolling off lips that crave another kiss.

His smile is crooked, and the short laugh he emits is arrogance and desire personified. "You didn't have to."

And in perfect timing, Cannon announces Rush to the waiting cameras and public.

It's only when he climbs the stairs and walks away that I exhale—and I didn't even know I was holding my breath.

He swaggers onto the stage to the roar of the crowd, which Cannon had drummed up, and he takes the mic, his voice permeating my every thought as I try to tell myself to forget about the kiss.

To forgo messing up this professional opportunity by acting on what I want with him.

So many people say women are weak for giving in when a man kisses her. They say we're weak when our knees tremble and when we fall under his "spell." I say screw that. I say, we're strong. That we're getting what we want one way or another. It can be by his taking or our owning it. There's a strength to it. A timeless and resolute beauty to it.

We're told we're bitches if we're too aggressive, and then we're told we're feeble and weak-minded if we fall too quickly. Or better yet, we're sluts if we crave the touch of a man. If we want to and like to have sex.

If we like to be made to feel good.

Well, I'm all of the above. I'm strong to a fault, I'm weak at times and will gladly own it, and hell if it doesn't feel awesome to tumble into bed with someone who gives as good as they get. From the first moment I laid eyes on Rush, I knew we'd end up a tangled mass of limbs and sheets.

The predatory look in his eyes, the gravelly grit that roughens up his delicious brogue—and the way my body reacts viscerally to everything about him—tells me that we're destined to explore our attraction.

In those few seconds standing beside the pool, I think I accepted it in my mind.

I chuckle because there's no denying it: we'll have sex. It will complicate matters, his brash arrogance will still irritate the hell out of me when all is said and done and ended, but damn, I'll be satisfied.

And right now, I'm okay with that. I can still be a professional agent, I can be a sexually charged woman, and I can feel proud of myself for both.

"Lennox?"

I'm startled from my thoughts, and make the most ridiculous sound when I look up to see Cannon looking at me from the stage, hand outstretched.

"C'mon," he says. "I'd like to introduce you to the public as part of the team."

"That's not necessary. Really. I don't mind being in the shadows."

Then again, maybe I should take his hand and be forced to stand under the spotlight. Maybe the public eye seeing Rush and me together would act as a deterrent for what is destined to happen next. Maybe knowing that Cannon, Finn, other clients, and my family are able to see the two of us together publicly, will prevent me from wanting to cross that professional line into personal.

What a mess.

Or not.

Who knew we'd end up meeting, working together? Who knew he'd become the litmus test on whether I succeed or not in my newly acquired goals?

While I'm back here concerned about public perception, Rush doesn't care what the public thinks of him.

Maybe I should take a lesson from him.

Maybe as long as I'm happy, that's all that should matter.

Chapter
THIRTEEN

Lennox

"THAT WAS AN INTERESTING PLOT TWIST," JOHNNY murmurs as he walks into the family room where I'm flopped on the couch in the most unladylike fashion with my heels discarded on the floor beside me. He sets a bottle of wine and a glass down beside me on the table. "Care to share?"

Eyeing him, I wait to see what other snarky comment he's going to make and when none comes, I shrug. "Apparently, we're both here for the same reason and didn't know it."

"I'm going to trust you on this but it's not adding up why an agent is in the mix."

"It's a long story."

"I'm sure it is." He glances at the screen of his phone. "In the meantime, I have Heidi waiting to be picked up and an eight o'clock reservation to get to."

"Heidi?" I ask.

"Flavor of the month." He laughs as he grabs his keys while I smile indulgently. Johnny is a good man, but such a player. I've had a front-row seat to the hearts he's broken over the years, even consoled a few of them in our college days, but that's just him. "One of these days, I just might find one I'm okay tasting for longer, but in the meantime, I'm taking full advantage of being obscenely rich and incredibly handsome."

"How about annoyingly arrogant too?"

"That too."

"You know the unbuttoned shirt thing went out in the seventies," I say as I eye the five inches of chest peeping out of this shirt.

My cell rings and when I look at the screen, my face must give away how startled I am when I see Finn Sanderson as the caller.

"Later," Johnny mouths as he kisses me on the top of my head before he moves toward the door.

"If you're calling me to apologize for being a dick, you can save your breath," I say by way of greeting when I answer.

He chuckles. "You really do love to play that whole woman scorned to the hilt, don't you?"

"Probably just as much as you like to play the dejected asshole thing." By now, curiosity has me sitting up, pouring myself a glass of wine because if Finn's calling me, I know I'm going to need it.

"You figured it out yet? My secret?" he says with a chuckle that grates over my skin.

"Secret?" I ask, taking the bait.

"Rumor is you couldn't wait to get to Los Angeles to grovel to Cannon and take his offer with the MLS only to find out it no longer existed. Oops. That must have been mortifying for someone like you."

"What are you talking . . ."

The guy at the airport. The one standing at the other ticket counter when I changed my flight. Finn knows because of him, and yet, the position no longer exists? What is he talking about?

"Look, don't be too mad. It was just a little underhanded tactic between agents—you know, like with Maddox last year."

"What does Hunter have to do with any of this?" I ask. Finn has totally lost the ball here. What the hell?

"This is about beating you at your own tactics. Decided I'd go after those potential clients you so beautifully described in your binder." His amused sigh ticks me off. "Names, phone numbers, emails, likes, dislikes . . . you keep great records but honestly, Lenn, you really should keep shit like that in a passcoded phone, not sitting in a binder for anyone to see in a conference full of hungry agents." He tsks. "Rookie mistake, Kincade, but then again, we shouldn't expect anything less of you, should we?"

How the hell did he get those details?

"You bastard," I grit between clenched teeth as I cringe at my own stupidity. But I'd been in a conference on sports ethics, *the irony*, when the phone call came, and I'd run out to the hallway to jot notes down on the players with the intention of entering them in my database when I got back to my hotel room. They were still in the folder. *So . . . he took a photo? This man is a complete and utter prick. What in the hell did Chase ever see in him?*

My eyes burn with frustration and anger I haven't felt in forever. Why is he telling me this? We're not in public, so there's no advantage to him. And yet . . . he's gloating.

"All's fair in love and representation, right?" he brags. "Those potential clients have been met with and wined and dined after you only met briefly with them because you thought you had bigger fish to fry. To think you've been made the laughing stock again. Only this time, in the City of Angels."

"What in the hell are you talking about?" I ask.

"The job with the MLS? The press conference today announcing Rush McKenzie? Cannon and I negotiated the deal last week for Rush to come on board. Part of those negotiations entailed explaining to Cannon why your services weren't needed there. I assure you, it wasn't anything personal."

I think I stare at my wine glass blinking several times as I try to process what he's saying. I don't even remember when I rose to my feet and walked toward the window to stare aimlessly at the view of the valley.

I don't see it though. No, I'm preoccupied, realizing how thoroughly gullible I was. *Had he made it a point to say all those fucking awful lies about me assuming I'd hear him? He wrecked my confidence and knew me well enough that he knew I'd call Cannon. That I'd ask for the job I'd turned down so that I could save face. And how I played right into every part of it.*

Oh, my God.

"Humiliation comes in all forms and ways, Lennox, and I guess you just got a clean dose of it." He chuckles. All I hear is condescension. "Hope Cannon was at least nice when you showed up. No doubt you were completely humiliated when he told you that your services were no longer needed." Does he not know I've been contracted for the position? "Did you finally understand there was only one reason he'd targeted you specifically for the position? You know, because he was interested in your other services?"

My stomach rolls at his insinuation. Again.

"You didn't put it together did you? Poor baby. I'd like to say I'm sorry, but I don't feel bad about it at all. Karma is in fact a bitch, and we both know which side of those two options you seem to fall into."

"You set me up." My first words are a whisper as the magnitude of everything hits me. The men standing directly in front of the exit. Finn's voice set to loud to ensure what he said was broadcast . . . just as I was trying to leave the conference room. Holy fuck. "You. Set. Me. Up."

"See? I knew it would take a few seconds for you to understand . . . and now that you have, I'm sure you'll be able to accept my *insincerest* apologies."

"You fucking bastard. You low-lying piece of shit. You—"

Oh my God.

He has no idea. He's so goddamn arrogant that he has no idea Cannon gave me the job, despite Finn's advice. All because I didn't go on stage tonight for the media circus. This is gold.

A slow smile crawls over my lips as I toy with what to say.

"Lennox? You still there? Please, continue. I'd love to hear what else it is you have to say."

"Hey Finn?"

"Mmm?"

"What was it you said about karma?"

"That it was a bitch."

"Remember that," I say and pause for a dramatic beat. "Cannon gave you lip service." I laugh. "Oh, did you not see me in the wings tonight, right behind the stage? Oops." I pause. God, I wish I could see his face. "Enjoy your newbies with low salaries, Finn, while I absolutely enjoy dining and schmoozing one of the highest paid footballers out there. You know, *your client*, Rush." His quick intake of air tells me I've made a direct hit. Perfect.

"You wouldn't dare." His threat is as empty as his voice is hollow.

"What did you say? All's fair in love and representation?" I chuckle at his silence. "Finn? This is about the time you hope all the shit you've said about how I persuade clients my way isn't true. Because if it is, you don't stand a chance holding on to Rush."

I end the call without warning, just as a litany of curses explode from the other end of the line.

Chapter
FOURTEEN

Rush

3 Weeks ago

"CHRIST." I SIT UP IN BED, LEGS HANGING OVER THE SIDE AS I SCRUB MY face and startle at the caller's name on my phone. Shit.

Rory.

He's the closest thing I've ever had to a little brother—the good and the bad parts of it.

Was moved back up to my team again—a reserve player.

Has finally been keeping his head down and nose clear . . . rather than let the drugs and partying win.

It's split seconds I have to hold those thoughts. Split seconds where the history between us runs through my head to remind me of the bond formed that day. A bond that changed my life.

"What's wrong?"

"Sorry to wake you, son," Archibald Matheson says.

"Is it Rory?"

His laugh sounds like pure exhaustion. "When isn't it?" But it tells me that it's nothing urgent and I breathe a little easier.

"What is it?"

"There are most likely going to be press camped out in front of your place when you look outside," he warns, and I rise immediately from the bed to take a look out the window. Sure as shit, they're there.

"Why?"

"Now that's a little more complicated."

"What did Rory do?" There's silence. "Archibald?"

"He's been seeing someone he shouldn't be. She's not in a very good marriage, unhappy with a husband who isn't exactly the nicest of men."

"Okay." I draw the word out as I pull on the back of my neck before looking back out the window to the trucks and cameras waiting for me to leave for my early morning training sessions.

"She's why Rory has straightened up his act. He's stopped the . . . *bullshit*," he says, his term for the drugs he pretends his son doesn't indulge in. The drugs that make a mockery of the law he'd been sworn to uphold. The laws made by the Parliament he's hoping to become an elected member of. "And he's focused on his fitness, his game, and the rest of his shortcomings. He's really turned everything around—"

"He has—"

"And it's all because of her, this woman. She's turned everything around for him."

"I don't see why—"

"This isn't the best time for there to be a scandal attached to the Matheson name, Rush. As you know, I'm standing for Parliament and it's a tight margin between me and the other candidate, so I could really use your help."

"Rory cheated with a married woman. Why would that reflect ill on you?" I ask, as my phone begins to start buzzing in my hand. Or maybe it already has been, but I've been so caught up in the conversation that I didn't realize it.

"I hate to even ask this of you."

"Ask me what?" I demand. "I'll help, any way I can, but I'm not sure what it is that I can do," I say, trying to make sense of what he thinks the problem is.

"There's a picture of them kissing on a balcony. It's all over the bloody place. Every newsstand, social media, the like."

"I'm sure you have a whole team at your disposal who can assist you in how to spin this."

"Yes, I do."

"But you're calling me."

"They think it's you."

The dread that has been creeping up my spine slams into me. "Me?" I laugh the word out, thinking this joke is anything but funny. "Funny."

"Rush . . ." His sustained silence owns my attention.

"Wait. You're serious. Are they bloody crazy?"

"Turn on your telly. Your computer. Your . . ." Before he can even finish, I have my iPad in hand and am staring at the grainy image taken from afar, trying to comprehend what I'm looking at.

"That's—she looks like—"

"Esme," he murmurs.

"Oh. Shit." The full weight of what Rory has done is out there and what Archibald's asking me to do hits me.

Esme.

Chart-topping singer who only needs one name to be known.

She's wildly famous and married to Seth Haskins.

My teammate and Liverpool's captain.

"That's not me," I whisper to no one in particular, almost as if I have to talk my own self out of believing it, because it looks like me.

Or rather it looks like Rory.

"I need to cash in that IOU, Rush."

"You're what?" Surely he's not—

"We've done nothing but help you ever since that day. We invited you into our home and treated you like a second son. We gave you everything you needed to set you up for success. You know I was well aware you were guilty that day. Not Rory. But this time, well, this time you take the rap for Rory."

"Sir—" And then it hits me. I know what he's asking, and my head shakes, rejecting any and every notion.

I was fifteen fucking years old, completely alone in the world, and this arse is holding a few desperate acts of a homeless kid over me . . . for his son.

No, for himself ultimately.

"If I hadn't let that officer take Rory that day, you would have missed out on that scholarship. Missed your chance. Missed *this* life."

My throat starts tightening up. He can't be serious. He cannot be fucking serious. Surely Esme will do the right thing and not pretend it was me with her. She knows I'd never touch a married woman. "But—"

"Your reputation can handle this, Rush. You can weather this storm because you're Rush fucking McKenzie—a footballer at the pinnacle of his game. Rory can't. He's been on the bubble for so very long between staying on the team or being cut. Something like this gets out? He'll be cut in an instant to protect Seth. But you, you'll probably be captain next year. Teams always forgive the antics of stars because they're afraid to lose them."

"I'm trying to process this, sir. Consenting to an affair is very different from a starving kid stealing food out of desperation."

"You're the rebel they expect this from. The man who brawls in pubs and changes women like you do your socks and doesn't give a fuck who sees or knows."

"That doesn't mean that—"

"I'll lose the election. My life's work down the drain. You know this town and how they love their LFC. You know anyone that messes with its chance at success is a villain. I can't run that risk. I can't. You know I wouldn't be asking you to ride out this storm if it weren't of utmost importance."

"Archibald." I clear my throat and my chest constricts as panic spreads.

"Rory told me Esme's leaving Seth. That they're truly in love and she can't handle Seth's abuse anymore." *Abuse?* Seth? He's a surly bastard without much of a personality who keeps his private life private, but abuse? "She's documented much of it. She—"

"You still have connections with the police. Can't you do something about that and fix the problem in the meantime?"

"I'm afraid I can't. The only thing to do is for you to step up. For Rory. For Helen. It'll blow over just as quickly as that thing you did year before last. Look how little that affected you."

The bastard in me wants to tell Archibald that his son needs to deal with his own problems. That he's spent a lifetime fixing Rory's mishaps to save himself and his political career the embarrassment of having a son who's trouble.

The fifteen-year-old kid in me who was starving and desperate for a way out remembers the promise I made when I signed my first contract.

The one that said I'd repay the Matheson family any way I could for giving me a life I wouldn't have had otherwise.

I look in the mirror across from my bed. My hair is sticking up all over the place and the darkness of my ink is stark against the white of my sheets.

Who knew that day so very long ago that I took a deal with the devil? Who knew he'd come to collect like . . . this? This is bollocks. Fucking arsehole Rory.

"Rush?"

Today is my payday.

The problem? I'm arrogant enough to think I'm bigger than this. That my star is rising so high and fast that nothing can touch it. That I can weather the storm for the man who gave me the chance when he didn't have to.

There's a fear too, but I push it away.

"If I do this, we're even." *I'll just ignore the reporters.* "There is no coming back for more." *I'll make no comment on the pictures.* "No favors." *I'll act as if it's any other fucking day.* "No more—"

"Of course."

"My debt is paid."

Chapter
FIFTEEN

Rush

"Do you know what bloody time it is here, mate?" Louie asks. "It's six in the fucking morning."

I laugh, his voice is just what I need to hear right now. Anything to keep me from heading back to the house and finishing what I started with Lennox earlier tonight.

Anything.

Anything . . . except another woman.

"Six? God forbid you actually see the sun rise every once in a while." I laugh.

"Moons are good. It means the party is still going strong. Sunrises, not so much. That means hangovers, training, and having to roll off whatever warm body I've found as a cushion for the night."

And as if on cue, a woman murmurs his name as a protest in the background. Predictable fucking Louie.

"Do you have a sec?"

My goalie and closest friend's laugh is deep and rich and tugs a smile onto my lips. "Unlucky for her, that's all I had in me last night," he teases.

"Jesus."

"Yeah. Of course. What do you need?"

"I'm here. You're there. Have you heard anything?"

"I've heard a lot of things. Question is, are any of them fucking true?"

My sigh is heavy. "Depends who they're from."

"Are the arsehole reporters still camping out at your gate? Probably. Is the story still selling tabloids? Of course, it is. We do love a juicy scandal here. Is Seth still a surly son of bitch who doesn't deserve Esme? Damn straight."

His sigh is heavy. He's seen the bullshit side of Seth before and he knows the real me. He hasn't asked for a single explanation, but threw a punch to help defend me when Seth came at me in the changing room. Thank fuck for Louie, the only mate who didn't need to ask if it was true.

"What about the club?"

"Still saying 'no comment.' Still giving the bullshit line that they're 'working on building the best team possible for next year.' As for your fate? Who the fuck knows? They have to weigh the benefits of keeping their proven captain or keeping you, the face of this new version of the team they've rebuilt. It's a shit decision."

"It is."

"Say something, mate. Anything. Do an interview with Piers Morgan. Get your voice out there. Your silence is killing you and we can't have that. You're too damn talented to be burying your career just yet."

"The gagging order—"

"Fuck the gagging order," he says. "It's like you have something holding you back when you should be fighting tooth and nail to keep your spot."

"Louie," the woman's voice comes through the line.

"I love you, mate, but—"

"But you've got to go give her your few seconds. I get it."

"Fuck you." He laughs.

"Later, mate."

"Hey, Rush?"

"Hmm?"

"You're the heart of this team and this team is your heart. You need to do whatever it is to get you back here. You have your reasons for doing whatever it is you did or didn't do," he says, walking a fine line and not asking for answers, "but if you're protecting someone or something, it's not fucking worth it."

He ends the call and I pause with my phone in my hand where I'm parked in Johnny's driveway. The darkened house sits before me, a shadow among the hills.

I'm unsettled. Restless. Uneasy.

It's not fucking worth it.

That echoes how I feel after tonight's event. It was interesting to say the least. I don't know what I expected when Finn talked me into taking this MLS gig as a means to lie low, but this wasn't it. A decorated stage where I talked to a small crowd about a game that is my life, but that clearly isn't much of anyone's here.

Is this what it feels like when you're on the downhill slide of your career? Car park events with a couple hundred people versus stadiums with tens of thousands?

I scrub a hand over my face and wonder if this is worth it? Yes, Archibald saved my arse all those years ago, but other than that, I made it to this level of football on my own. My skill. My sacrifices. My love for the game. Do I hate the slander against my name, that I'll be known as a *homewrecker* and *bastard?* Yes. But can I face losing my career due to loyalty to a man whose son hasn't changed since he was a lad? *No. Fuck. No.*

Will this not die a quick death like Archibald said it would?

Chapter
SIXTEEN

Lennox

My mind runs the conversation with Finn over and over in my mind and each time it replays, my anger sparks anew.

I know I should revel in the fact that I might get the last laugh in this whole fucked-up comedy of errors, but I'm still hurt that he would do it in the first place.

And angry.

So goddamn angry that my bare feet might as well have worn a hole in the carpet from where I've paced back and forth. The city has sparked to life beyond the windows, glittering dots in the land of dreams.

I'm too busy stewing over Finn and his bullshit.

This is on me.

Totally on me.

And what the hell is in it for him? Why would he advise Rush to come here unless it was for some endgame tactic?

I'm primed, pissed, and have had too much wine to avoid second-guessing or overthinking my next movements.

When I hear the front door downstairs slam, I know Johnny's out, so there's only one person it can be.

I'm down the stairs and striding into the kitchen in seconds. I don't give myself time to consider how tired he looks. The tie undone and hanging around his neck. The beer bottle he's holding up to his lips and drinking without a breath. His hair going every which way from the hands he's run through it.

What I see is his shirtsleeves rolled up, displaying the dark ink of his tattoos beneath.

What I remember is the taste of his kiss and the need to have more.

What I know is the want and the need to use him to take the hurt and pain away.

I'm too selfish to think of anything but that as I walk across the kitchen and take him by surprise.

My hands are fisting in his shirt as my lips find his, the sound of the beer bottle clinking to the counter—glass onto marble—the only other noise besides his surprised gasp.

He lets me take the lead as I deepen the kiss, pulling him against me. Our tongues touch. Our groans amplify. It takes everything I have to push him away, to break our connection, but I have so much to say.

"Your agent is a condescending prick that is doing you no favors," I growl, giving a yank to his shirt to reinforce my comment, and just when he starts to reply, I slant my mouth over his and take what I need once again.

The kiss is laced with greed and lust, and all I can focus on is the feel of his body, the trace of beer on his tongue, and how very angry I am at him for just being him.

"We can't do this," I murmur in between kisses. Over and over. A nip of his bottom lip. "This is wrong." A gasp as his hand fists in my hair. "Unethical." His hand on my lower back pulling me against him, so I can feel how hard that beautiful cock of his is. "We need to stop." A grind of his hips against mine. "Rush?"

It's his turn to break the kiss this time. He twists his hand in my hair and pulls back ever so slightly so our faces are inches apart.

"In case you haven't noticed, I don't give a fuck about the rules." He dips down and tugs on my bottom lip with his teeth before leaning back again so his eyes are front and center, lids heavy with lust. "I care about the here and the now and the taste of your kiss and hopefully the grip of your pussy should we keep this up. So . . . fuck the bloody rules."

I've always been shit at self-control.

Always.

And right now, I know there is no turning back. There is no saying no. I knew the minute I met Rush McKenzie I was going to break the rules for him, and the laugh that falls from my lips and echoes around the kitchen sounds just as crazy as the notion.

Emotions are complicated, nasty things.

That's why this is the perfect way to do this. Without thought and on instinct. If we just dive in head first, scratch that itch, neither of us will be able to complain about it.

It will just be pleasure.

That's all it will be.

"Careful, Nox," he murmurs. "You're playing with fire here."

I lean in closer so my lips are at his ear—his body tensing in anticipation is a seduction all in itself—and whisper, "You ready to burn with me, Rush?"

I see the muscle feathering in his jaw as our eyes lock again, our desire making the decision before our reason can. Our excited breaths hit off each other's lips as our chests heave against one another's in a battle for the small amount of space separating us.

And then in that split second, we collide again as if the air between us is on fire and we need to smother it to put it out. Our bodies become one as we use the anger and desperation and lack of control to fuel our every moment. We begin removing clothes—items are discarded without a care to where they are being tossed—because right now there is a need to touch his skin, to map his tattoos with my lips, to add my own marks with my teeth.

We don't take the time to admire each other's bodies in this state—misted with sweat, smelling of arousal, and tense with a carnal necessity. We can't. We're too consumed by the moment and each other.

Our lips bruise as we kiss like our lives depend on each and every connection we make.

We don't discuss where we're doing this or how. We just move in sync. He's lifting my ass onto the kitchen counter and propping my feet up on the stools below.

He dips his fingers into me with one hand while his other holds my neck, and I lean back into it.

"Rush. God. That feels . . ." My words are eaten by the moan I emit when his lips find that hollow spot just beneath my jaw and his fingers slide in as far as they can go before he starts the motion all over again.

I sag against his hand as his groan fills the room, prompting me to scoot my ass closer to the edge to give him unhindered access.

My eyes close and lips part as I let him prepare me in the most pleasurable way for the thickness of his cock that is ready and waiting.

He works me up so that between the friction of his thumb and the manipulation of his fingers, I'm a wet mess, which is more than ready to be pushed over the edge he's built me up to.

Our lips meet again, and this time it's my hands fisting in his hair, it's my hands reaching between his thighs to grab what I want and tell him I want it right now. And regardless of the violent desperation that tinges our kisses, Rush makes sure that his hands have mapped every surface of my body, leaving goosebumps laced with anticipation in their wake.

It's almost as if he's marking me to make sure every time someone touches me from here on out, I'll remember this—his hands, his touch—and the havoc they wreaked on my senses.

It's exhilarating and exhausting because all I want is him in me, owning me, pleasuring me.

"Lennox. I need . . . you. Please. You ready?" he murmurs with his lips against my breast, those eyes of his looking up at me.

"I thought you'd never ask," I tease as he moves to where his pants are half hanging on the wine rack and fishes his wallet out. Within a few moments, he's jacketed, those sexy forearms of his on perfect display as he rolls the condom over his dick.

But it's when he looks up at me that I lose my breath. Rush stands there with shadows playing over his body and face, chest heaving, and eyes roaming over all the places his hands have been until they land between my parted thighs.

His hand slides up and back over the length of his cock as he takes a step forward and stares at me sitting here—legs spread, body begging, arousal glistening on my inner thighs. If I ever needed to paint a picture of everything that is desire, it would be Rush McKenzie in this moment.

The muscles in his neck are taut. His body an incredible work of art, but it's his eyes that own every part of me. The look *in* them and the way they look *at* me.

"I think you're going to hurt me, Lennox, and yet, I'm a glutton for punishment." He murmurs the words through a knowing smile before rubbing the crest of his cock ever so slightly up and down my slit.

I tense in pleasure, in anticipation, in everything that's anything, when he pushes the first inch of that glorious cock in. My moan is simultaneous. The arching of my back is too as I lay back on the counter so I can give him access to devastate me completely.

"Look at you. Feisty." He takes his free hand and places it right between my breasts. "Gorgeous." He runs it over and cups each breast. "Willing." He drags it slowly over my abdomen. "Wanting."

And on the last word, he pushes his way into me. My mewl meets his guttural groan as he sheaths himself root to tip within me. The burn of the stretch is pleasurable. The sight of him with his head thrown back and fingers digging into my inner thighs is one to behold.

"Rush. Please," I murmur as I tighten my grip around him, desperate for him to move and pleasure me.

And as if on cue, Rush does just that. He gives me a few strokes to prepare me and then with one thumb rubbing my clit and the other hand gripping the curve where my hip meets my thigh, Rush dives right into a punishing pace fed on lust and greed.

Our bodies connect again and again. The only sounds in the kitchen come from our skin slapping, our breaths gasping, and satisfaction as we moan and groan and beg and plead with each other. *Faster. Harder. Right there. Oh my God. Yes.*

In the moment, I know I'd think less of him if he were gentle or timid. It would take away from what this is. Hunger. A need. A desire to take and sate and use sex to feel whole, when you're never supposed to use it to do that.

Gentle is for romance. This is pure lust in its truest form. No niceties are needed. No small talk. Just hands gripping flesh and hips thrusting against mine so I can feel and concentrate on how his cock scrapes over every single available nerve inside me. It's pleasure and pain. It's salvation and revelation. It's so right while being so very goddamn wrong.

But Jesus, who would ever say no to this? To him?

With each thrust in, he pulls my body so I slide atop the counter and slam into him with the same force he's using. My nerves sing. My body soars. My eyes roll back and my legs go tight. And then it's his name on my lips, Rush, over and over and over as my orgasm hits me.

It's a lightning strike of bliss. One that rolls in waves through some parts of me and jolts against nerves in others. I try to still so I can absorb its strength, while needing to move because it's so powerful.

He lets me own it, take it, revel in it for a few moments so my climax isn't overshadowed or ruined by his.

It's the smallest of gestures that crosses my mind ever so faintly in my post-orgasmic haze, but it's there.

And then just as quickly, when his restraint snaps and his groan rumbles through the kitchen, it's forgotten as he takes what *he* needs from me to reach his high.

"Lennox. God. Fuck." Each word is accented by a jerk of his hips and a tightening of his fingers into my flesh.

He falls on top of me—sort of. His face is resting against my abdomen, lips pressed to my skin, and his fingers find and lace with mine at my sides.

We're both panting, both taking in the moment.

"I don't think that was part of the contract," I murmur, as I free my hand from one of his and run it through his hair.

He chuckles. "I'll make sure Cannon writes an addendum to your contract to sanction this because, woman, you can't expect to give a man something like that and then tell him it's not part of an ongoing contract."

Chapter
SEVENTEEN

Lennox

"You've been avoiding me," my dad accuses as I stop, mid-stride on my jog (if you can call it that) up the long winding hill that leads to Johnny's house.

"I've done no such thing." *Yes, I have.*

"You're in Los Angeles?" He already knows the answer.

"Yes." I hate that I feel like a little girl about to get scolded, when I know that's not how my dad operates. Rather, he lets the disappointment or concern in his voice lead the way.

"And you took the deal with Cannon?"

"I did." I walk toward the edge of the road, the guardrail at my knees, and put a hand on my hip as I wait for his response.

"Did you ever think to call and talk to me about the reasons I thought the job wasn't a good idea?" There's a click over the connection and I can picture my dad perfectly. He's just risen from his desk to shut his office door so he can have some privacy.

That's one admirable thing about him. As a single dad of four girls, he always made sure we had his undivided attention when needed . . . and obviously, he realizes that I need that right now.

"Did you ever think to consult me on the Chicago offer before turning it down?" I counter.

His sigh is long and telling. He sounds tired, and yet I struggle with the notion that he's getting older, and that the things that used to excite might just be the same things that now plain wear him out.

"I have my reasons, Lennox." And the way he makes the comment leaves no room for discussion, and I'm once again the scolded child. Silence weighs across the line. "You want to tell me what's going on with you?"

"Nothing. I'm fine."

He chuckles and the sound brings tears to my eyes. I hate it. Why is it that no matter how old you get, you still need your parent's assurance and approval? "Okay. You can lie to me. You're an adult, so it's your prerogative. But I have four daughters so I know the words *I'm fine* mean exactly the opposite. Just know when you want to talk, I'm here."

"How come you haven't given me any new clients to chase, Dad? How come we had this big talk a few months back about needing to go after Finn's clients to strengthen the business and you haven't trusted me enough to go after one?"

"This has nothing to do with trust, honey, and everything to do with timing."

"And yet Dekk, Chase, and Brex are being sent all over the place as you're turning down invites for me to speak at conferences. I'm suspect to your timing excuse."

"I have my reasons for the conference as well. Chase told me you were hot under the collar about that."

"What is the reason?" I ask.

"I'm worried about you."

That's not an answer. It's a deflection in perfect Kenyon Kincade fashion. "I'm a big girl. I can take care of myself."

"As you always have, but that doesn't take away my need as a parent to tell you I'm worried about you."

I wage an internal war over being mad at him for not giving me straight answers but still caring about me. It's a stupid war, but one I wage nonetheless.

"Why?"

"Sometimes I wonder if I pulled you into this business and you agreed out of obligation, not because it's what you love to do," he says. I feel like I just took a dagger to the chest. His words perfectly explain how I've been feeling lately, and yet, I do love my job. "Where you used to be gung-ho and dot every "i", now you cut corners and take unnecessary risks.

You're the kid in school cutting class while your sisters are turning in their assignments on time."

He gives me a moment for the words to sink in, to pause rather than go on the defensive about being compared to my sisters. I hate that while every part of me wants to buck at what he's saying, he's actually right.

I have been cutting corners and thinking more about me than my job. I have been dreading my days at work, and the thrill has virtually died.

And yet, I still love what I do.

"You've never forced me to do anything I don't want to, Dad. I just . . . I'm getting restless, I guess. Maybe I need a challenge or a change of pace, but that doesn't mean I want to quit."

"Your mother used to get like that." His chuckle is soft, reminiscent, and it fills me with equal parts sadness and joy. How much I crave to be like her or to have some connection with the woman who I feel fades from my memory more and more each day. "Sometimes I forget how much alike you two are. She'd look at me every once in a while, with that soft, beautiful smile of hers and say, 'I need a change, Kenyon.' I never could say no to her. Before you guys were born, that change meant a secluded beach house or crowded tourist attraction for a few weeks. After we had you guys, it meant I'd come home to furniture being rearranged or a room being painted a completely different color. Her restlessness drove me crazy at times, but it's part of the reason I loved her so much."

"I had no idea," I whisper.

"In the early days, I worried she'd feel that way about me. That I'd be the thing she needed a change from. I asked her about it one time, and she just threw her head back and laughed before pulling me in for a kiss and saying, 'You are who quiets the restlessness, Ken. That's how I knew you were the one.'"

I'm standing on the side of the road in the Hollywood Hills with tears streaming down my face, hating that this precious piece of the past was all I needed to feel connected to my family again.

Sure, I'm upset about Chicago and everything that has made me feel insecure over the past week, but it's my family. They're all I have.

"You okay?" he asks as I sniff again.

"I'm here recruiting a client, Dad."

"Oh." There's surprise in his voice, and I can picture him sitting up straighter in his mammoth office chair, the silver of his hair glinting against the fluorescent lights.

"I wasn't at first. It was more of an, *I need a change, Kenyon,* type of moment," I say and smile. "But an opportunity has presented itself and if I can land this client, it'll make up for all the mistakes I've been making lately."

"Lennox. You know I don't expect—"

"It's Rush McKenzie." I know if I hadn't cut him off, that name alone would have right there.

"Your partner in the MLS assignment?"

"Partner is a loose term," I say and then go on to explain Cannon's expectations by bringing me on board. When I finish, silence weighs on the line as a car zips past me. "Dad?"

"Do you think you're up for the task? I mean, he's a huge name in the middle of an even larger scandal. Often times, those types of clients come with as big of rewards as the consequences."

He doesn't even know the half of it.

I shift my feet and feel the delicious soreness from last night when I do, and then internally cringe at the details I'm omitting from my father.

"I understand."

"There's no room for error with him. He's sitting center stage with the sports world watching. He broke the one code athletes live by—don't screw with a teammate."

"But I don't think he did," I say out loud for the first time.

"You've known him a few days and have come to that conclusion, huh?"

"Yes," I assert. "I think he's all persona. He may be a rebel, but something tells me he's smart enough not to fuck with a winning team dynamic."

"You know that's not a popular opinion, right?"

"Since when do I care about popular opinion?"

"It's a touchy situation for an agent. One more wrong move from him, and while he might survive the fallout, everything and everyone around him will be blamed for it."

"By the way you're trying to talk me out of it, I'm beginning to feel like you don't think I can handle it."

"That's not what I said."

"But he's Finn's. Isn't that the goal here?"

"The goal is to build upon what we already have at KSM. To take the pieces he's chipped away at with his dirty tactics and restore."

"In other words, steal." I laugh.

"I know you can't see it, but I'm shaking my head right now."

"I figured."

"There's something else, isn't there? Did something happen at the conference?"

Tears fill my eyes, and I hate every shred of degradation I feel, and how it surfaces from the undisguised compassion in his voice.

"No." Yes. I'm silent for a moment, grateful he doesn't press. But if he did, what would I tell him? That I need to do this for me? That I need to know my skill sets include more strength of character and resilience than short-lived beauty? Contrary to what pageants ever sold to the contender. To me.

And don't start me on the other accusations, especially after I slept with Rush.

"No, Lenn? That's it? Because that no sounded an awful lot like there's more to the story."

"I need to do this, okay? The change of scenery. The challenge. Who knows what I'll find?"

I can almost see his nod as he takes in my argument. "Who knows?"

"Thanks for calling."

"Next time don't avoid me."

"Yes, sir," I say through a laugh. "Bye, Daddy."

"Hey Lennox?"

"What?"

"If you had told me you ended up in Los Angeles because you needed a break without any mention of recruiting a client, I would have been completely fine with it."

A lump forms in my throat as I struggle to hold the tears back. Because this man, this incredible yet flawed man, just gave me the words I desperately needed. Our family is far from perfect. Often, we bicker more than we laugh. But right here, right now, my dad showed me why I am who I am.

His love for me and his confidence in me is unconditional.

But I want more. I want his confidence in me to be unshakable.

"Love you, Daddy."

And when I hang up, I know one thing with absolute certainty: I can't and won't screw this up.

Chapter
EIGHTEEN

Lennox

I'M OUT OF BREATH, AND DECIDE WHEN I FINISH MY RUN AND ENTER the house, that I need to do better, be better. I crossed that line—scratched that itch last night.

And what a glorious scratch it was.

But the problem with scratching itches is when you do it too much or for too long, it begins to swell and hurt more than feel like relief. It becomes a sore you try to ignore.

It becomes a permanent scar you can't get rid of, and I already have enough scars to begin with.

That's how I look at men, relationships, and sex. It's okay to start with, but then I need to distance myself soon thereafter.

And after talking to my dad today, I know I need to do just that—take a huge step back. Not only for myself but for the promises I need to fulfill for my family and for *myself*.

At least, that's what I tell myself as I go in search of Rush. The problem is I find him right away.

He's sitting at the nook table, gym shorts on, shirt nonexistent, hair all over the place, with a whole feast of takeout food spread over the kitchen counter. A ridiculous plate of pancakes and syrup is sitting in front of him with about a quarter of it gone, and the look of absolute bliss blankets every line etched in his expression.

Last night comes back to me in snapshots. The sex on the kitchen counter. His broken voice calling my name as he climaxed. The silence afterward, as we tried to figure what happens next. The eating of Johnny's ice cream straight from the container as we sat and watched crappy reruns on the television. Falling asleep on the couch, because I was afraid of saying I was going up to bed and wondering if that meant I was going alone or with him.

Then, waking up alone.

But when I enter the kitchen and see him sitting there, I'm hit with a straight punch of lust. The kind that makes you stagger and stop, questioning the things you're about to say.

But I know I need to say them.

"This is . . . this is absolute heaven, the dog's bollocks," he murmurs when he sees me, glancing up at me from over a forkful. "Pancakes are a culinary wonder."

"Says the man who probably eats beans on his toast most days." I grimace.

"That's beans on toast to you, and nah, too many carbs," he says around a mouthful, before offering me a wink as I point to his plate laden with carbs with a perplexed expression on my face. "Do you want some? I had a ton of breakfast delivered for us."

"So I noticed." I glance at the heaps of food and wonder if he's expecting an army of people to show up, because there's no way that the three of us can eat all that.

"On second thought, don't eat. Save the pancakes for me." He chuckles as he leans back in his chair, letting his eyes roam up and down the length of my body when I stop short before him, hands on my hips, and resolve deep in my bones.

"We need to talk."

"I thought we were talking."

"We can't do *that* again." There, it's out there. I said what I needed to say but hell if my body is revolting against me saying it.

"That? As in incredible sex, type of *that*? Because if that's the nonsense you're talking, you can just head back out that door and forget you came in here." He waves with his fork, his smile wide, but then it begins to fade when he meets my eyes and sees that I'm serious. "You're not kidding, are you?"

I shrug. "It's unprofessional of me to be working side by side with you, represent you and the league in a sense, and then . . . be sleeping with you at night."

"According to who?" He sets his knife and fork down and crosses his arms over his chest.

"According to ethics. According to everyone who thinks I use my looks to gain clients. According to—"

"Hold up. What about using your looks to gain clients?"

"It's a long story," I sigh and shift on my feet. "And it doesn't matter. What matters is this—you and me. We can't do this anymore. We had an itch, we scratched it, and now we're both satisfied."

"Satisfied?" He snorts. "Speak for yourself."

"I'm serious. I'm representing my family business while working this contract. If someone were to find out, it wouldn't just look bad on me, but it would also look bad on Kincade Sports Management."

"Then we won't let anyone find out."

"That's easier said than—"

"Than what? Than it's no one's fucking business who you sleep with?" He stands and takes the few steps toward me. Every part of me reacts to his nearness, and I dislike myself for it. He lowers his voice. "Are you saying you didn't enjoy last night, Lennox? Are you telling me that the scratch marks down my arms aren't real? You and I both know it was good. That it would be even better next time. A little fun never hurt anyone."

"Exactly. We had a little fun. It can only get more complicated from here and I loathe complicated. I think you've had more than enough complicated in the past month to last you a lifetime." I take a step back but he takes one forward, so I gain no space between us. "I'm sorry, but my mind is made up."

"Why? You're not my agent, and you're not recruiting me so—"

"Work up an appetite, did you?" a disheveled Johnny asks, striding in with his sunglasses on, hair a mess, and wearing completely mismatched clothes.

Rush glances Johnny's way while I stand there staring at him, wondering if I was just saved by the bell.

But I know I wasn't. This conversation still needs to be had with Rush.

"Help yourself to breakfast," Rush says. "I really wanted some pancakes."

"Thanks, dude," Johnny says and then looks at us one more time, a piece of bacon stopping halfway to his mouth, as he does a double take.

"Christ. Seriously?" He emits a dramatic sigh when he takes his sunglasses off and flinches from the bright sunlight. "I knew I smelled sex last night when I came home."

"What?" I laugh the word out, cheeks heating.

Johnny looks from Rush to me and then back again. "The two of you are a pheromone blast if I've ever seen it. Couldn't you guys have waited a bit?" He groans and then plops onto the barstool at the island and starts pulling food onto one of the paper plates that Rush left out. "Now it's going to be like a rabbit den around here with you two fucking each other everywhere. This is not what I signed up for."

I fight back a laugh. Rush doesn't. "You're the one who vouched for both of us so at least we chose wisely."

"I didn't vouch for shit." He goes to the fridge and grabs a beer, the crack of it opening echoes around the kitchen as he sits back down. "What I do vouch for is those grins you both have on your faces."

"There's that," I murmur.

"Don't you have any shame?" he asks me.

"Says the man hungover, and probably hiding someone tangled in his sheets upstairs."

"Her name is Heidi," he says around a mouthful of food, "and no, she's not in my bed. I knew if she woke up and saw Rush, that she'd dump my ass after realizing he's way hotter. I figured I'd mitigate that awkwardness by sending her off before you guys woke."

"Well," Rush says, "can't say I'd blame her for thinking that." And he gains a glare from both Johnny and me.

"Thank you for sparing us from Rush's big ego," I add.

"This is really good." He looks at the bag of the take-out. "I'll have to try this place again." Another bite. Another sip of beer. "All I ask is that you two fuck monkeys don't dirty up the surfaces in the house." Rush and I slide a glance at each other. Johnny freezes. "Fuck, man."

Rush eyes the island where he's sitting, and Johnny shoves back, his stool hitting the one beside it with a clang.

"Really? My kitchen counter?" he screeches.

Rush chuckles. "Nah, mate," Rush lies. "Your bed is pretty comfy though."

Johnny glares at me, and I can't hold back my laughter anymore. "We did not have sex in your bed. Lord knows what we would catch if we did."

"You guys are assholes," Johnny says as he sits back down to his food again. "Just don't be"—he motions his hand all around—"you know. Let me catch you or some shit. That is not something I want to walk in on."

"Should I be offended?" I tease.

"No, the last thing I need to see is that fucker's dick. I'd be left with an inferiority complex for the rest of my life."

"No worries there," Rush says leaning his hip against the island and crossing his arms over his chest, as if it's an everyday comment on how inferior men feel beside him. "When you walked in, Lennox was telling me why we can't be shagging anymore anyway."

I stare at Rush, pissed that he's trying to involve Johnny in our discussion, no doubt to have him take sides.

"She's smart," Johnny says and points his fork at me. "She's trying to let me keep my sanity."

"I was telling her I just don't think that's going to happen," Rush says, that smile of his as devastating as ever. "Why turn down a good thing?"

He hooks an arm over my shoulder, and I physically remove it by stepping away. Being close to him is not what I need right now.

"It's not happening again," I say and grab a piece of bacon.

"You sure about that?" Rush asks.

"I am," I say and sigh. "On that note, I need to take a shower and get ready for work."

"In my bathroom?" Rush asks.

"No, in mine."

And with one last look his way, I saunter out of the kitchen, leaving the two of them and their testosterone alone.

The funny thing is, despite having sex with Rush, the magnetism didn't fade.

It always fades. It always loses its luster.

So why, as I climb the stairs one by one, do I admit to myself that this is going to be much harder than it should be?

That working with Rush and keeping my hands off him is going to be a difficult challenge.

Chapter
NINETEEN

Rush

SHE'S BEEN AVOIDING ME.

She can say she isn't. She can pretend to be busy with the hundreds of calls she takes every day. One moment she talks some athlete off the ledge of doubt, and then the next she's like a bulldog as she negotiates what she wants with a team.

It's impressive.

It's a turn-on.

Anyone who says they don't like a woman who owns her confidence has to have a little dick and not much sense. Because Lennox . . . hell, Lennox is a complete and utter badass.

It's definitely sexy.

And it's also a pain in my arse because Christ, that woman and her pussy have left their mark on me. Maybe not so much a mark—other than the scratch marks—but a hunger.

But isn't that the problem? I've had her and know how good it is. Unlike all the other fuckers wondering if she's as fucking sensational as she looks.

I raise my hand because I can vouch—she is.

I've had her. I want her again.

Maybe telling me she's off limits has fed that fire.

Or maybe I just want her.

Either way, while I admire her restraint, her reasons are shit. And I'll tell her that the first chance I get when she's not surrounded by Cannon or the other bastards vying for her attention.

"She's definitely not a hardship to look at, is she?"

Speak of the devil. I glance at Cannon, notice his eyes looking the same place mine are.

Lennox is standing in one of those business suits she wears—navy-blue trousers, a matching jacket, and a soft, silk camisole beneath—and a pair of nude high heels. Her hair is back in some kind of thick braid with a few escaped pieces framing her face. Her sunglasses are on and her phone is pressed to her ear as she paces back and forth in the tunnel leading into the stadium. She's gesticulating as she talks, and her laugh can be heard across the pitch.

"Nah, mate, not hard on the eyes at all," I murmur as every part of me revolts at the fact that he's watching her.

"You can thank me for pulling her on board for this project. Finn tried to talk me out of it, you know, but can you blame me?"

Why the fuck would Sanderson do that? And surely Cannon hired her on skill and merit, not because she's hot—

"I had dinner with her last night. She's definitely enough to challenge any man. Good thing I like challenges."

My hands fist reflexively. *Like hell you'll be touching her, arsehole.* "I wasn't aware the two of you were a thing."

"We're not." He shrugs and emits a laugh that is one hundred percent arsehole. "At least not yet anyway."

"Good luck with that. Heard she's already smitten with someone else."

"Mr. McKenzie? We're almost ready for you," one of the public relations people says to me.

"Okay. I'll be right there." I glance from her to Cannon before walking the short distance to where Lennox is pacing.

She's finishing up her call when I approach, but when our eyes meet, I can tell by the sudden slouch of her shoulders and shock in her expression that I'm right: she's definitely avoiding me.

"You're here," I state as she closes the distance between us. She smells like sun and coconut oil. Like sex and desire. Like exactly what this man needs and wants.

"It's my job to be here," she says, looking anywhere but at me.

"Are you going to stand there on your phone and ignore me like you have the past few days or are you actually going to pay attention?"

"I'm not avoiding you. I'm a busy woman and this isn't my only responsibility."

"You're avoiding me. It's the tattoos, isn't it? They either scare women away or make them flock to me in droves?"

"Droves?" She breaks a smile. "I doubt it's the tattoos," she murmurs, but through her sunglasses I can see her eyes dart down to the winding mess of ink on my bicep.

"Then it must be the size of my dick. Though I can't say I've had many complaints when it comes to that."

"If you're trying to get me to like you, that's not the best way to do so—by telling me I'm just one notch on a bedpost filled with many."

"I'm? As in present tense? So you're still thinking of us in the present instead of the past." I lift my eyebrows.

"You know what I mean," she says and rolls her eyes.

"I do know what you mean, and no, you're not a notch on a bedpost. Far fucking from it, but mission accomplished—I got you to talk to me. And face it, you miss me. You said we couldn't, but I'm beginning to think you still want to." I lean in closer and whisper, "Don't worry. I know you see me and every part of you says yes, but being the sensible woman you are, you're trying to do the right thing. Play by the rules. I get it. I do. But, Lennox, sometimes it feels good to be oh-so-wrong."

Her quick intake of air tells me there is more between us left to explore. Like the bed. The pool. So many surfaces. So damn many.

"I admire your persistence. I do. And I never said I didn't want to sleep with you again," she says glancing around to make sure no one else hears her. "I said I can't, that it's not professional."

I hum a noncommittal sound and then bring a hand to the back of her neck as my lips find hers. It's brief, but I take advantage of her momentary shock to take more of what I so desperately want.

And just as soon as I do, I break the kiss and step back, my grin slow to spread, because I don't want to give her the satisfaction that I'm chasing her. The other part of me is dying to show her that her game's not working—that I still intend to have her. And the jealous, fuck you part of me, wants to make sure that Cannon sees me so he can wonder what the hell is going on.

"What . . . What are you—"

"Time to go to work," I say with nothing more than a wink and a laugh as I leave that gorgeous, confused face of hers behind without explanation.

And I do go to work. The line of kids and adults alike stretches through the concourse of the stadium. Liverpool gear is in their hands and at the ready for me to sign when they reach the front of the queue.

"Thank you, mate," I say to the young lad in front of me.

"I want to be like you someday," he says. "I mean the footballer part. Not the other part. My mom says she'd string you up by the balls for doing what you did."

"Hank!" his dad gasps, mortified at the comment, and tries to stifle his laugh.

My own smile is hard to fight as I look at this ten- or eleven-year-old kid and know what a smart-arse I was at his age.

"I'm so sorry," the dad says. "I don't know—"

"It's fine," I say and hold my hand up in a no offense gesture. It's no worse than the implications I've been given all day with every question from the press. "You know the hard thing about being a footballer, Hank? It puts you in the public eye when the only thing you care about is what you leave on the pitch. Even worse, sometimes things are said about you— things that aren't true—and it doesn't matter if you speak up about them or not, because people are going to believe what they want to regardless. Do you understand what I'm saying?"

"Yes, sir."

"So you need to train every day. Your footwork, your skill moves, your shooting. And you also need to get tough, because there will always be criticism, always be rumors that aren't true, and people trying to tear you down. The only thing you can control is you. So train hard, stay in your lane, and shrug off the negativity. Okay?"

I reach across the table and bump fists with him, but when I glance in my periphery, Lennox is standing there, head at an angle, and eyes fixed on mine. There's something in the look she gives me that says she heard me, and that she understands.

It's the oddest feeling because in this Rory-Esme-lying shitstorm, I haven't experienced nor expected that someone who doesn't know me would consider that I didn't do it. Until now. Until Lennox's smile.

"Yes, sir. I'll train hard. I promise."

"Okay then. I can't wait to play with or against you someday. Bye, Hank. Enjoy the game."

His dad nods in appreciation to my chill response after what was said. Hell, it's not the kid's fault. He's only repeating what his arsehole parents said.

I watch them walk away and then I turn to face the next in line, and before the kid even says a word, I know his story . . . or a version of it.

I know, because it's like looking in a mirror at a younger version of me. His hair is longish, his cheeks are hollow, his eyes are wide with excitement at meeting me, but there's a depth of sadness behind them that I can't explain. I just know. It's exhaustion from always feeling like you're less than. It's a weariness that comes from worrying if you ate too much of your breakfast this morning because you were starving, and therefore didn't leave enough for your mum, since there was only one serving. It's a tiredness over the fear that someone's going to find out that the dirt beneath your nails is because your water was cut off. That it will be noticed that your clothes are a little too big, because you got them at the local Salvation Army on a handout for the homeless day.

It's on his mum's face too. The desperation to be seen as a mum who gives her all.

I'm bone-tired from working two jobs, but I'm here so he can see his hero.

I'm trying to be both father and mother so he can have a better chance at life.

I'm hoping that by meeting you, he'll get the drive and hope to want more than I will ever be able to give him.

Just as my mum did for me in countless ways, like calling in sick to wait in an endless line to meet legendary footballer, Ian Rush. The same footballer I idolized and would lie and tell my teammates I'd been named after.

The pitch was the only place we were all equals. The green of the grass was where I was Rush McKenzie, whose footwork and determination the other boys envied. It was the place where they forgot I was the kid no one really knew.

The pair of them hit me in every part of my past and what's brought me to this future, and I struggle with what to say.

"Hi. And who might this be?" I ask as I meet his eyes and then his mum's.

"I'm Scottie," he says in a timid voice as he worries his hands in front of him.

"Hi Scottie. How are you today, Mum?"

"We're very good, thank you." She darts her eyes to the line behind her and then back to me. "We don't have anything for you to sign. We can't—" Her voice breaks off as she motions to the merchandise stand to the far left of us. I know she means they can't afford to buy anything for me to sign. "But you're his favorite, so I had to make sure he got the chance to see you since we'll most likely never get the chance to see you play in England."

My smile is plastered on my face, as I swallow over the lump of emotion lodged squarely in my throat.

I've seen mothers like this one a few times over the years, and mostly due to the rush of the event, I haven't stopped to consider the extreme hardship my mum suffered. I recognize the look in her eyes, because I saw it for years in my mum's. But I can also now see something with startling clarity.

This mum is probably around the same age my mum was when she died. When she cried her final tear because she wouldn't be there for me anymore. And this mum's the same.

She'll never give up on her son. She'll push and push because of her love for her little boy.

God, it's times like these that I want to make more of a difference.

"Do you play?" I ask Scottie, when I can finally push words from my mouth. He nods. "How old are you and what position?"

"I'm thirteen and I play center mid." His voice is so very quiet.

"A very important position. That means you're steady and dependable when needed and aggressive when warranted."

"Yes."

"I'll tell you what," I say, then I pull my jersey over my head and take it off. "I think this would fit you better than me."

Chapter
TWENTY

Lennox

WHO IS THIS MAN?

His comment to the little boy with the red hair and freckles galore about not believing everything that you hear, and the look he gave me, is the reason I'm still standing here. Still staring.

That's why I'm watching him when I should be stewing over *that kiss* he planted on me in public—*public*—where everyone and their brother could have seen it.

And that's how I catch the change in his expression—the softness—when he pulls his jersey over his head and signs it for the little boy who's staring at him like he's his hero, with a mom beside him who has tears welling in her eyes.

I take a few steps forward instinctively but am unable to hear what he's saying when his voice lowers, as if they're the only two in Rush's world right now. The little boy looks at Rush with disbelief etched in every line of his face.

Rush starts to look around as if he needs some help, and when he sees me, he motions me closer.

"Did you need something?" I ask.

"Yes. Um . . . my friend Scottie is going to be my guest for the exhibition tonight." Scottie's jaw drops open and he glances at his mother, who looks just as surprised. "Can you help me find someone to get him and his mother some gear and out onto the field? I'm thinking they can have a spot on the end of the dugout with the rest of the team."

"No. Way." Scottie can barely get the two words out as his arms are halfway stuck through the jersey as he puts it on.

Rush turns to him, his smile genuine, and nods. "Yes, mate. If that's okay with you and your mum?"

"Yes. Of course. Are you sure?" Scottie's mom asks, almost as if she's not used to anyone doing something like this for them.

"It's my pleasure," Rush says and then looks back at me while Scottie is all but bouncing out of his shoes. "Can you find someone to help me with that, Lennox?"

"Definitely." I nod, and our eyes meet for a brief moment. I don't know Rush well enough yet to be able to read into whatever emotion is swimming in his eyes—compassion, understanding, a gentleness I don't expect—but all are definitely there. "Scottie and Mrs.?"

"Daphne," his mom says with a quick smile.

"Scottie and Daphne," I say. "Why don't you guys follow me and we'll find someone who can get you guys all set up?"

"Sure," Scottie says.

"I can handle that for you, Ms. Kincade." I'm startled by the woman from the MLS public relations team, who steps up beside me and motions for Scottie and Daphne to follow her.

"Thanks," Rush says with a smile. "I'm also going to need another jersey too."

"I'll get that taken care of right away," she says putting her hand on Scottie's back and steering them to our left.

I watch the trio as they walk toward the inner part of the stadium. Scottie is bouncing and talking excitedly, while Daphne takes one more glance back to where Rush is now talking to the next person in line. She has the softest of smiles on her lips, and I swear I see a tear slide down her cheek.

Anyone looking at the scene would think this was a planned event. Some well-placed public relations for the bad-boy soccer player whose reputation has taken a hit.

But I'm on the inside of this well-oiled MLS machine, and I know this wasn't a stunt to garner good press. It was Rush McKenzie showing a softer side I don't think many have seen before.

A side that he's not supposed to have. Not because I don't want him to be a good guy, mind you, but because I know I'm losing the battle with my resolve.

I know if I see much more of this nice, caring Rush, I'm going to cave.

How can you not want to be with a man who treats a kid like he's gold?

And how can you push a man away when you think everyone else has him pegged all wrong, and you're obsessed with figuring out why he's not trying to prove otherwise?

Maybe that's why I stick around and watch the rest of Rush's meet-and-greet session when I have a million other things to do, like follow through on two new athlete prospects as well as finalize a few negotiations.

Perhaps I figure if I stand here long enough, there will be something he does that will sour my opinion of him. I've seen it a hundred times, where athletes walk out of these junkets after an hour because it's beneath them, or when the line never ends, they become short with the fans.

But not Rush. I'm more than impressed with how he takes time for each and every kid as if they were the first ones in line. He always has a smile and words of encouragement.

And my inability to leave backfires. By the time he finishes and strolls over to me, before he heads to warm up for the exhibition game, I'm even more attracted to him. Not just because he's stunningly handsome, but because you learn a lot about someone in how they treat others—and he treated everyone with grace and gratitude.

"Hey," he says. "You're still here."

"As are you," I say, angling my head to the side, wondering how tired he is from being "on" for the past four hours. Now he has a hard nine-ty-plus minutes of soccer.

"You're staying for the match?"

"Nah. Soccer's not my sport."

"Exactly. That's why you need to watch me play. And the proper terms is *football*." He winks.

"Football. Soccer. Same difference. It's not my sport," I tease.

He sputters over a cough. "What, love? Did I just hear you properly?"

I nod, even though the smile I'm fighting says otherwise. "You did."

"What do I need to do to convince you otherwise?"

I cross my arms over my chest as I stare at him and roll my eyes at myself for melting at his boyish grin.

"I'm a hard woman to convince of anything, Rush."

"Are you throwing down the gauntlet? Because I'm pretty sure you just dared me to convince you that football is exciting. And I'm pretty competitive . . . so once I convince you of that, you know I'm going to succeed at convincing you of another very important matter."

Our grins match and our eyes hold, as people hustle around us to get things picked up before the crowd is let through the gates for the exhibition match. The connection we share is still as strong as ever, but how ridiculous was I to think avoidance would weaken that?

It hasn't.

Not with him standing here with the sunlight on his face and those eyes owning every emotion of mine—confusion, desire, defiance, want.

"This is the part where you tell me what it is you want, Lennox. This is where you explain to me why your words are saying one thing but your eyes are saying something completely different when it comes to us."

"You need to get ready for your game."

"Only if you stay and watch."

I laugh. "I'm sure Cannon would be really thrilled if you cut out on this extensive production because of me."

"I don't give a toss about Cannon, Lennox." And the way he makes the comment tells me he's not joking. "So you'll stay because you're dutiful and sensible, and definitely wouldn't want to rock the boat. I'll stay because I'm going to get a hat trick and dazzle you with some fancy footwork. Once you're impressed, we'll talk about the rest."

"I think you suffer from a serious lack of self-confidence," I say drolly despite being utterly charmed by this man.

"I'm going to win you over yet, Nox," he says as he takes a step back. "Like me, football is an acquired taste. Once you have it, you can't resist sneaking a little in every chance you get."

"Definitely lacking self-esteem." I can't help but smile.

"Make sure you're sitting front and center. I wouldn't want you to miss a thing."

And without another word, he jogs toward the underbelly of the stadium with two of Cannon's "lackeys" following to make sure his every whim is taken care of.

I watch until he fades from sight and the only thing I can do is laugh. Arrogant ass.

This is the part where I should be telling myself that over my dead body am I staying, because I don't want to give Rush the satisfaction of being right.

But if I'm dead, then I wouldn't be able to experience all that there is to Rush, and no matter how many times I tell myself I'm holding out . . . he seems to have found a weakness of mine.

Him.

The question is, what am I going to do about it?

The answer? *Stay and watch.*

Of course, I do. I watch each pass of the ball, each set made, every shot taken, and secretly marvel at Rush's natural talent.

The entire time though, his comment keeps running through my head, almost as if to help justify my weakening resolve.

It's no one's fucking business who you sleep with.

And he's right. It's not. But I also know public perception and the professional bias that comes from it. That thought leads to Rush and what he's going through back home with Liverpool. After some digging, there are quite a few rumors about his team captain. None of them paint him in the most flattering light.

So if Rush was having a fling with Esme, maybe it was because those rumors about Seth and his controlling—and possibly abusive ways—are true.

If that's the case though, why does Rush stay quiet? Why does it feel like Rush is taking this hit as if it's a duty rather than because he's guilty? *And if he's with her, why is he pursuing me?*

"Goooooooooaaaaaaaaaaalllllllllll!" the announcer screams a millisecond before the entire stadium roars. I jump up in unison with them, my hands in the air, my voice going hoarse. "Number thirteen, Rush McKenzie, just made an incredible shot, ladies and gentlemen. That's his second of the night."

Rush high-fives the rest of his teammates in this pseudo-All-Star game with the best players from around the league competing against each other, before turning to me and pointing with a huge grin just like he did after the first goal.

The next thing he does is run over to where Scottie and his mom are sitting on the bench, high-fiving him before all the guys proceed to ruffle the hair on the top of Scottie's head.

My smile feels permanent. I truly am enjoying myself.

It's not like I ever doubted he could do it. There's a reason he's often talked about in the same circles as Messi, Maradona, Ronaldo, and even Beckenbauer.

I thought I hated this sport—the long breakaways, the low scores, the endless back and forth. After becoming fully immersed in this game, I'm beginning to think I disliked it because I didn't have anyone to root for.

But right now, watching Rush own the field every time he touches the ball, I see it differently.

His skill is phenomenal. Footwork that runs circles around the others. A cockiness that says he knows it and plans to exploit it every chance he gets. A grace that can be likened to a dancer's but with the aggression of a fighter.

If the roar of the crowd here is invigorating, I can only imagine what a game is like sitting in a seat somewhere in England where the crowd capacity is three times what is here tonight, and every touch Rush gets on the ball is either revered or reviled.

When his third goal is scored toward the latter part of the second half and his hat trick is accomplished, he simply turns my way, arms out, and takes a bow.

I throw my head back and laugh.

It's all I can do, because Rush McKenzie just successfully convinced me that soccer is an exciting sport.

So much so that I can't remember the last time something—or someone—mesmerized me to the point that I didn't pick up my phone to take a call.

And my phone had been ringing.

But I wasn't answering.

No. Instead I was falling a little more in lustful like with the tattooed newcomer putting on a show for me. Because this man wears his heart on his sleeve for those he believes deserve to see it. *And I absolutely love that.*

Chapter
TWENTY-ONE

Rush

11 Years Ago

"C'mon, mate. You have to celebrate. It was a fucking hat trick," Rory says, hand on the door, phone in the other, and a pair of the most gorgeous boots tied by the laces and hanging over his shoulders.

It sounds stupid because I have boots. Practical boots that get me through every training session just fine . . . but Rory's are a smashing black and red with a hint of white, top-of-the-line pair like the professionals wear. They look like luxury for your feet, which is ridiculous but true. Hell, for a kid always having to scrounge through used bins to find a pair of boots to fit me, I'd give anything to be able to drop three hundred quid on a pair.

I'll have a pair like that someday when I sign with Liverpool. I know I will.

"Thanks, but I'm fine. You guys go out without me." That and I have no money to go and celebrate with. Sure he'd spot me the cash, but my pride is stronger than my need to fit in with the guys. Besides, they don't all like me just yet.

I see the glances and the rolled eyes when the coach compliments me. I feel the tackles that are a little too hard during training and given out of frustration because this new guy—me—is threatening to take their spots.

"Us guys aren't going anywhere. I'm talking about going to my mum and dad's. They phoned and told me that you're coming home with me so you can celebrate properly."

"Oh." I think of Archibald Matheson and his constant presence around the pitch. His barrel laugh and quick comments to the coaches and other parents. And I think of how just two months ago he stood on that sidewalk outside of the shop and saved me in a way I'm not sure he even realizes.

"My mum's cooking is way better than the shit you're getting here," he says as my mouth waters. I'll never complain about the food I'm provided with because the memory of hunger pangs is too recent, but home-cooked food? I can't remember what that actually tastes like. "Besides, she isn't taking no for an answer. It seems my mum and dad love you more than me." His laugh echoes through the empty hallway, and I can't tell if it's annoyance I hear or hurt, but one thing's for sure, it sounds fragile. Something he seems to be more and more as of late.

"That's not true."

"Whatever, mate. I don't care. Let's go."

I sit there and stare at Rory—the one who feels like the only friend I have—and wonder why I'm hesitating. "The rest of the guys. They'll think—"

"Fuck what those bastards think. They're just worried because you're kicking their arses on the pitch and making them look bad. Besides, I told them you're with me. I have your back, Rush. That means they won't say a word since they know my dad turns a blind eye or makes any trouble they may get in go away over at the station." He nods, our eyes meet, and I wonder what it is he sees when he looks at me, because it sure as fuck is something different than when everyone else does.

When I don't stand, he strides forward to kick my foot. "You'll be fine soon enough. Hell, a hat trick tonight helped with that seeing as everyone loves winning."

"And hurt, seeing as I played the entire game," I say.

"And?" he asks with a raise of his eyebrows and a shrug. "C'mon. She's waiting and I'm starving."

*

I place the napkin in my lap and look up to find Helen Matheson staring at me with wide eyes. "So? Did you like it?"

My eyes all but bug out of my head. "Yes. I'm sorry. Did I not say I did? It was"—Wonderful. Incredible. Homecooked—"my new favorite meal."

She claps her hands as Archibald chuckles. "I'm so glad," she says as if she were nervous that I was actually going to complain. "After the game you played today, you deserved something special."

I spare a glance across the table to Rory and feel awkward. "Rory kicked arse—did great today too. I think he's going to make a fine defender if they end up keeping him there."

"Rory will do fine wherever he plays so long as he keeps practicing," Archibald says dismissively as he takes a sip of brandy. "But you, Rush. You were magnificent today."

Shifting in my seat, I feel uncomfortable at the praise, but I offer a smile or comment when proper during the rest of the meal. Rory even makes a face at me at one point and we erupt into laughter.

But it's only when the meal is done and Mrs. Matheson walks out with a cake lit with candles that I do a double take when they start singing, including me. She laughs as she puts it down in front of me. And when the singing ends, they all look at me expectantly.

"We know it's not for two weeks, but we wanted to help you celebrate your birthday properly," Helen says. "Happy birthday, Rush."

I blink at her . . . and swallow back tears. It reminds me of the last time my birthday was celebrated. It was my twelfth birthday and my mum was healthy and happy. She'd picked up an extra job waitressing that I kept telling her she didn't need, but when I opened my present, I understood why. She'd bought me a Liverpool shirt. We'd cried together when I opened it.

It's the last great memory I have of her—before treatments and hair loss and pain. Before she lost her jobs, because she missed so much work from being sick. When we cuddled together in that tiny flat, so I could keep her warm and try to make her laugh through the pain.

"Rush? Son? I'm sorry, I didn't realize this would upset you. I promise I'm not trying to take over for your mum."

I'm so fucking embarrassed by the tears that I shove away the one tear I let slip down my cheek with the back of my hand as fast as I can.

"No. This is . . . it's good. Fine." I feel like an arse. "It's just . . . I can't re-member . . . It's only ever been my mum and me who celebrated my birthday."

"Not anymore. Any friend of Rory's is family to us," Archibald says in that deep baritone of his.

"Go on, make a wish," Helen says.

When I close my eyes, I wish the only other wish I've ever had other than to save my mum: I wish to play for Liverpool F.C. someday.

And it's only after I blow the candles out and Rory grumbles how full he is that Helen hands a wrapped present to me.

"What birthday is complete without a gift?" Archibald says as Rory smirks in his seat across from me.

"You've already done more than enough. I can't accept anything else."

"Go 'head, mate. I promise you'll love it," Rory says.

I open the package and stare at the same set of boots that I was madly wanting hours before. Bloody hell. What do I say?

"I can't—this is too much. Thank you, but—"

"Nonsense, son. One of the best footballers I've seen play in a long while deserves to have the best for his feet," Archibald says.

"These are expensive. Thank you, but like I said, I can't accept them."

"You can and you will," Archibald says with a finality that silences the room. "Tell him, Helen. Tell him what you asked me earlier this week."

Both Rory and I look back and forth from his dad to his mum before Helen finally speaks. "We want you to think of this place, this house, our family, as your home. Rory's never had a brother before and Archibald says you're without a family. That you need a steady family to help you on the field as well . . . and we want you to know, we've really loved having you here the few times Rory has brought you home and"—she smooths her hands down her thighs as if she's nervous—"I'm rambling. I don't mean to and I don't want to overstep, but we want you to stay here with us over the holidays and when you have breaks from the academy or any time things get too crazy where you're staying."

My head spins at the offer. At the sense of normalcy and home and warmth I feel when I'm in this house. At having someone like Rory in my life who looks out for me.

"I don't know what to say."

"Say yes," she says, eyebrows raised and hope in her eyes. "I always wanted to have two boys. It was my dream, but I was unable to have any more children after Rory and so . . . I don't know, but when Archibald suggested this, I thought maybe this is God's way of giving me two boys." Her smile—there's something about the warmth in it that reminds me of my mum in this moment. I'd do anything for it to remain so I can remember her a little bit more.

God, I miss her.

God, I miss . . . a sense of belonging. Of not being alone.

I clear my throat. Uncertain what to say.

"I'm good with it, if you are, mate," Rory says with a nod.

"Sure, yeah. I don't know what to say other than thank you . . . but I still can't keep the boots."

And by God, when Rory and I left there two hours later, I had the box with the boots in them stuffed under my arm and my head a whirlwind of thoughts.

"Come with me?" Rory asks when the sidewalk splits and I take a step toward the dormitories.

"Where?" I ask.

"To have a smoke."

"You know I don't smoke."

"Not that kind of smoke, Rush. The other kind that makes everything speed up and feel good." He shifts on his feet, shoves his hands in his pockets, and lifts his brows as I stare at him in shock. He's a policeman's son. I don't know why I figured a policeman's son would never do that. "Go drop your boots off. I'll wait here for you."

"Nah. No thanks." I finally break free from the shock to respond. "I have shit to do."

"C'mon, don't be a sod, Rush. If we're going to be brothers, mate," he says with a wink, "it's time you know all my secrets." His laugh floats through the night.

"No judgment here," I say.

"Sometimes I just need a release to deal with 'em. Being perfect can be daunting." He cuffs me on the shoulder. "Good thing you can be that for both of us now." Another laugh as he takes a few steps backward. "You sure?"

"I'm sure." I force a smile and watch Rory jog the opposite way, wondering how the fuck he can give one hundred percent on the field tomorrow after getting high tonight.

How he could disrespect his parents by doing that shit after everything they've done for him?

Everything I would give anything to have.

Chapter
TWENTY-TWO

Lennox

"Ms. Kincade?" I turn to look over my shoulder to where Cannon's assistant is standing with her hands clasped in front of her and a soft smile on her face.

"Oh, hi, Maggie. I didn't see you there. What is it?"

"Mr. Garner is looking for you. He says the presentation will start soon and he wanted to make sure you were by his side."

"Oh, yes. Sure." I look back to the general managers of two MLS teams I was just speaking with. "If you'll excuse me. I definitely want to finish this conversation after dinner."

"Perfect. I'm more than interested to hear your thoughts on the state of the league," one of them says.

"He'll meet you backstage momentarily," Maggie says as she points to a small hallway that leads toward the back of the small conference area.

"Great. I'll run to the ladies' room and then meet him there."

Tonight's function is Cannon's attempt to wine and dine potential advertisers and sponsors by having them all in one place with the coaches and management of each team in the league. Of course, Rush is the big draw—as well as the ever-constant murmuring over whether he's here to play for good—and he will be unveiling the league's new marketing plan for the coming season.

Lucky for me, I haven't had much contact with Rush though, because that man is absolutely stunning in a black tuxedo. Like stop-and-stare, pick-your-jaw-up-off-the-floor stunning.

I make my way toward the back of the ballroom of sorts and startle when I look up to see Finn standing there.

"Look at you all dressed up and with nowhere to go," he says with that condescending grin on his lips.

"Go to hell, Sanderson." It takes everything I have not to barrel through him—because he's the last person I want to see right now—but I know I need to play this cool. His unexpected appearance tells me he's worried about me stealing Rush.

Good. He should be.

"I'm sensing some hostility, Lennox."

"And I'm sensing an agent who's a little fearful that his plan to oust me from a project failed and now he's worried that I just might steal his prized client away."

"I don't have any prized clients."

"Ouch." I twist my lips and stare at him. I know this game. Downplay your athlete as not important to make the temptation to steal him that much less. "I wouldn't let Rush hear you say that."

"Talking about me to him, I presume?"

"I have better things to waste my time on than talking about you." I give him a killer smile. "Now if you'll excuse me, I have a job to do."

"I guess the question I should ask is if you've slept with Rush yet?" His words stop me in my tracks just as I move past him.

What the hell?

I'm shocked at how brazen he is but when I turn to face him, my expression shows nothing of the sort. "Excuse me?"

"Well, you sleep with clients before you steal them—maybe as a way to steal them because that's all you have to offer them? So if you haven't fucked Rush yet, then I have nothing to be worried about." The look he levels me with is pure condescension and it takes everything I have not to haul off and punch him.

"When did you become such an asshole?" I narrow my eyes as I try to comprehend.

He shrugs. "Can't blame an agent for coming to see for himself whether you're up to your usual."

"I mean, I used to actually like you. Did all that money and power you've gained over the years not compensate enough for how small your dick is?"

He chuckles loudly as I take another step toward the door, and I know his lack of a snappy comeback means he's secretly freaking out that my sister, Chase, said something to me about him—or lack thereof.

Perfect.

Serves him right.

But it doesn't do anything to quiet my scattered thoughts as I walk down the hallway toward the restroom. Did he really just say that? Did he—

I yelp as someone grabs my arm from behind and pulls me into a small room off the main hall. But my fear doesn't last long when Rush's lips smother the sound as he pushes me against the door he just closed.

My hands pound against his chest in reaction to being scared to death, while my lips react and take the kiss he's owning my lips with. The kiss I've craved and thought about over and over despite telling myself I can't have.

There's hungry desperation in it. Carnal desire. When his tongue touches mine, I feel it all the way from my fingers to my toes.

And his hands. I missed the feel of them. How they touch me with equal parts reverence and urgency.

As much as I want to beg him not to stop, I inhale a shaky breath when he does. We're standing inches apart, the need and want and lust we feel for each other more than apparent in the ragged sounds of our breaths filling up this small, darkened room.

"Rush." *Get your thoughts about you, Lennox.* "We can't—I can't do this." *Finn could be outside this door.*

"We just did. And we still can." He laughs as confusion blankets his face.

"No, we can't. Argh!" I step around him and take a few steps to gain some distance and hopefully my senses.

"Why can't we?"

"Because of Cannon. And Finn. And . . . We just can't."

"What the fuck do Cannon and Finn have to do with who either of us sleep with?" Then almost as if something hits him all at once he staggers a step back. "It's Cannon, isn't it? You want Cannon instead of me."

"Oh my God. *No.*" I laugh, completely taken aback by his assumption. "It's not because I want Cannon. It's . . . it's complicated, and I have to go right now because of course, I have to stand out there with Cannon and introduce you to the guests. To top it off, I don't want Finn to see us leave here and—"

"Finn's here?" he asks, clearly surprised when I nod. "Then I guess you better start talking fast."

"Rush." His name is a sigh of resignation.

"Tell me why, Lennox. Explain to me why a chemistry as strong as ours—the kind that snaps against each other's every time we're in close proximity—should be ignored?"

"We don't have the time to flesh this out—"

He steps in front of the door. "Yes, we do."

I stare at him, hands on my hips, and know he's not going to back down until I explain what he truly needs to know. "This whole thing— you promoting the league for a short time while the Premier League is off-season and as a means to get you away to let everything die down there—is all a ruse. He's trying to wine, dine, and impress you to stay here."

"Any intelligent person could assume that," he says. "It's smart on his part." He pauses as if he's going to say something else but then pauses. "That's not what you're hiding from me, though."

"Cannon lured me here under the guise that I would consult with him on how the league could offer better packages to their players. He wanted more structured benefits and compensation to keep them happy, to ensure they'd want to play here versus be lured overseas."

"Fat chance." He snorts.

"Exactly, but once I signed the contract, he informed me that my in-centive-driven purpose in this role is to recruit you to stay here."

"Okay." He draws the word out, his expression pensive. "So we can't sleep together because why?"

"Because Cannon has it in his head that I need to be your agent. That I need to steal you away from Finn and represent you myself. He feels that if you're with me, he'll get what he wants: his shiny star to hang the league's success on." I emit a frustrated sigh. "He thinks I'll be his puppet, for lack of a better term."

"He definitely doesn't know you then." Rush chuckles. "Because the woman I know would never let anyone own her or her decisions."

I'd love to pause and let that compliment sink in, because what Rush said gives me joy. He believes in me, but I can't let that affect the fact that sleeping with him still causes an issue.

"Thank you. But can you see how this is a problem all around?" I ask while Rush stares. "It's a bad move if you ask me."

"What is?" he asks. There's an intensity to him right now that unnerves me. I'm not sure if he's going to be angry with me or . . . I don't know, but I begin to stumble over my thoughts.

"Cannon hiring me for the league. The you being here part. The me being here to steal you makes matters ten times more complicated when I've already slept with you."

"You mean, *am sleeping with you.*"

"It was one time, Rush. We got each other out of our systems," I lie.

His chuckle tells me he knows it is. "Funny. I sure as hell haven't gotten you out of mine and truth be told"—he crosses the short distance between us, and runs the back of his hand down the side of my cheek—"the way you just kissed me tells me there's a whole lot more you want to get out of our systems."

"Finn's out there," I deflect. "The last thing I need is him seeing us leaving this room together. He's a smart agent. I'd be concerned if my client was working side by side with another agent, too."

"I hope I make myself clear when I say that no one determines or deters who I sleep with other than me."

His words are a stark reminder of the mess he left behind back home.

"Rush, it's words like those that give the press the fodder they need to annihilate you. That's how you ended up in the States." He squints at me in anger briefly, but then it's gone, because he can see that I don't believe it's true. "If I thought you had a girlfriend back home, I wouldn't have slept with you in the first place," I whisper.

At that, I see a small—*relieved?*—smile form on his gorgeous lips. One that doesn't help me not want to kiss him any less. He leans forward and kisses my forehead, lingering. And I know he's heard my faith in him.

So, I continue. "Rush, this is where I live. This is my job. My professionalism on the line. My reputation. And—"

"So then we don't let them know. We've been hired to do a job and we're doing it. That's the bottom line. Anything beyond that is out of their realm."

"It's not that easy. Do you know what it would look like to other athletes if word got out? That I sleep with potential clients in the hope that it would win them over to sign with me? I mean, there's so much more to the equation." I think of Finn's accusation minutes ago and know the only way Rush will understand is if I tell him, but I also want to take the high road. The last thing I need to do is to poison him against his agent because I have personal issues with the prick. "You might get away with doing whatever you want, whenever you want even if it's trouble, but you still get paid. You still have a public pushing for you because of your incredible talent. Me, on the other hand? I look like a tart who fucks her way to the top."

I wish I knew what was going on behind those eyes of his.

"You're my tart," he says with a half laugh before his expression softens and grows intense as the other part of what I said hits him. "You said I had incredible talent."

It strikes me in the moment that this grown man, gruff in so many ways, just stopped in his tracks for simple praise. Almost as if everything else is white noise.

"Surely you know that," I say through a laugh.

"It's not something I hear from people who matter to me." Our eyes meet, hold, and I open my mouth and then close it, uncertain how to respond. He truly isn't used to hearing it. "And Finn?" he asks, changing the topic before I can ask the questions I'm sure are fleeting through my eyes.

"What about Finn?"

"Does he know about Cannon's master plan to force me to stay here and never go back home?" He smiles this time, although I can tell he's still processing.

"I have no idea what he knows or doesn't know. He tried to prevent Cannon from hiring me, so I can assume he has an inkling why I was brought on board."

"Do you know Finn well?"

I huff out a laugh. "We have a history of sorts—no, not the kind you're thinking of," I say when he looks startled, and I realize my poor choice of words. "He definitely has his opinions about me, so what I think of him doesn't really factor into this conversation."

"I can respect that."

"I should get out there. Cannon's probably wondering where I am," I say but Rush doesn't move out of the way.

"Is Cannon right in his thinking?"

"About?"

"If you were my agent, would you talk me into leaving the Premier League and staying here?"

"I'm not your agent though," I say, trying hard to keep my opinions to myself.

"Humor me."

"Rush," I groan and look at my phone to check the time. Cannon is definitely going to be looking for me.

"What would you advise?"

I straighten my shoulders and look at Rush, the athlete, instead of Rush, the man I want to experience again, and I speak the truth. "I'd tell you you're crazy to even let the idea of staying here pass over your lips. You're at the top of your game, the pinnacle of your career, and you'd be selling yourself, the sport, and your fans short. I'd also tell you that you should have never come here in the first place."

"Really? Why's that?" he asks as if he's surprised by the comment.

"Because coming here looks like you're running. By not staying there and facing the press and your teammates, it gives the appearance that you're guilty of fucking Seth's wife behind his back." Rush cringes at the harshness of my words and his reaction surprises me. "You haven't said a word otherwise, so everyone is making assumptions. Assumptions that I think are total bullshit. You know I don't think you did it, but for the freaking life of me I can't figure out why you don't say otherwise."

He stares at me, and for the briefest of moments, I think he's going to break his silence on the subject. There is a look in his eyes that tells me there's so much more that I don't know but true to fashion, he just gives the subtlest of nods.

"Finn says I have to be quiet because of the gagging order the management put into place after a fight broke out in the changing room."

"That's why you've been silent?" I emit a huff of disbelief. "I don't buy it. Since when have you ever managed your career by the assumptions of others? That's what bugs me about this whole situation, Rush. That's what eats at me. Why were you told to come here? To save face on negotiations that don't sound like they're being made, or to do a favor, and for what purpose?"

"You're the first person who's said anything like that to me."

Oh, this man is killing me. How can someone so gruff and strong and opinionated be gentled by simple words of truth? *And how can he look at me with such deep affection as if he's craved that? Needed that?*

"The real question is, what is it that you want? Just you. Until you answer that question, everything is going to feel way off."

And this time, when I go to walk past Rush to go meet up with Cannon, he lets me without saying a word.

Chapter
TWENTY-THREE

Rush

THE REAL QUESTION IS RUSH, WHAT IS IT THAT YOU WANT?

I stare at Finn sitting across from me. He's leaning back in his seat, a cigar is burning in his ashtray, and a pint is sitting half-drunk beside him. He's partially buzzed, but that's not stopping him from dishing out advice that I'm only half listening to because ever since last night, Lennox's words are on repeat in my head.

"Word around the league is that you're killing it, McKenzie. Charming the investors, rallying the supporters, and there's an uptick in ticket sales for the upcoming season."

"I feel like a sham."

His eyes whip up to mine. That definitely got his attention. "What do you mean, you feel like a sham?"

"People are buying these tickets because they think I'm staying to play here when I'm not. I haven't given any indication that I am, but by simply being here, it's the conclusion they've drawn."

"And that's a problem, why?"

"Because it is. They remember when the MLS started and the LA Galaxy signed David Beckham to play in the States. Cannon is giving the same impression to fans when it comes to me and it's bullshit."

"C'mon," he says and waves a hand in indifference. "You're selling them the idea of it. That doesn't mean it's going to be the reality."

I think of all the families who are spending their hard-earned money for tickets. I think of Scottie and Daphne, and how she promised him before they left after the game that he'd get to see me again. I didn't have the heart to tell her otherwise—to upset him after an awesome day where she told me she couldn't remember the last time she saw him so carefree, so much like a kid should be. So yeah, I'm the arsehole who left it to her to tell him eventually.

What's worse is I know she's already trying to figure out how she can split her money—paying a utility bill late, some groceries, hell if I know— to bring her son to one of my games. I've been there. I've watched the worry on my mother's face as she calculated and robbed Peter to pay Paul, because the days when the younger version of me was happy were so few and far between that she did whatever she could to see it again.

Just like me, just like Scottie, there are so many more like us out there whose parents will spend the money they don't have in order to perpetuate a dream. In order to give their child the best chance in life.

"Cannon is lying to them," I say.

"It's part of the game. We all play it."

"But I don't." I sit forward and lean my forearms on the table as I wait for him to meet my eyes. "When I'm in my Liverpool kit, I'm not playing any other game than the one on the pitch against the opponent."

"If you think that, you're fooling yourself, Rush." He takes a sip of his beer and lifts a chin toward a table full of women who keep looking our way. "You're constantly playing a game. With the public, reinforcing their perception of you. With your endorsements, and what they're wanting you to sell. With your teammates, and who you want them to think you are—the motivated, aggressive athlete or the guy who'll stab them in the back and sleep with their wives."

I stop with my glass halfway to my lips and stare at my agent. How funny that Lennox, a woman I've known for a whole two weeks, is all but yelling at me that she knows I didn't touch Esme and my own agent, who has known me for years, is saying shit like that.

When my agent retired four years ago, he told me Finn was the best. He promised me that if I wanted someone who would push both my career and increase my sponsorship deals, then Finn Sanderson was the man.

But right now, I sit and stare at Finn and wonder if he's ever really taken the time to know me other than when a significant negotiation was about to happen that would thicken the lining of his pockets. Because I'm not feeling any of the love or trust when it comes to him like I did with my previous agent. I'm not seeing faith in me or even concern to hear me. I expect an agent to mitigate problems—that's what they do—but I'm not seeing *my* agent fight for me the way a woman I've known only a couple of weeks is willing to fight . . . and that's a problem.

"So happy to see you addressing my concerns," I say sarcastically.

"C'mon, man. You know I didn't mean that last part. I was just joking." He huffs out a breath in annoyance when he sees it still hasn't set right with me. "You're getting paid to stand there and look pretty. Are you going to argue with that?"

"Yeah, I'd much rather be back home with my trainers and coaches and preparing for the next season. It's not the money. It's the premise you pushed me here under."

"I didn't push you anywhere. That's fucking nonsense. I guided. You agreed. End of story."

I throw my hands up. "It feels dirty, mate."

"How dirty does over one hundred million dollars sound?" His eyes meet mine, his brows lifted, as he runs a finger over the rim of his glass. "Because that's what is possible here. A long term contract. Bonuses. Endorsement deals. They want you and they want you bad."

And there it is.

The pitch. The promise. The reason he showed up in Los Angeles when he never shows up—unless Lennox is right, and he's here because he's afraid I'd switch agencies to hers.

And telling me he's negotiating a hundred-million-dollar contract is definitely something an agent would do to get you to stay put.

"You have nothing to say to that?" he asks.

"It's a lot of money." I nod. "Are you throwing the bait out there to see if I'll bite or are you telling me something I should already know?"

"You said you're enjoying sunny California."

"Have they made me an offer or are you blowing smoke up my arse?" I ask, wanting to know and not wanting to know. That's a shit ton of money. It matches what I already have in the bank, more than any person could ever spend, and yet . . . I balk at the idea.

It would be like selling every part of me to something I didn't believe in wholeheartedly.

"Numbers are being tossed around, comments are being made. I simply want you to know it's happening so you have time to figure out if this is what you want or not."

No.

"Was this the plan all along, Finn? Did you have this all worked out with Cannon ahead of time, waiting for my next screwup to talk me into it?"

"You're a highly demanded football player. Whether there was this little snafu or not, you were being talked about. But you being you, isn't that enough of a reason for the MLS to want you?"

No. My head spins. I feel like I've been maneuvered into this. Hell, was this all a setup? Rory and Esme? The photographer? Everything? Was this a way to twist my arm? I don't trust Cannon for a bloody second, but I at least trusted Finn.

Could he? Is this?

What the fuck?

"You're jumping to conclusions." Finn holds his hands up. "I can already see it in your posture. Chill out, man. None of this was planned. Shit happened, and now it might present another opportunity for you to further your professional career."

"Furthering my professional career would be winning the World Cup for England. Getting the Golden Boot. Having a few Premier League championships under my belt. Not coming here where football has been trying to get off the ground for over a decade and is still failing."

"It would be a way to make a name for yourself in a whole different place."

"I like my name attached to Liverpool F.C. just fine, thanks mate." I pause for a beat before looking back to him. "It's the only place I've ever been, and I'm perfectly happy for it to be the only place I play for a while. I'm not washed-up yet."

"Rush." My name is a frustrated sigh. "No one said you were."

And yet if I played here, that's exactly what would be implied.

"Don't discard the possibility. It's a great opportunity."

"Of course, it is. I mean, is this in my best interest or yours? Because

I'm thinking any opportunity where you get ten percent of one hundred million is definitely in your best interest."

"Now you're just being a dick."

I shrug nonchalantly because he's right. I am being one, and I fucking deserve the right to be when this is my life we're talking about here.

"Any news from the club?" I ask. It's the only thing I care about, because the longer I'm here—save for the pleasure of seeing Lennox and her long damn legs every morning—the more I miss home. The gray skies and cobblestone streets. The green of Anfield's pitch, and the sound of the guys harassing each other in the changing room. The feel of my bed and the taste of my bloody tea instead of the weak shit they have in the States. Proper beer in pubs where you go to hang with mates, rather than swanky bars like in LA where you go to be seen. "The transfer window will be closing next month and I need to not be transferred."

"Management is still figuring things out."

"And you know this because you've talked to them directly or because you've been hung up on by Millie at the front desk after she informed you, 'we'll call you when we know something'?"

"Why are you in such a shitty mood? Huh? I got you away from the media frenzy and the club drama there and now we're here." He motions his hands to the sunny sky above and the beach in sight to our left. "Are you really complaining about being in Los Angeles?"

"No, I'm complaining about my agent trying to sell me a pint of piss and trying to make me believe otherwise."

"For your information, I've been talking to Patrick. Several times in fact. You happy?"

"And?"

"And they're trying to figure out how the fuck their team captain is going to play with the man who was supposed to be the new team vice captain"—he points at me—"you, without punching each other out in the middle of a game."

"I told you it wasn't me, Finn."

"And I told you it damn well looks like you in the photo, so in case you can give me something else to present to the team to say otherwise, you're the one who's looking bad in this situation."

"Shit."

"You fucked up—big time—and a manager doesn't want a problem-child messing with their team chemistry."

And there he goes again. "You're my agent. Aren't you supposed to be telling me you're fighting as hard as you can to get me where I need to be because you know the truth?"

"I am fighting."

"It doesn't seem like it." I look back to him. "You told me this would blow over."

So did Archibald, Rush. And despite his blasé attitude when he asked me to take the hit, Archibald still calls or texts every few days to make sure I stay the course. To remind me how he's seen me as another son, from taking me in, educating me, feeding me, taking me on family holidays . . .

But he's a father figure who lets another son stuff his own future and then calls in a marker . . .

He messages me to tell me the story has fallen back in the pages and is slowly dying.

Good.

Fucking great.

But that doesn't mean it's been forgotten by my club and team. Or by Seth.

That's the part I underestimated when I agreed to this narrative.

That's the one thing I can't change.

A chance encounter. My stolen meal lost under the boots of some interfering policeman. The man who sent his son with the policeman to learn about *real life* and *responsibilities* . . . but then sent that same son an easy get-out-of-jail-free card eleven years later. Quid. Pro. Fucking. Quo. *All so Archibald Matheson can ascend to his own throne.* Easily done, because it costs him nothing.

Was it worth it?

That's what brought me to this moment. To this quid pro quo.

Was it worth it? I stare at Finn and repeat Lennox's question in my head.

I have much to prove that it is—wealth, a place in sporting history, the chance to play a game that I love, and make more money than I ever dreamed I could. I'll never have to worry about being hungry or cold or unclean again. I didn't go to jail that day, I didn't miss the scholarship, and I didn't spend the rest of my teen years growing up alone because of them. The Mathesons became a family where a seat at the dinner table was always set for me.

Then there's Archibald. A man I possibly hero-worshipped, until I saw how his career came before his family. How rising through the ranks—and his need to feel important at all costs, including supporting my career—was accomplished mostly to the detriment of his flesh-and-blood son, who still hasn't grown the fuck up.

Rory. My brother. Often someone I consider my best friend.

And Helen. She made space for me in her heart, not replacing my mum of course, but certainly filling the large hole Mum left since she died.

She's spent so much time trying to right Archibald's wrongs and shortcomings. She's fought so hard for Rory's success—not professionally, but emotionally—as she has mine.

How could I let her down now?

Despite their weaknesses, they've never turned their back on me when almost everyone else had. Sure, I know Archibald did it to attach his name to the closest thing he could find to a rising star . . . but she did it out of love. She did it because she cared. And part of that has helped me be the man I am today.

So that's why I can do this.

He first saw me.

That's what brought me here.

She first loved me.

That's why I can hold out on this.

He became my brother. One I won't abandon.

But then my debt will be paid in full. End of story.

"How about you get a royal pregnant? Then everyone would be so excited that you'd be forgiven." He chuckles.

"Funny," I say dryly before becoming dead serious. "I don't want to leave the team, Finn. I don't want to be transferred. That's where I belong and I'm good enough, sought after enough, that my agent has the right to tell my team that. Seth is good, but he's on the tail end of his career while

I'm in my prime." I take a sip of my designer lager and when he doesn't respond, I continue. "I'm getting calls left and right. Media asking for interviews and the like. I'm beginning to think I should talk publicly."

Maybe I'm baiting him about breaking the gagging order. Maybe I'm seeing what he says compared to what Lennox suggested. I know I have no plans to speak to the press, but perhaps I'm trying to figure out where his true allegiance lies. His paycheck or his player?

And he fails miserably when he answers.

"It wouldn't be smart to go against the gagging order. We should stay the course." *We should stay the course.* Archibald's words . . . exactly. He lifts his finger to the server for another round that I no longer want to sit here and drink with him. "And in the meantime, you should soak this shit up. The sun, the surf, the women who will eat up those tattoos and that accent of yours."

"Yep," I say, mind completely disengaged at this point. I want to tell Finn to piss off, but I'm knackered and can't be bothered.

"Where are you staying again?" he asks the question I dodge every time he asks.

I don't think it's the best time to mention I'm staying with Johnny . . . and Lennox. That won't go over well at all.

"I already told you last time you asked, a friend's house."

"Good for you. A bit of advice, Rush," he says, leaning forward as if he's going to tell me the secret of all secrets. "Enjoy all that this city has to offer and tell me it wouldn't be a hardship to live here."

Chapter
TWENTY-FOUR

Lennox

"Fucking hell," Rush says as he saunters into the family room where I've set up shop on one end of the couch. My laptop is on my legs, a few contracts are on the cushion beside me, and a bottle of wine is half gone on the end table opposite me. "I have stamina." He winks, adding that grin I've been trying to ignore. "You know that, of course, but this press thing is bullshit."

"Meaning?"

"Meaning, how many meetings and press briefings and circus shows do I have to go to where I smile wide and stand there beside Cannon but don't say anything other than sing the MLS's praises. These people don't love football. Not like back home. They think they do but they have no desire to put the funds and the marketing in to make it what it could be here in the States."

I look over to him where he stands, sweats on, shirt off, and welcome the distraction as my eyes were about to go cross-eyed from all the fine print.

But now I'm definitely alert at the sight of him and the visceral punch he gives me each and every time. It's almost as if my body knows how good he is and is trying to shock my head into forgetting.

"That is kind of what your job description is, though." He levels me with a glare that makes me chuckle. "Poor baby. Rough day at the office, dear?"

He presses his fingers to his eyes before running a hand through his hair. "When do the questions ever fucking end?" he asks and sighs. "What about Esme, Rush? Are you going to be the chink in the Liverpool armor, Rush? Hey, Rush, who do you think the team is going to keep—you or Seth? The transfer window will be narrowing soon so who do you think, Rush? Such bollocks," he says as he moves toward me and begins to gather up all the papers on the couch beside me.

"Hey, what are you—" And before I can finish what I'm saying, he plops down, head on my lap—where I've just pushed my laptop out of the way—and his feet are extended over the armrest. "Rush!"

I look down to find him looking up at me with that sheepish smile and those thick lashes framing his pale, unapologetic eyes.

"Excuse me?" I ask in mock exasperation, which I've given up feeling when it comes to him.

"I just needed to be with someone nice who doesn't ask me a million questions," he says in a sleepy voice, closing his eyes as he snuggles in and gets comfortable. "Someone who isn't judging or questioning or wondering while I stand there with a smile plastered to my face, pretending it doesn't affect me, since I'm the face of a whole bloody league."

It's the first trace of Rush's frustration and I'm glad to see it. A part of me wonders if it stems from what I said to him at the event the other night. The function where I spoke my mind when I swore I wouldn't. I couldn't help myself. Not after Finn and his bullshit. Besides, anyone who's not affected in some way or another by the event he left behind needs to have an emotional overhaul.

And of course, he just pigeonholed me with that whole speech. Because while we've been skirting around each other over the past week with Finn here in LA, I can't help but remember the look on Rush's face when I told him I didn't think he slept with Esme. The widening of his eyes. His lips opening in shock.

The question is what or who he's covering for and why.

"They're naturally curious, you know. Everyone is." I tread cautiously, and when he doesn't open his eyes or respond, I continue. "You haven't given a single statement about the matter. To anyone. If you did, it might clear things up for some people."

"I told you, the team is under a gagging order," he murmurs.

"And I told you, there are ways to work around that," I say, "but the fact that you carry on like business as usual when you left a wake of trouble behind you has people curious." And probably, very disappointed. The comments on his post from his massive following on social media reflect just that.

"Next topic, please."

I don't hide my frustrated sigh as I study his face. The way his lashes fan over his cheeks and the dark stubble from not shaving this morning. I so want to lean over and kiss those lips. There's an ache, a need, that seeing him, having him touch me causes. It hasn't left since that first time he kissed me.

Change gears, Lennox.

Save your sanity.

I reach out and run a hand through his hair. "I was working here, you know."

"I know, but you're also working with me, and since I seem to be getting the short end of the stick on your attention as of late, I figured I'd insert myself right where you can't ignore me anymore." He opens his eyes to meet mine.

"I've hardly been ignoring you."

"Then why am I the only one lying horizontal right now?" His grin widens, which is a welcome sight after the worry etched in the lines of his face moments ago.

But as much as it's a welcome sight, I emit a sigh. It's all I can do. The man most definitely wins an A for effort and being relentless over the past week.

Between walking around in those damn LFC sweats that ride low on his hips to making sure to occupy every single space of the house I'm in, he's definitely determined to wear me down until I cave.

If I'm on the phone pacing with a client, he plops down, props his feet up right in my path as if I'm not there, and starts scrolling on his phone.

If I'm working at the dining room table on the computer, he turns a game on, any game, and commentates to drive me crazy.

If I'm in the kitchen, he hops up on the island right where I'm preparing food, taking samples of whatever I'm preparing.

I've held out, I'm proud that I have, but the more he's around and the less I'm around the outside influences in my life that were making me feel inadequate, the more I'm beginning to agree with him that it's no one's business who I sleep with.

"You have to stop doing this," I scold.

"Doing what?"

"Thinking my time is your time."

"But isn't it your job to make me happy? So essentially your time is my time." His grin is back and when I avert my eyes, I'm looking at his chest. The intricate tattoos cover his left shoulder and down to his wrist. They're a mosaic of images and words, the most substantial one a compass of sorts that all the rest revolve around, and I study each one while he watches me do so.

"Do you have something against wearing shirts?" I murmur.

"Yes. As a matter of fact, I do. It's a shame to wear them when the weather is as great as it is here. You should try it sometime."

"We're not as free here in the States when it comes to women going topless."

"You should be. I won't tell anyone if you take it off if you don't tell."

"Funny."

"Tell me something, Lennox."

"Hmm?"

"Why are you here? There's more to it than just the MLS. I've heard you on the phone with your sisters and dad. You miss them."

My smile is soft as a swell of emotion hits me, and how right he is. "I do."

"Care to expand?"

"Only if you care to?"

Our eyes hold for a beat, a silent challenge highlighted with an undertone of sexual tension that neither of us can deny. His heartbeat pounds under my hand I have resting atop his chest and in this moment, I know my defenses are all but nonexistent.

"You're upset."

"Sometimes family does that to you even when it's unintentional."

"What happ—"

I press my finger to his lips moments before shifting so my lips can replace it. He stills for a beat when our lips meet, and as I use my tongue to coax his mouth to part.

There's hesitation.

"What are we doing here, Nox?" he murmurs against my lips.

A tenderness we've yet to experience, but that is so very welcome, especially when he uses his nickname I only hear when we're alone.

"I'm kissing you." I slip my tongue between his lips again.

"I thought there were rules."

Another touch of lips. A soft groan when I gently tug on his lips before I lean back to answer him.

"There are."

"You're breaking them."

His eyes darken as we stare at each other, our breaths feathering one another.

"I'm taking lessons from you."

And this time when I kiss him, I don't stop. I revel in the moment. In him. In needing this human connection with a man I know will make me feel good. A man who won't be able to hurt me.

We both know this will go nowhere.

We both have lives to return to in a matter of weeks. So despite the warnings I've given, the promises I've made to myself, I act on that ache deep within—both physically and emotionally—to be connected with someone when I feel so very untethered from everything else.

He breaks from the kiss and when he studies me, I wonder what he sees. The inadequate agent trying to do right by her family or the hard-headed agent who's trying to make a place for herself in a world where nothing is as it seems? Or the woman who's trying to do both while carving a little piece of life for herself in the midst of it?

"You haven't asked to be my agent," he whispers.

"Presently, I have more things on my mind than who's negotiating your contracts."

"Like?"

"Like kissing you." I lean down and tease his lips.

"Oh," he says, and I smother the sound with my kiss.

His hand reaches up to the back of my neck to pull me closer, yet he lets me take the lead on this. My action creates his reaction. My sigh is only accented by his soft groan.

And so we kiss. Our tongues meet and flutter over one another's. Our hands roam gently over one another despite our awkward positioning.

But there's an intimacy to the kiss, a longing sated. The hunger is still there between us, the dire lust, but the urgency we've typically exhibited is on hold while we connect in the simplest of ways.

My body heats from his touch. My mind goes blank, save for allowing me to appreciate and savor this rare moment of tenderness from a man who's all about action and distraction.

The best part about it all is that he makes no move to take more. He allows me to take what I want and not hurry whatever this is along.

Sure we've had sex before, but there's something about this moment, about each meeting of our lips and sigh of contentment that fills some part of me I wasn't sure was missing or needed until now.

I really like kissing this man.

The front door slams and while I jolt back into a seated position, Rush stays right where he is, groans dramatically, his dick flying full mast against his sweats.

"Seriously, Johnny?" he says as keys jingle and footsteps fall on the floor. "Can't a man snog a woman and not be interrupted by the other man who owns the damn house he's letting them stay in?"

I laugh, as I scoot out from my seat so that Rush's head falls to the cushion, while gathering my contracts and papers that had fallen during our kissing.

"When I agreed to the two of you staying here, I didn't think I was going to have to sterilize the whole house from your infectious lusting," he says as he strolls into the family room. "Wow. A football game on the telly and a hard-on in your pants. Let's hope that hard-on was for you, Lenn, and not the game."

I hold up my middle finger to Johnny, conscious that for the first time in my life, I'm embarrassed about getting caught in this position. Considering the fact that Johnny and I were roommates in college, we've both caught each other in compromising situations, but there's something different about this time.

Something that unnerves me, and it's not until I collect my things and am heading up the stairs to Rush and Johnny's banter in the background that I realize what it was.

Rush made me feel. In the moment, our kissing was incredible, but now that I've been able to step back, I realize it was too tender and too reverent. I usually shy away from anything that makes me feel like that.

Pleasure and desire and lust are what I prefer. It's what I bury my heart beneath. It's what I swear I want, but for some reason I've let Rush dig down to.

Shit.

Well, lucky for me there was Johnny.

Lucky for me I was saved by the bell.

Chapter
TWENTY-FIVE

Rush

THE BREEZE IS COOLER TONIGHT, AS IT WHISPERS UP THE CANYON and through the trees surrounding the house.

On any given night the view is one for the ages, but tonight it's even better. Lennox is standing at the edge of the patio, hands braced against the railing, face held up to the sky.

And almost as if she's tempting every part of my willpower—that was tested with that snogging session earlier—she's in an all-white bikini with a sexy chain wrapped around her waist that's glinting off the moonlight. Her hair is wet, and water runs down every inch of her body.

I take in the curve of her arse, the length of her legs, how you can all but see her skin beneath the wet fabric . . . and have to stifle a groan by the sauna that I just stepped out of.

Who is this woman and why is she owning way too many of my thoughts? It's more than her body. That, in and of itself, is devastating, but add in her no-nonsense attitude on the phone when she's on business calls, and there's no denying sexy is an understatement when it comes to Lennox.

But, what am I going to do about it?

I understand her side of things—why she's saying no and the corner she's backed into on this. And I also have to be aware of the fact that maybe I do want her as my agent. Someone who believes me and tells me straight versus looking at me as a damn paycheck is a fucking rarity.

My fingers itch to touch her. To claim her. To have her.

And yet, I don't keep women around long, I never have. So what does that mean when you've shagged and discarded a woman who you might want to be your agent? How the fuck does that work?

"I know you're standing there, Rush," she says in that husky rasp of hers before looking over her shoulder to where I'm standing. "Are you enjoying the view?"

"It's a beautiful night," I murmur as I walk out from behind the shadows. "The stars. The view. The—"

"Me," she says and turns to face me.

I whistle. The woman is more than enough to bring any man to his knees. I take in the whole of her. The intensity of her eyes. The delicate curve of her shoulder. That chain that rests right beneath her belly button.

And I was right. That wet, white swimsuit clings to her skin so that even by the pool light, I can see the dark pink of her nipples through the fabric.

She's bathed in complete confidence—that only makes her sexier—and owns everything about me in the moment.

"Yes. You, Nox," I say as she crosses the distance and steps into my personal space. Without hesitation, I reach out and run a hand down the side of her abdomen before twisting my fingers in that damn chain and tugging her gently into the shadows with me. "You are a sight for sore eyes."

Her breath hitches, and there's something different about her now. Earlier she was soft and . . . seemed vulnerable for lack of a better term, but right now, she's a straight-up siren. Her eyes are telling me the same thing her body is, and I cannot complain about them finally aligning.

I run the backs of my fingers down her cheek, as our gazes lock in the moonlight. "We've been skirting around whatever this is, Lennox, for way too long."

"Around what?" she asks in a rush of breath.

"This." I rub my thumb back and forth over her bottom lip. "Us."

She's so damn close. Her lips. That body.

"You mean our business partnership?" She lifts a lone brow and smiles.

"Nothing about us says business. Not our first meeting. Not our first fuck. And definitely not that kiss earlier."

I think I catch a wince when I mention kissing. Interesting. The iron princess let down her guard earlier, let me see a different side of her, and now it's firmly back in place.

Can't say I mind one bit though.

This—the self-confidence, the forwardness—isn't a hardship to be on the other end of.

"Then what exactly does this," she says, and mimics the same motion I made between the two of us, "mean?"

"That you want me just as much as I want you."

"That's a little presumptuous, don't you think?" she asks while her fingertip trails a path along the midline of my chest.

My muscles flex in reaction. My dick grows hard. And when she keeps going south, I grab her wrist and hold it still.

She wants to play this game? Tease and tempt?

I'm more than willing.

"You and I both know that's a lie," I say in a whisper. As I kiss the inside of the wrist I'm holding, my chuckle carries through the night. "You know as well as I do that you want me again, Lennox. That you see me, that you watch me, and when you do, your body aches and your pussy grows wet, and all you can think about is how I taste. How I feel." I lean in and tug on her earlobe gently, her back arching when I do. "Don't worry, the feeling is mutual." I lean back, and those eyes of hers flutter open to meet mine. "What are you going to do about it?"

"You're trouble, you know that?" she says, but her eyes dart to my lips and then back up.

"You're right. I am. And drama follows me as part of the package, but we're not talking about that. We're talking about pleasure. About release. About the confidence to know what you want and to take it without caring that you do."

"Is that so?"

"It is." A smile toys at the corner of my mouth.

"Hey Rush?" A lick of her own lips.

"Hmm?"

"I thought you were the type of man who takes what he wants."

Fuck. This woman. This moment. Her dare.

"I am. *I do*. But, darling, for a woman who keeps telling me no, it's only fair that I wait for you to say yes."

Lennox leans in, the heat of her breath hits my ear, and all the blood that isn't already pooling to my dick, heads there. "Yes." It's one murmured word, but it also heralds the sound of my control snapping.

I groan. It's all I can do, as I pull on her wrist so she steps inside the sauna at my back.

The room is dimly lit with a rope light, which goes around the underside of the benches that span every wall as well as the top where the wall meets the ceiling. The benches are made of hemlock and the front wall is made of glass that you can see out from the inside but that no one can see in.

"Rush, what—"

"Turn around and face the wall, Lennox," I order, just as she's about to face me. I know she likes to be in control, so this is either going to unnerve her or turn her on—me taking completely over. "Brace your hands on the back of the wall."

"What if I told you—"

"Do as you're told, Lennox." My words are a warning, and I wait to see what she does. How she reacts.

With a look over her shoulder and her eyes locked on mine, she takes her time walking toward the bench before taking one hand and bracing it on the paneled wall and then the other.

"Spread your feet wider."

She doesn't respond. Her lips part as I see goosebumps begin to chase over her bare skin.

"Look forward, darling. I've let you play with me long enough. I'm in control now."

She does obey, and it's such a damn turn-on. I study her in the dim light and debate which part of her I want to touch and taste first. Which part I want to savor, and which parts I won't be able to because I'll be gone beyond reason.

Time stretches to let the anticipation build as I slide my shorts off.

Each second feeling like a minute, each minute like an hour. Our breaths are the only sound in the room.

"There will be no need for these," I murmur as I pull on the ties at the sides of her bottoms, one by one, until the fabric falls to the floor. I do the same to the top.

She gasps when I reach out and run a single finger up and down the length of her spine, before I step up behind her so my body ghosts hers in a whisper of a touch.

She starts to turn to face me in reaction.

"Uh-uh, Lennox. Hands back on the wall. Leave them there." I trail a line of open-mouthed kisses from the edge of her shoulder to just below her ear. "This is killing you, isn't it? To not be in control? To not get a say." I scrape my teeth ever so gently there as my dick presses against the crack of her arse, a tsk in warning given when she tries to wiggle back against it.

"If you want that, you'll do as I say."

Her groan is an aphrodisiac.

I run my hands over the length of her body before finding my way between the V of her thighs. She's already wet, ready, as if she's trying to beat me at my own game to lose control before we even get started.

But I won't let her.

I can't.

She leans her head back, a moan escaping her lips as I slide my fingers into her slickness, tucking inside her so she bucks her pussy into my hands.

"You filthy girl. You love that, don't you?"

Another moan in response. Another grind of her ass against my cock.

I work her up so her moans are loud in my ear and her muscles tighten with each push in and pull back out. And when I feel her about to fall over the edge, I take my hand on her neck and push her forward. "Stay like that," I murmur as I step back to get the most gorgeous sight of her bent over, ass and pussy on display with her own arousal glistening her inner thighs.

My hand's on my dick, stroking its length, as I drop to my knees, and take my first taste of Lennox Kincade. Her cry fills the small space as I slide my tongue up her slit then back down before burying it inside of her. Before owning every inch of her. Before licking her and pleasuring her with my fingers until her legs buckle and my name falls from her lips over and over as I bring her to the brink.

I can feel her contract around me. I get lost in the feel of it as her ragged breath matches mine.

Every part of me begs for my turn as I rise to my feet.

"Again," she murmurs when I'm no longer touching her, her hand off the wall for the first time as she reaches back for me.

My chuckle reverberates, as need owns my thoughts, and greed fuels my actions.

"Hands on the wall."

"Only if you fuck me," she says in a broken voice.

"We're getting there." I laugh, but then groan as she jolts when I slide the head of my cock right at her opening.

Every part of me tenses. I try to fight the violent desperation to take her with abandon. To pound into her. To chase my own bloody pleasure now that I know she's found hers.

My hips thrust ever so slightly into her. Her warm, wet heat grabs my cock inch by inch, until I bottom out and see stars.

Fuck.

Heaven.

Hell.

Just fuck.

My hands grip the sides of her hips as she flexes those muscles around me. Once. Twice.

"Lennox," I warn, as her chuckle fills the room.

She's in control now. She owns me in this moment. With her pussy. With her confidence. With how damn good she feels.

And I snap.

Control lost.

My hips slam against hers. I thrust over and over in a punishing pace encouraged by her words. *Oh my God.* Harder. *Yes.* Right there. *Faster.* Don't stop. *I'm coming again.* Rush. *Rush.*

And when she tightens around me this time, I lose the battle but win the damn war. I empty myself into her, my hips jerking, my vision going black, her name a groan of bliss on my lips.

I gather my hands around her waist and hug her against me, my cheek resting just above her shoulder blade while we wait for our hearts to decelerate. And when they do, we both shift onto the bench to let that post-orgasmic haze settle before figuring out where we go from here.

Or at least, that's what we should be doing, but I'm just replaying every damn minute of what happened through my mind again.

"That was . . . incredible," she murmurs.

"It was. I'll . . ." *Never look at a belly chain the same way again without thinking of you.*

Without thinking of her—*this*—and what just happened. Without wanting it to happen again.

But the words die on my lips, because that's too much right now. Too much to think about. Too much to wonder about.

"We can't do that again," she pants, and I give as much effort as I can to my laugh. "This was a mistake." But she doesn't move. Instead her fingers find mine and lace between them.

"Is that so?"

"Mm-hmm." She doesn't even have the energy left to form words.

"Was it that bad?"

"Horrible. Terrible," she says with amusement in her tone.

"So when can we do it again?" I tease.

"Give me about thirty minutes to fortify."

This time my laugh is so loud that it reverberates off the walls. And then, I open my eyes and see Johnny walking toward the sauna.

"Oh shit. Johnny. He's coming." I don't give a fuck about being in the nude, but fuck if I want him seeing Lennox stark naked.

Lennox is up scrambling for her bikini as I throw on my shorts and meet him before he can open the door.

"Not exactly a place you want to go into right now, mate," I say offering him a shit-eating grin.

"No. Noooo!" he whines and postures himself like a toddler about to stomp his feet. He stares at me in disbelief. "Jesus fucking Christ. Really? C'mon, Rush. Can't you guys use a bed?"

"You're just jealous we're getting some and you have your hand tonight."

He makes an unintelligible noise that makes me laugh. "It's not funny." He jabs a finger at me. "It is not. I'm going back inside."

"Good choice," I say with a nod, enjoying the scent of Lennox still on my face.

"I'm sending you the bill to disinfect that damn sauna. Every pretty penny of it."

"It was money well spent." My laughter echoes through the night especially when he raises his middle finger and disappears into the house.

Chapter
TWENTY-SIX

Lennox

How does a woman recover from something like that? A dominant man. Some incredible sex. Laughter to end it with.

I snuggle deeper beneath my covers as Rush's laugh echoes from somewhere in the house where he and Johnny are playing pool.

But I'm here, in bed, alone.

I needed space. Time to distance myself. Time to reiterate to myself that this is what I needed.

Some mind-blowing sex to erase the confusing emotions I felt earlier after kissing him.

Not Rush, and the tender kissing from earlier tonight.

Just the Rush who demanded I hold my hands against the wall as he owned my thoughts as much as my body. The man who gave me the physicality I needed to set me right.

Because I don't get close to men. We have fun, we have sex, I move on.

That's why I went to bed without a second glance Rush's way. There was no invitation to my bed, no inkling that I want more.

And oh, how I want more.

Just a quiet exit so it's clear I'm not the girl who needs to be held and coddled afterward. Sex is sex. Love is love.

And only one of those I subscribe to.

Then why am I staring at my ceiling, wishing Rush was warming the spot beside me?

Chapter
TWENTY-SEVEN

Rush

5 Weeks Earlier

THE DOOR OPENS AND RORY'S SHOCKED EYES MEET MINE. HE STEPS back immediately, hiding behind the panel of the door in case there are paparazzi who have followed me.

"Are you out of your mind?" he asks, all but pulling me inside and slamming the door at my back.

I take a few steps and turn to face him. "I could ask the same of you."

Tension thickens the air between us, as I'm sure he wonders what he could possibly say to make this better.

Nothing.

There's nothing he can say for fucking up, no, complicating my life like he just has. I think of the two decoy cars I had to deploy from my house so the press followed.

I want to clobber him.

I want to find the truth.

I want to hate this fucking IOU—a complicated punch I wasn't ready to receive. Anger. I'm so fucking angry.

"Rush." A shrug. A sigh. "I don't even know what to—"

"Do you love her?" It's the one question I need an answer to. It's the one thing that matters.

"Ah, Rush McKenzie. Who knew you were a romantic at heart?"

"Cut the crap, Ror. This isn't funny. You're fucking with my life. I don't care if you or your dad think my career can handle the consequences, it's total bullshit. Complete fucking crap. And if you think for one second you're going to be prancing around like Prince Charming while I'm—"

"She's the love of my life, mate." Rory looks at me, eyes huge, an apology written in everything about him—posture, expression—before he nods. "She made me want to live again. She—"

"What do you mean she made you want to live again?" I laugh in disbelief. "You have all of this." I hold my hands out to the massive house we're standing in. "A football career—"

"Barely."

"A family who loves you—"

"Duty and love are two different things," he says. "I assure you there is no such thing as a perfect son, as I can attest to that."

"Rory," I sigh. "I'm not following you right now. I'm taking the damn fall for you, so forgive me if I want some answers."

"You don't get it, do you?" He gives a frustrated grunt as he paces into the next room and I follow. "My dad. Constantly living in the 'why can't you be more like Rush?' shadow that my dad demands. Never living up to what he wanted of me."

"Bollocks." *Fuck, I could use a drink.* There's a dull pounding behind my eyes, and I don't think it will be going away any time soon. "What does any of that have to do with Esme? How does you fucking Seth's wife have anything to—"

"When I tell you she made me want to live again, I fucking mean it," he shouts.

"You're my oldest mate. Doing this—" And that's when it hits me. It's now that I really hear his words.

"Rory?" My voice falls as I struggle to comprehend. As I look at a man, and question how I didn't know he was so debilitated he'd want to take his own life. "What the fuck are you talking about?"

"How would a guy like you understand?" he says and rubs his temples.

"I'm not in the mood to be fucked with, okay? Don't throw implications like that around if you don't fucking mean it." I'm in his face in a second, looking at the closest thing I've ever had to a brother, and I know it's true. I know . . . "Why?"

He shrugs as shame worries into every line etched in his face. "You don't know what it's like to be me." His voice is barely a whisper, and I grab onto the back of his neck and force his eyes to meet mine.

"I don't care what's going on in that world out there," I say and motion with my free hand. "I am and always will be here for you, brother." I don't move, can't. All I can think of is *what if?* All I can wonder is how he could ever think he was alone.

Because when I say he's the closest thing I've ever had to a brother, I mean it. He could have thrown me under the bus a million times when we were younger. When I was trying out for the academy, he could have told the guys I wasn't just picking up their rubbish to be nice, but was saving the bites of protein bars left in their wrappers so I could have something to eat for dinner. He could have said I was the one who "accidentally" picked up the wrong jacket after training and took it home with me so I'd have a little warmth in that freezing cold shed only to return it the next day and apologize for grabbing the wrong one. He caught me doing both and didn't say a word.

He could have raged and told his parents not to include me in their lives, because why should he?

But strangely, he let me into his family instead.

We talked shit. A lot.

We talked women. Even more.

We talked football. More than anything.

So how did he get here?

More importantly, how did I not know he had?

"I am always here for you," I reiterate.

"I know." His voice is hoarse as I grab him and pull him into a hug. My mind reels. How have I been so selfish with my own life that I didn't realize he was floundering? How have I been on the pitch, in the changing room, and not seen it? Sure, there were the drugs I knew he dabbled in here and there, because Archibald confessed knowing about them to me, but not this. Not suicide.

I take a step back and clear my throat to rid it of the emotions clogging it. "Make me understand. I need to understand."

"I can't make you understand, Rush. I can't let you walk in my shoes nor understand what's in my head. I can't explain the daily grind I felt just to wake up, put clothes on, and pretend everything was normal when I was silently dying inside. All I can do is tell you I was a day or two away from doing it—my plans were made, my letters were written—when Esme walked into my life."

Scrubbing a hand over my face, I head toward his kitchen and help myself to a drink. I need something to help me process this.

"How'd that happen?" I ask and then wince as the whiskey burns when it goes down.

"It was after a training session about five months ago. I was sitting in my car after I'd been told the club was considering cutting me for poor performance and fuck, mate, I was in a bad state. I was just about to pop some Oxycodone to take the edge off—"

"Bloody hell, Ror. How can you take that shit—"

"I'm off it now. I swear I am. But I saw Seth . . . saw Seth and Esme arguing. It was dark out, but they were beneath the lights while my car was in the shadows near a tree. He fucking hit her, mate. Hauled off and clocked her, and I just watched—stunned. She's Esme, pop princess and wife of Liverpool's captain, and he punched her in the stomach like it was something he did every day."

What a fucking arsehole.

"Ror—"

"I'm not kidding, mate. The wanker hit her and then strolled to their car, got behind the wheel as if nothing had happened, and waited impatiently for her to get in. As they drove out of the car park, she looked my way—tears on her cheeks, and shame, so much shame in her eyes as they passed by."

"You didn't get out? You didn't say anything?"

"No. I wish I had, but I was halfway to being high and the last thing I needed was our captain to let the club know he'd seen me using."

"So what happened next?"

"I fell down the rabbit hole. Remember that week I was sick and missed training?"

"You weren't sick?"

"No. I was drunk and high and one day in the middle of it all there was a knock on the door at about eleven o'clock at night and there she was, Esme. She had a black eye and had been roughed up. She told me I was the only one who knew anything about it, that she'd seen me that night so she knew I knew, and she needed a place to stay until Seth calmed down some. And that's how it all started."

"Fucking hell, mate."

"I know it sounds like bullshit, but it's true. She helped me get counseling and pulled me from the depths, and I was there for her because she didn't want the press to know and somehow . . . we fell in love. She helped me turn my life around, Rush. I'm fitter than I have been in years, my head is clear, and I'm going to therapy regularly to learn strategies to live with the depression. I have my bad days, but how can I not love my life now?"

"Why didn't you go to the police? Your dad? Why—"

"She begged me not to."

"You could have at least gone to your mum. Helen would have helped you. You're her everything."

"I've fucked up so many times, Rush, I couldn't stand to tell her I was using again. I couldn't crush her like that when she's been the only one who has ever had faith in me. When she's helped me too many times before." Tears well in his eyes and between the sight of them and his words, I feel like I've been hit with a knife in the chest. "I couldn't disappoint her when I feel like that's all she's been when it comes to me as of late."

"That's crap. She loves you."

"Yes, but love doesn't fix the hurt you've caused. It just makes it ache a little less."

His words are so very true.

"And now? Now what are you going to do?"

He sighs as he stares at me. "She keeps telling me she's going to leave him but the timing has to be right. She's busy getting her legal matters in order so that when they split, she doesn't get screwed."

"And if she doesn't leave him? How are you going to handle that?"

"She will. I know she will."

I stare at my oldest friend and know he believes it.

I study him, identifying how fragile his recovery could be. Would he be able to stand up to the scrutiny I'm under right now with the press and the media and the bullshit of this story?

Or would he fall back under the veil of depression and despair he pulled me away from all those years ago? Because I know what it's like to hit rock-bottom. I know how destitute you feel when your life falls apart and you wonder why you get up each morning. I know.

Chapter
TWENTY-EIGHT

Lennox

"DAD SAYS YOU'RE GOING AFTER RUSH MCKENZIE."

I stare at the face of my sister, Brexton, on the computer screen and don't try to hide the surprise, although since when does anything ever stay a secret for long in our family?

"Well, I'm glad Dad's telling everyone about something that may or may not happen."

"If you'd bother filling out and replying to our internal status memos, you could tell us yourself," she says.

"I see them but I don't really think I need to respond, seeing as you already know who I'm recruiting. If you have any questions, ask Dad. I'm sure he'll let you know."

"Tell us yourself. When did you last attend our weekly meeting?"

"I'm in California," I say drolly.

"No shit." She laughs. "That's why I FaceTimed you so you could see that we're in the digital age and these big square things we work on all day long actually allow us to talk to each other like we're in person." She rolls her eyes. "Next excuse, please."

"It's not an excuse, I'm just busy."

"As we all are." She lifts her brows as if to ask me what else I'm going to say, but I know she's the queen of back-and-forth, so it's better if I just let it be.

"So which one of you groaned or snorted when Dad announced I was going after Rush?" I ask.

"Meaning?"

"Meaning, I know you guys, and I bet there was a discussion, a few snide comments, and a few hands raised to volunteer to try to recruit him yourselves." I sit back in my chair at the kitchen table.

"Can you blame us?"

There's honesty in her voice I want to ignore but can't. How can I when I'm struggling with my own identity right now? I have preached for weeks that I won't sleep with Rush, and then I all but ask for it in the sauna the other night.

And want him even more now.

How do I vow to my sisters that I'm not going to screw this up when I can't even keep my own word to myself?

Talk about having an identity crisis. Who would have ever thought that having sex with Rush would be considered a downfall?

"Look, I've let you guys down in the past. I know I have. I'm trying to make this right by doing my part to gain a big-name client to the firm."

"We don't see what you see, Lenn. We don't feel that way about you at all. Is this about Chicago?" she asks.

"This is about a lot of things," I say without elaborating.

"Because Chicago is you making a mountain out of a molehill when you don't even know the half of it."

She stares at me through the connection, and even though she's only two years older than me, I bristle at her *I'm older, I can say what I want* attitude.

Because Chicago is a big deal. It frustrates me that none of them can see things my way. They're not on the same receiving end of altered assignments. I do try to hear what my dad said. That it's not about talent but desire for the job. But old habits are hard to break . . . clearly. *When did I lose my self-confidence? When did I feel so judged by my own family?*

And yet here I am in Los Angeles, doing exactly what I'm not supposed to be doing—mixing business with pleasure.

"You're a pain in my ass," I mutter.

"Always. That's what big sisters are for, right?"

This time I roll my eyes in response.

"He's just your type, you know. How are you going to manage that when you're working side by side with him? When you're trying to tell—"

"What do you mean he's just my type?" I laugh, thankful to have the house to myself right now. All I need is for her to know we're sleeping in the same house on the heels of that question, and she'll know the truth.

"He's edgy, unapproachable, good-looking, and a little rebellious. Add to that the fact that he's only here for a short while and that's your dream."

"That's such bullshit." I laugh, but she remains serious as she studies me. "What?"

"Name the last guy you dated who you knew would be around longer than a few months."

"What are you talking about?"

"Bradly. That's who I'm talking about. Remember the torrid affair you had with him when you knew you'd be trading him to the other side of the United States? Then there was Hiro, who was leaving to play baseball in Japan. All your men have time limits on them, Lenn. All of them. So see? Rush is the perfect plaything for you since he'll have to return home soon."

Jesus, am I really that predictable? Do I really actually do this?

"What's your point, Brex?"

"My point is don't *fuck* the clients." She laughs. "And don't fuck potential clients either."

"Did you tell Dekker that when she was sleeping with and recruiting Hunter?" I ask like the impetuous, little sister that I am.

"Please tell me you're not asking for justification?"

But there is no justification needed because the other night has replayed in my head like a fantasy over and over again. Rush. His dominance. The way he made me feel. The way I want to feel again.

"I can't force him to switch to KSM," I say.

"Agreed, but that doesn't mean you can't show him how his agent isn't doing his job. I mean, Finn's blatant incompetence might cost him his career. That should count for something."

"Incompetence?" I ask.

"He's a prick who's out for himself and always has been. We both know that." She takes a sip of her coffee and looks at me. "Vic was there, you know."

"Where?" I ask, suddenly surprised at her change of topic and out-of-the-blue mention of her fellow agent-friend, Vicktor Malachi.

"At the conference in Vegas. He watched Finn's whole made-for-movie show to humiliate you in front of the other agents."

My shoulders sag and I hate that tears fill my eyes, but it's almost as if it's worse having someone I love know how I was humiliated.

"It's no big deal," I say, forcing a smile to pretend it didn't cause the tears it did. The subsequent questions about my actual abilities. "I got the last laugh in the end though. I got the contract with MLS when he thought it was nonexistent."

"He's an asshole and we all know it. Just watch your back, because I don't trust Cannon and Finn for a second." When I don't speak, she continues. "Rush would be a great add-on to the KSM team, but more than anything, we'd love to have him aboard simply to fuck with Finn."

"Good to see you have an order of importance."

"We may bicker like hell, but we always have each other's backs." And there's something in the way she says it that makes me smile and miss them, when I didn't think I did.

"I've heard he's a real bastard, you know. Great to the fans but a prick to his agents, teammates, the like."

"Who are we talking about?"

"McKenzie," she says.

"Rush?"

"Yeah."

"I can't say that I've seen that side of him yet," I say.

"Are we talking about the same man, Lenn? The man slept with another man's wife. His teammate's no less. And then rather than face the music, he ran to LA where it's sun, relaxation, and no doubt other brainless bimbos to screw."

I bristle at the comment and hope it doesn't show on my face. "Yes, I forgot. You've been perfect in all of your dating exploits, huh?" I say with a tinge of sarcasm and leave the comment hanging there as my sister shifts in her chair. She opens her mouth and then closes it.

"Don't you dare explain away that it was different," I say.

"It was. I mean—there were things people didn't know about our situation."

"Exactly," I say pointing my finger at the screen. "And we don't know the whole story about Rush and Esme's either."

"His silence is deafening, though."

We stare at each for a beat as I nod in agreement. "Hey Brex?"

"What?"

"Never mind." I shake my head and play it off.

"No. Tell me."

"It's just . . . have you ever done something for all the wrong reasons only to wonder if they were right all along?"

"Should I ask you what in the hell you mean by that or should I just nod, tell you I love you, and that I'm sick of you being that far away from me?"

I smile. "The latter. Definitely the latter."

"Have a good day, Lenn. I miss you regardless of what you think . . . and we love you."

"Love you too."

"And good luck."

I stare at the darkened screen when the connection ends and think of everything she said to me. She's right. *Don't fuck with the clients.*

But what if I already have?

What if—

"She's right, you know."

I yelp and almost fall back in my chair when I hear Rush's voice. "You're here. You're home. I didn't hear you come in." The words tumble out a million miles an hour.

"I am." His grin is wide as he watches me fumble with the pen in my hand and wonder how much he heard.

"She's right about what?" I ask as he moves into the kitchen, running shorts on and chest misted with sweat as it still labors for breath from his run. How stupid is it that the mere sight of him has that ache building between my thighs?

"All of it." He leans his hips against the kitchen island. "That I'm a bastard. That I'm selfish. That I'm not an easy client to deal with."

I angle my head and meet the truth in his eyes. "Nah. I think that's what you want people to see, to believe, because that protects them from getting close to everything you hold dear."

He looks out the window for a moment and I wonder if he's going to refute me, but the fact that he doesn't tells me I might be right in my assessment.

The man is an enigma. Every time you get too close, he shifts focus elsewhere. Normally I'm fine with this because the less I know, the better.

But there's something about him that makes me want to know more. There's been something about him from the first moment I laid eyes on him that won't allow me to let it go.

"And how did you manage to skip out of today's promotional extravaganza?" he asks with a flair of his hands and a roll of his eyes.

"You're really not enjoying this whole thing, are you?"

He twists his lips for a beat before meeting my eyes. "I'm a football player. Being on the pitch is what I love, not talking about it."

"Over the years I've learned that love of the game means different things to different athletes. What is it about socc—football that you love?" I ask as I turn and face him completely. That soft smile that ghosts his lips tells me everything I need to know. He's not in it for money or fame.

It's his one true love.

"It's hard to put into words and when I do, I sound like an idiot."

"Try me."

And for the first time since I've known Rush McKenzie, he blushes. It's adorable and sexy all in one confusing breath. Something I need to attempt to forget.

"It's stupid really, but it's what saved me." He twirls the set of keys in his hand and focuses on them. "Times were tough when I was young and footie was the one thing I was good at. It was the only thing that made kids look at me admirably instead of with pity, or like I was the weird one."

"Kids can be cruel. I wore glasses and had four years' worth of braces, so I understand feeling like the weird one."

"You? Ugly?" He laughs as he takes a seat opposite me and then pulls my chair so my knees slide between his spread ones. His hands are on my thighs. There's something so very natural about the moment that I swear my stomach flips when he looks up from my legs to meet my eyes. "I love the game because it is who I am. I can transition to this figurehead that Cannon wants me to be later in my career, but not now. Not when the game is like a drug to me, sparking me to life, begging me to be better at everything I touch. A better footballer, a better teammate, a better idol for kids, a better everything."

I stare at Rush and know with absolute certainty that this is not a man who would cheat with his captain's wife. This is not a man who would throw away his career on a stupid move. This is not a man who should have been vilified so instantly without a defense. *Surely his teammates, those he's close to, can't believe this lie either.*

"There are moments on the field when the crowd is chanting, the air is thick with anticipation, and my blood is coursing with adrenaline that I just know I'm going to do something incredible. It's almost as if the moment elevates my game."

"The moment and all the hard work you put in," I say. My research over the past few days has shown me that Rush is known for his endless dedication. He's typically the first one on the pitch and the last one to leave. Impressive for a man who most would assume doesn't care about a thing in the world other than himself.

"Perhaps. Then again, maybe I'm just one lucky bastard who has gotten a few breaks now and again."

"You don't need to play it down around me. I live in a world where I want athletes who are good to know it. That way they know their worth and will never sell themselves short."

"And what about those who are awesome players but arsehole people?"

"I've come across those a time or two."

"Do you represent them or do you out them for who they are?" His eyes turn serious, and for the first time, I'm not certain if we're still speaking about him.

"It's not my place to out them, but if they're assholes, then their colors are true enough that the world will see in time."

He falls quiet, his eyes dropping to stare at his thumbs moving back and forth on my knees. "They do always end up outing themselves over time, don't they?"

When his eyes lift to meet mine, there's a gravity in them that unexpectedly adds heaviness to the moment. "Rush?"

His smile is there, but more forced than sincere. "You never answered my question," he says. "How were you able to get out of that boring shit-show today?"

"I had meetings."

"With your sister?"

I shake my head. "That was just the last few minutes of my day." I blow out a sigh. "I've been avoiding her."

"Why?"

"Long story."

"Do I have anything to do with that long story?" He angles his head to the side and waits for a response.

"Of course you do. We always talk about the athletes we're recruiting or are on our radar to want to recruit." It's not the whole truth, but at least I'm not lying completely.

Our gazes hold as if he's not sure he believes me or not, but then nods after a beat. "What else did you have to do that enabled you to escape Cannon—and his fifteen handlers—telling you what to do every five seconds? How did you avoid being stared at like you're an alien?"

"Or maybe they're staring because you're incredibly handsome and talented?"

"That too." He winks and we laugh.

"Let's see. I negotiated a deal for a baseball player, worked on a trade for an NBA star, and then finalized some endorsements for one very over-enthusiastic, Olympic gymnast. Oh, and how can I forget the two hours on the phone stroking various athletes' egos to make sure they know I love them and no, their careers are solid and they shouldn't be worried."

"Busy day."

"Busy indeed." He pulls my chair even closer. "But you missed one thing."

"What's that?"

"There's only one thing you should be stroking, Kincade," he murmurs as his eyes darken with desire.

"Is that so?" I ask as he leans forward and captures my lips with his.

"Definitely." A kiss. "You're contractually obligated. Remember?" He quirks an eyebrow, a half-cocked smile on his lips.

"Then by all means, let me make sure I fulfill it."

Our lips meet as our fingers entwine.

It's crazy to me how easy it is to kiss him. To be kissed by him.

Rush McKenzie is doing things to me that I'm not used to. Random kisses in the kitchen. Distracting me when I'm working.

And strangest of all, *I want* to get to know him better.

But is that only because I know he'll be going soon?

Chapter
TWENTY-NINE

Lennox

RUSH JINXED ME.

After I teased him about having to play the part for Cannon and the MLS, I've been dragged to each and every event over the past few days. A benefactor rah-rah session at the Santa Anita Raceway. An interactive fan experience at Banc of California Stadium, where Rush partook in running drills with youth players. A board meeting, where I discussed comprehensive compensation packages that might lure players away from other, more successful leagues. And on, and on.

That's a lot of face-to-face and smiling with random people when I'm more used to the one-on-one aspect of negotiating and sealing deals.

The only upside to the exhaustion? Rush. Being with Rush. Laughing with Rush. Waiting for those few stolen moments where I look up and meet his eyes across the pitch or room or wherever and see that soft smile of his.

An even better upside? Knowing everyone in that room wanted to be the one going home with him, and technically, I was.

And now? Three glorious days off from the MLS grind. I have my own clients to tend to, but I can do that from Johnny's little piece of heaven of a house and backyard.

That's why I startle when Rush comes strolling into our bathroom while I'm mid-brushing my teeth.

"Get dressed," he says, his grin wide and mischievous.

"That was the plan," I say around my toothbrush.

"No. I mean, get dressed, I have somewhere I want to take you." I glance his way in the mirror to his boardshorts and plain black T-shirt.

"Where?"

"That's the best part. Nowhere in particular."

"What?" I ask as he backs out of the bathroom.

"Ten minutes, Nox. Better get that fine arse of yours moving."

Fifteen minutes after hearing a horn honking from the driveway, I stroll out the front door, purse under my arm with my bikini inside, since he had board shorts on, and stop to a halt. There's Rush sitting behind the wheel of a bright red, convertible Mustang, engine revving, grin as wide as can be.

"What are you . . ." My words fade off and I laugh as I lift my phone to take a picture of him. Right now, it's the most relaxed I've ever seen him. Smile wide, eyes alive, and so excited. "You sure you can drive that thing? I mean, aren't you on the wrong side of the road?" I tease.

"I'm skilled. You can vouch for that."

This man does things to my insides. "You're getting your wish. To drive a classic American car."

"I am." He stretches across the car and opens the door. "Hop in. Come for a ride with me."

"Where are we going?"

"Wherever we want."

And we do. Rush navigates through the endless traffic of Los Angeles' freeways out to the Pacific Coast Highway until we're traveling north. The congestion of the city makes way to the winding road that follows the coast. The ocean is sparkling to our left as we fly with the sun on our faces, the wind in our hair, and with Rush's hand on my thigh.

It feels like freedom after being confined in a sense to Johnny's house for so many weeks with only the contract with MLS, my work, and his training as part of our everyday routine.

There's even something liberating sitting beside Rush and not being able to talk. The wind whipping around us as we drive simply allows us to enjoy each other and not feel forced to fill the time with nonstop talk.

I'm not sure how much time passes before we exit the freeway in the outskirts of Santa Barbara County. I glance over to Rush and notice for the first time that he's watching the GPS on the dash. I never realized there was an address input into it.

The street we pull down is lined with trees and the brine of the sea is in the air. Our eyes meet briefly before he looks at the addresses of the houses to our left and although it's a second, I know he's up to something.

But I don't say a word.

I wait for him to pull up to the gate, punch in a code that has it swinging open, and then turn the engine off once we've driven through.

"Are you going to tell me what we're doing here?" I ask when he just looks at me with a mischievous grin.

"A little R&R."

"R&R?" I laugh. "What are you talking about?"

"This is ours for the next two days," he says nonchalantly as he climbs out of the car and rounds the hood to where I'm staring at him with surprise on my face.

"What do you mean for the next two days?" I stare up at him to where he's standing with the door open.

"You told me you didn't want anyone to know that we're doing whatever it is we're doing . . . so, now," he says and waves his hand around us, "no one will know. We have a private beach, a secluded house away from everyone—"

"And no food or clothes or toiletries or so many things." I laugh the words out, stunned at this gesture.

"The fridge is fully stocked as per my request to the owner, and who needs clothes? We have a private pool, and I'm sure there are those fluffy white robes if you want them. Toiletries were also on my request list. Remember I share a bathroom with you so I know what you like, and when it comes to the so many things part—"

"You're serious, aren't you?"

"Johnny deserves to have his house back to himself for a few days," he says as he takes my hands and pulls me up and into him. "And, darling, I really want you alone for a few days so I don't have to worry about getting caught every time we have our horrible, unsatisfying sex."

"It is terrible sex, isn't it?" I ask and savor the tender kiss he places on my lips.

"Dreadful." Another kiss. "You come. Then you come again. Then I come. It's completely unsatisfying."

"I'm glad you have this all planned." That, of course, is a gross understatement. I'm astounded. To think that this man thinks he's a bastard. Selfish. A hard client to deal with. Well, aren't all clients? They should be since it's their life they are advocating for. But the rest? No. He's nothing like the man people think he is.

Like I said to him the other day, I think it's the façade he wants people to see. *And yet, he's selflessly brought me away. For R&R.* No one has ever done something like this for me. And I'm shocked. In awe.

"This is the part where you tell me how incredible I am, I repay you with some wine and cheese, and then later some dessert with my tongue buried between your legs."

"Oh."

Well, no woman is going to complain about that, now is she?

"Exactly. Any more thoughts on the matter?" he asks.

"I think we should go inside and practice our horrible sex."

"Practice does make perfect," he murmurs before we laugh and go explore our new place. "Or in our case, it makes it perfectly horrible."

Chapter THIRTY

Rush

"I'm still in shock you did this." Lennox looks at me from across the deck. She has my T-shirt on and nothing else, its dark color accentuating the tan on her very long legs. Ones that I've been between the better part of the afternoon, and I'm definitely not complaining about that. The breeze is blowing through her hair and the sun is at her back as she takes a sip of wine.

She's a sight to behold and for the first time since I've been in the States, there's something—or rather someone—who might make me sad to leave and go back home.

"We both deserved a break."

"I think poor Johnny deserved a break from us too."

"I think he's going to disinfect the entire house while we're gone." I laugh and grab a cracker and slice of cheese from the table beside me.

"Nothing could ruin my good mood today," she murmurs and twirls around, some of the wine sloshing over the top of her glass. "Oopsie." Her giggle floats across the patio, making me smile, and I realize she's a bit tipsy. "Party foul."

"It happens to the best of us." *God, she's bloody gorgeous.* I pat the spot beside me on the chaise lounge. "Come sit with me."

She eyes me coyly, her smile carefree. "I thought I wore you out."

"To sit, Nox." God knows she did wear me out earlier. "Just to sit and watch the sunset."

"In that case then," she says and skips over before plopping down and snuggling into me. "Perfect. This is *absolutely* perfect."

"It is," I say and press a kiss to the top of her head as I pull her in tighter.

Business-savvy Lennox is sexy. Bedroom-vixen Lennox is every bloke's dream. But tipsy Lennox is equal parts adorable and amusing, which makes me want to lean forward and kiss her senseless.

"I needed this," I murmur against the top of her head. "Somewhere to go without people knowing or watching or wanting something from me. You have no idea how much I needed this."

How much I needed you.

The thought takes a second to register and when it does, I push it as far away as possible, because I don't need anything. Or rather, I don't need anyone.

I did once.

And after she died, I vowed I'd never let myself need anyone again.

We sit in silence as the waves crash onto the shore and the sun dips slowly toward the ocean.

"You gave me the sunset," she murmurs almost dreamily out of no-where. "No one's ever given me a sunset before."

"That's ridiculous. Surely—"

"Shh," she says and presses her lips to mine. "Let's enjoy it."

She lays her head back on my chest.

No one's ever given me a sunset before.

I'm not sure why that one comment hits me so hard, because Lennox Kincade deserves more than just sunsets. She deserves sunsets and sun-rises and everything in between.

And as if on cue, her phone rings a distinct tone that has her scowl-ing. "Except for that. Go away, Dekker," she grumbles.

"I don't mind if you get it."

"Well, I do," she says with a huff before walking over to where her handbag is, carrying it back to where we sit, and then unceremoniously dumping the contents of it onto the chaise beside us. The contents she fumbles through makes me laugh: a purse, a makeup bag, a baseball with signatures all over it—which I'm sure has some value but instead is just thrown in there like most women would a scrunchie. Oh, and there are a few of those too, along with business cards and pens, but it's when I see her toss a mobile phone to the side before picking up a second one that I laugh.

"Two mobile phones? Are you that important you need two?" I laugh.

"It's a long story," she mutters and waves a hand my way as one of the mobiles rings again. "There!" She pushed the button on its side with a dramatic flair and then the ringing stops immediately. "Problem solved. Interruption handled."

She looks up at me with the biggest, cheesiest grin before she resumes her position cuddled to my side.

"Is there a particular reason you're not talking to your sister?" I ask.

She snorts. "Lots of reasons."

"Like?"

She shakes her head, and even though I can't see her eyes, I swear she's rolling them. "Because they always seem to be perfect and I always seem to be . . . me."

"And what exactly is that? Gorgeous. Intelligent. Feisty. No nonsense. Sexy. Fun."

"But why did you lead off with gorgeous?" she asks with a bite to her tone.

Warning bells sound in my head. "I wasn't aware it was a crime to tell you that you're gorgeous. Especially when you're sitting like that," I say motioning to her leg draped over mine, my shirt hitched all the way to her hip, those inquisitive eyes irritated, and her lips pouting at me. "I assure you it wasn't meant as an insult. Quite the opposite, actually." Her sigh in response is heavy. "You want to explain what me calling you gorgeous has to do with why you won't pick up the call from your sister?"

"It's complicated."

I throw my head back and laugh. "You're talking to me, remember? King of complicated as of late."

"Working with your family is complicated."

"I can imagine. I bet there are some fun fights there."

"Between four sisters?" She snorts.

"Do you like what you do? Does it make you happy?"

"Yeah." She says the words, but there's something that glances through her eyes that tells me otherwise. Perhaps it's the same something

I've caught in snippets when I've walked in and she's having a conversation with one of her sisters. There's snark to her tone. Almost a combination of hurt and irritation that she plays off the minute she notices I see it.

Just like she did right now.

"That doesn't sound too convincing."

Her smile softens. "When you're one of five in a family business, sometimes it gets a bit crowded. Opinions. Dibs on clients. Everything." She chuckles but that spark is still missing. "But yes, I'm happy."

I twist my lips and nod. "I can imagine that at times it feels like you've lost your identity in a sense. You're one of "the Kincades" rather than Lennox Kincade."

"I'm sure psychologists would say it's classic middle-child syndrome," she murmurs and then rests her head back against my chest, this time lacing her fingers with mine.

"I'd say it's more that you feel you've become part of the scenery at KSM. Camouflage if you will."

"Camouflage?" She laughs the word out.

"Yeah. In a sense. You all fit into this puzzle that works and fits in all the right places, but every once in a while, you want to be an edge piece versus the middle piece. Every once in a while, you want to wear the crown and step into the limelight instead of being part of the court standing in the background." I squeeze her hands. "You've lost your crown."

She laughs. "That sounds ridiculous. You know that, right?"

"It might, but it also hits you because it rings true."

"Rush."

"It's the same for me. I love playing football. It's my passion, my life. The best part about it? I'm part of a team. I can blend in. I can support them. But I also love being selfish sometimes. Taking the ball down the field and doing it for myself. Hogging all the glory and owning it rightfully. There's no better feeling than that moment when the ball hits the back corner of the net and the crowd goes bloody wild."

"You never blend in on the field, Rush. You stand out every time you touch the ball."

"Just like you do."

"What?" she asks with disbelief. "You're crazy." But when she looks up at me with tears filling her eyes, I can tell what I've said means something to her.

"It's okay to want the crowd to go wild. It's okay to break away every once in a while, and be selfish. There's no shame in it. Your work at KSM is yours, but not. Make it yours. Find what you need when you need it to make the crowd go wild. Until you do, darling, you'll never be happy."

She looks up at me and for the first time since this conversation, her smile rings true. "Who knew Rush McKenzie was a secret philosopher?"

"Hardly."

She leans up and presses a kiss against my lips and tugs on parts of me that typically lie dormant. "You've given me more than you think, Professor McKenzie. I used to be in the spotlight, on the stage. Taking the limelight. I know the allure. Not sure I want that anymore." That last bit is but a whisper. "Where was I? Oh, I know." She giggles. God, she's fucking cute. "You've given me several orgasms, copious amounts of wine . . . and an escape. And now kind words that I needed to hear."

"And I've given you the sunset."

"Yes. You have," she says and runs her fingers up and down my stomach absently.

And we stay like this until the sun dips and the colors stop dancing across the sky to make way for the stars.

Chapter
THIRTY-ONE

Lennox

THE COOL MORNING AIR BLOWS IN OFF THE OCEAN. IT'S THAT GRAYISH time of the morning where the sea and the sky look like they're one color, and there is no way to tell where one ends and the other begins.

I'm sitting up in an amazing expanse of bed with the comforter pooled around my waist in this luxurious beach house that Rush has rented, and I'm not sure why I feel so unsettled. I should be asleep, I should be snuggled up beside him, and when I turn to look at him over my shoulder and study him, I know exactly why I feel unsettled.

It's him.

It's Rush.

The sight of him makes my pulse quicken and stomach flutter. That happened when we first met, but this is different. That's supposed to fade—hell, it typically dissipates after the first date for me most times—but with him, it just keeps growing more intense.

Have I slept in the same bed with men before? Of course, I have. Have I wanted to? Not really. I don't like cuddling or the small talk. I'm not a fan of feeling forced to be something I'm not—the grateful girl because the guy picked her.

That's bullshit.

They should be the grateful ones . . . and yet when I look at Rush, I feel grateful. I feel . . . things.

Things I don't know how to process, nor do I really want to, because they're not something that can be on my radar.

And yet when I look back out at the ocean, I can't help but feel . . .

relaxed. Appreciated. Wanted. Heard. It's the oddest combination of things and yet what I needed all the same.

"Hey." Rush's sleep-drugged voice fills the room the same time he rests his hand on my lower back.

"Good morning," I murmur as I turn to look at him over my shoulder. There are pillow creases on his face and his scruff is darker than normal, but it's his eyes—the crinkles at their corners, the clarity in them for just waking up—that hold me rapt. "Sleep good?"

"The best."

"What're you doing? It's early."

"Just enjoying the peace. It's not often I get to sit and just be."

"I understand that."

I turn back to the surf and its crash coming in through the French doors we left open from our second-story bedroom. "So did your American car live up to the hype?"

"It did. There's nothing like a fine piece of Americana planted firmly between your legs."

"I'm thinking I should be offended by that comment." I turn to him and lift a brow, and it's met with a devilish grin.

"Not in the least, darling," he says and then falls silent as his fingertips dance over the dimples in the small of my back. "It is stunning, isn't it?" He adjusts the pillow beneath his head so he can sit up higher and enjoy the view. "Sunrises are my favorite."

I go to speak and then close my lips as last night comes back to me. *No one has ever given me sunsets before.* Oh my God. Did I really say that? Did I really sound like a sappy Hallmark card while under the influence of wine, sex, and chocolate?

I cringe and hope maybe Rush was under the same influence, but know damn well he wasn't. Instead, he gave me a speech about crowds and crowns that struck so many chords in me that I even had a ridiculous dream about riding some stupid chariot in the middle of a stadium where the crowd cheered when I lifted my crown.

Yes, Rush is messing with my head.

The question is, what am I going to do about it, because whether I want to admit to it or not, I'm okay with it. The panic and sudden arm's length I hold men to when they get too clingy hasn't happened yet.

I'm sure it's coming.

It has to be.

"Johnny told me you lost your mum. Do you mind me asking how old you were?"

His directness shouldn't surprise me by now, but it does. It's a topic many people shy away from and when I turn to meet his eyes, there's nothing but sympathy and compassion.

"I was thirteen."

"I'm so sorry."

"Don't be." I play it off like I always do with a shrug. "It was a long time ago."

"Long time ago or not, it still hurts like hell. I was fifteen when I lost mine."

"I had no idea." Turning to face him, I reach out and take his hand, feeling like an ass for thinking about only myself. "I'm so sorry."

"Like you said, don't be."

"Brain aneurysm," I say about my mother's cause of death. "Yours?"

"Cancer."

My chest constricts at the thought. The one thing I've always felt lucky about is that my mother died quickly. There weren't months on end where she suffered, or endless waiting for the inevitable. It was quick—unbelievably so—almost to the point that it was hard then and now for me to believe she's gone.

But I can't say that to Rush. I can't be grateful for how mine died and then ask how long his suffered. I can't tell him that any shrink would have a field day with me and say I probably have trouble forming attachments with men because the minute I feel anything beyond the superficial lust, I run to prevent more hurt.

And even though my mind processes that thought, I lie back down with him, my head on his chest, and both of us looking out toward the horizon beyond.

Fading memories fill my head and make me smile and long for my mother all at the same time.

"I always worry I'll forget the sound of her voice. The smell of her perfume. The feel of her arms wrapped around me, her laugh."

"You'll never forget her. And just when you think you have, she'll be in one of your dreams again, and you'll experience her so you don't. And you also have your dad to help remember for you."

His words bring a bittersweet tear to my eye, and I think of the conversation I had with my dad a couple of weeks back about how much I was like my mother. "What about you? What do you miss about your mum?"

He runs a hand up and down my arm. "It's been too long for me to miss anything. Too many things have overshadowed that time in my life."

I look up at him. At his strong jaw and thick lashes, but he keeps his eyes on the sky. "Didn't your dad help keep her memory alive?"

Rush's expression remains as guarded as his voice, which lacks any emotion when he responds. "I never knew my dad."

"I'm sorry. I didn't . . ." My words fade as I insert my foot in my mouth and scramble for something to say in its place. "The two cell phones."

"Two mobiles—oh, in your handbag." He laughs. "What about them?"

"One is my mother's. It doesn't work but I can't get rid of it. I mean, it's not like I think she's going to call me on it or anything—hell, it's not even charged, but I carry it with me still. I don't know if I think it's good luck or because it's something tangible of hers I can hold on to, but regardless of how stupid it is, I can't get rid of it."

"It's not stupid at all. I understand that."

"Sometimes I even charge it so I can listen to the voice memos she'd left herself." I haven't told anyone that. What is it about Rush that makes me trust him so implicitly?

His chuckles softly beneath my hand. "I understand that. For the longest time after my mum died, I carried around a medallion she gave me after she got sick. It was unexciting, except for the intricate compass etched on its front that she swore would bring me good luck. When I asked her what was so lucky about it, she told me that no matter where I went in life, it would always help me find my way back to what was right. That's the first tattoo I got. Right here." He points to above his heart. "It's her compass so I'd never lose my way."

I sit up on my elbow and trace the intricate lines of the design on his chest, knowing how important it is to feel like you have something to hold on to. "It's perfect."

"Just as you carrying her mobile is perfect for you." He shifts all of a sudden so that he's half lying on, half lying off me. "You know what?"

"Hmmm?" Those eyes win me over again.

"I think we need a morning swim."

"We do?" That is not what I was expecting.

"Last one in has to cook breakfast." Rush jumps out of bed, and I follow right after him.

Our laughter echoes off the halls as we chase each other down the stairs and through the house.

We don't think about suits or towels or anything else as we jump off the patio into the sand. The sky is lighting up with streaks of color that soften the dark ocean water. We both yelp as we hit the cold morning water, but just as quickly, he reaches out to me and pulls me against him.

The last thing that crosses my mind before his lips make me lose my thoughts is that Rush just gave me a sunrise to remember too.

Chapter
THIRTY-TWO

Lennox

"Was that terrible too?" Rush asks as he reaches out for me and pulls me through the warm water of the jacuzzi until I'm almost sitting on his lap, my back to his front.

"Horrible," I say. "A huge mistake."

"You seem to keep making mistakes and having horrible sex with me."

"Dreadful ones." He chuckles and shifts me on his lap so he can kiss me.

I startle momentarily at how used to this I'm becoming.

This feels too much like a thing, like we're a thing . . . and I'm not sure what to do about it.

"You okay?" he asks, his smile fading, and I nod. The irony is while I'm silently freaking out, I'm also secretly reveling in everything about this weekend and him.

The way he made me coffee in the morning so I'd sit with him while he had his cuppa, as he called it. How when we sit near each other, his hand always finds its way to me somehow—fingertips tracing up and down my spine, a hand on my thigh, a finger tucking a strand of hair behind my ear. How he knows nothing about baseball, and how adorable he is trying to figure out its rules.

So many things that make me want to push myself back. But I find myself snuggling in a little closer.

Like right now. He's wrapped his arms around me and set his chin on my shoulder from behind.

"I'm fine. I'm just dreading going back to LA tomorrow," I murmur as I stare at the lights out on the ocean—some sailor somewhere trying to get home to his family—while we soak up the last night of our stay here.

"So am I." Rush's fingertips play idly over my bare skin beneath the bubbles. There's a comfortable ease to us here that I'm going to miss when we go back to Johnny's and remember that we're not supposed to be together. And as if on cue, he asks, "Is there a reason you haven't asked me to switch over to KSM and let you represent me?"

"Several, but the main one is that I'm not working right now, and therefore I don't want to talk about work."

"I can respect that, but I also think we need to talk about it at some point."

I take his hand in between both of mine and play with his fingers as I try to figure out my next words to say. "Are we going to ignore that I've done a lot of talking this weekend and you haven't done much?"

"I've done plenty." He chuckles. "I've called your name. I've called God several times."

I turn so I can punch him playfully in the shoulder. "That's not exactly what I mean."

"Then what do you mean?"

"If I were to ever be your agent . . ." Shit. I twist my lips and try to figure out how to say what I need to say. "Look, I'm not a spill-your-heart-out kind of girl, Rush, and yet when it comes to you, I've spilled more than is normal for me. So—"

"So you're expecting tit for tat."

"Not necessarily, but I don't like feeling . . . exposed. Vulnerable. I guess that's the best way to describe it."

This is not working. I'm fumbling big time.

"And why's that? How did I make you feel vulnerable?"

"There you go turning the conversation back on me again."

"What is it you want to know?"

"Nothing. Everything. Something."

He laughs. "Talk about giving me the third degree. I've told you. I come from a shit upbringing. No dad, Mum died, and then I got the scholarship at the academy at age fifteen, signed my first contract at sixteen."

"All things I could have looked up and most likely found on the

Internet." I sigh. "If you lost your mom, then who were you with until you received the scholarship? Family?"

"No one." His smile doesn't reach his eyes. "When I mean times were tough, I mean times were really tough. I got by and did what I had to do until I got the scholarship."

"Oh my God. Rush. I had no idea—"

"Look. I don't need your pity. I had some luck on my side. I had a teammate's family take me in. It all turned out in the end. It's not worth talking about."

"I'm not giving you pity. I'm just—"

"So, what is it you want to know?" he asks. This clearly makes him uncomfortable. "That I hate sushi, and tequila is the one alcoholic drink I refuse to touch? One bad night was enough for me with that shit. That I like loud music and started out knowing how to use my fists more than my feet? Or is it that I like my schedule and routine, and being here in the States makes me feel out of sorts, so while I'm enjoying my time here, I can't wait to get back?" He lifts me from his lap and shrugs as he moves to the other side of the spa. "Is that good enough, because we all don't have mums and dads and memories galore that form us. My memories are of training and then more training."

"Or maybe it's that I'm sharing your bed but you haven't said a word about the Esme situation and whatever the hell happened to cause it."

And in that split second, I know I made an egregious error by the immediate stiffening of his spine. So of course, I try to overcorrect. "It's only natural for me to ask. I mean, don't I—"

"Don't you what? Have I asked you the names of the people who've occupied your bed, Lennox? Have I asked you for details about your sex life and how each man has come into it?"

"Rush—"

"I thought we were enjoying each other. I thought you knew the kind of man I was or else you wouldn't have pursued this—whatever this is— with me."

"That's not what I meant. You took it all wrong," I say, scrambling to fix the assumption he made. How he assumed I was asking about if he slept with Esme instead of . . . instead of . . . I'm not sure what I was asking other than I want him to confide in me what happened, who the photo is of. I want to feel like he trusts me as much as I've blindly put my trust in him.

But before I can get the words out, he speaks. "I should have guessed." His sigh that follows is like a dagger in my chest.

"Figured what?" I ask, immediately on the defensive.

"Is that what this was all about? You. Me. *This?*" he asks throwing his hands up.

"What are you—" And then I realize what he's asking, and I'm dumbfounded by it. "You think I'm sleeping with you because I want answers? For what, Rush? You think I'm being paid by Seth or LFC or someone to get the truth out of you? Then what? I'm going to sell the sordid story to the tabloids and make money off it?" I climb out of the spa, pissed at the insinuation, and turn to face him. "I can make my own money, Rush. I don't need to make it off selling athletes' stories, so screw you for even implying it."

"That's not what I was saying."

"Isn't it?" I shout. "Maybe you're so used to people fucking you over that you don't know what it looks like when someone is actually trying to help."

"Help with what though?" he asks in too calm a voice. "The last thing I need is someone I'm sleeping with to hold my hand, Lennox. I've got plenty of people for that. You're—" He runs his hand through his hair and mutters an obscenity. "Never mind."

"I'm what?" I ask, heart in my throat, as I wonder if I'm going to like or loathe the answer he gives me.

"You're the one person I feel like I can be myself with. The one person who . . ." His sigh is so heavy it drowns out the waves. "I'm doing what I have to do. Okay?"

"For who, Rush? Who are you doing it for, because it sure as shit isn't for you? Quit hiding behind some stupid club gag order and just tell me the truth."

"No," he says unequivocally.

"Don't you trust me?" It's the worst question I could ever ask given the expression in his eyes.

"I don't trust anyone."

"What a sad way to live," I say reflexively and see the slightest wince, before his guard goes back up.

"Now you're insulting who I am?" The words come out in a laugh.

"No. I just . . . is it so wrong to want to help you? Is it such a bad thing to see you suffering for something I don't think you did and for the fucking life of me, I can't understand why?" I throw my hands up.

"It's none of your business."

"Got it. So I'm good enough to fuck, but not good enough to open up to. Perfect. Classy."

He pinches the bridge of his nose and rolls his shoulder. "Those are your words, not mine."

Oh, for fuck's sake. Why can't he tell me?

Why can't he see I'm more than a pretty face? Trust in me. Why am I not even enough for his truth?

I need him to be the good guy I think he is instead of this asshole who's standing before me trying to pick a fight.

"So you want people to believe you're fucking her with no remorse. Good to know." I start to walk away when the low, frustrated grit of his voice rings out.

"I've slept around my share, Lennox. Even done some things I'm not proud of, but I'd never sleep with a married woman, let alone a teammate's wife."

I turn to face him and when our gazes meet, his eyes are burning with emotion that is all but boiling over. "Then explain the picture to me, Rush. Tell me how the hell there's photographic evidence that you did."

"Why does it matter?"

We stare in silence as the cool breeze chills my wet skin. His honesty equally hurts and fortifies my heart.

"I don't understand. If that image isn't what it looks like it is, then why in the fuck are you silent about it? Why the hell—"

"Drop it," he demands. "Can you please just drop it?" This time his voice is softer, almost begging, and my last thought before I turn to walk away and do as he asks, is that there's a whole host of pain in his eyes.

I wish he trusted me enough to let me know what it is.

Maybe I could help.

Or maybe I could sit by silently and hold his hand to let the man, who thinks he doesn't need anyone, know that someone is there.

Because I want to be that person. He said he doesn't trust anyone, but I want him to trust me. And honestly, I want to trust him too.

Because I'm slowly beginning to need him.

Chapter
THIRTY-THREE

Rush

I WATCH HER SLEEP.

She's lying across the bed. The sheets have fallen around her so they're positioned just below the swell of her breast, and one hand is resting on top of her heart. Shadows from the moon outside play across her face, and her hair is fanned out on the pillow beneath her.

Jesus.

My chest constricts as I try to figure out why the fuck there is a heavy lump in my throat.

We fought, I had every intention of setting her straight, end of story.

And yet it isn't.

Far from it. She asked a simple question she deserves an answer to. A simple question that I would want to know if I were in her shoes.

What exactly is this between the two of us? Before Lennox, a question like that would have had me cutting my losses and moving on.

Isn't that why I slipped, though? Am I hoping she'll hold out until she realizes she's right? That I really am the man she thinks I am?

But I didn't chase, I didn't give her the answers she wanted, and I didn't give her the man she deserves.

Instead, I sat downstairs with a beer in my hand feeling like shit when every part of me wanted to come up here and tell her my story from beginning to end. The starved boy chasing a dream. The man who stepped in, giving him the chance at the academy, to the cashed-in IOU . . . and the necessity to ride this thing out for Rory's health. *For my brother's future. Because he never gave up on me.*

I want her to know that I'm protecting others, that I am the man she thinks I am . . . and not the selfish bastard everyone thinks I am.

I stare at her and panic hits.

Wouldn't it be easier to walk away, chalk us up to some stellar sex, and then blame our demise on the moment being ruined? But standing here watching the rise and fall of her chest, all I want to do is slide into bed beside her and hold the fuck on.

Lennox quiets the shouting in my head. She placates the rebellion that fights from within. She makes me wish I'd never agreed to this thing with Rory so that there didn't have to be lies and secrets between us.

There's something about the way she looks at me, the way she treats me. As if I'm Rush McKenzie the man, instead of the football phenomenon everyone else fixates on.

But how can she know me? How can she get me like she does when all we're supposed to be is a quick fling to help pass the time?

I sit on the bed and face her, my fingers reaching out to brush a piece of hair off her face, to touch her a necessity.

Just a fling, huh?

She stirs, those eyes of hers flutter open, and she immediately turns her cheek into my hand as if it's the most natural thing in the world. Almost as if there's an instinctive trust in me.

I'm not sure why it gets to me when she does it, but it does. That lump in my throat grows even bigger.

"I'm sorry." We both say it at the same exact time. Her lips—that I desperately want to lean down and kiss—turn into a ghost of a smile.

"I'm sorry, Nox." And I don't think I've ever spoken truer words.

"I didn't mean what I asked. I phrased it wrong. You don't owe me any explanat—"

"Shh," I murmur. "I do. And—I . . . sometimes you do things because you have to. They're not always what you want to do, but they're the right thing to do."

"Help me understand. Why would you—" Her confused sigh finishes her sentence for her. "How could you risk . . . how could you let people think you did something like this?"

"It doesn't matter what people think about me. I learned a long time ago that people believe what they want even when the truth is looking them straight in the face."

Like I am you right now.

"But it does matter. It's a battle worth fighting. Finn. Your publicist. Your lawyers. Your teammates. They should be screaming at the top of their lungs, vouching for you, setting everyone straight."

"I gave up hoping anyone would go to battle for me a long time ago," I whisper as I run my thumb over her bottom lip. "And I'm okay with that. The only person you can completely depend on is yourself."

"You pay these people," she says, disbelief ringing in her tone. "They better fight for you."

She doesn't understand, and I'm not sure how to make her. "I'm a kid from the wrong side of town who got a chance of a lifetime and ran with it. Everything I've done I've had to work and fight for myself." I lean down and press a kiss to her lips, needing her touch. Needing that connection. "That's not going to change now. I've got it under control. It'll all work out."

"Rush."

I deepen the kiss to distract her, because what else can I say? That the only father figure I've known—who I thought was in my corner—betrayed my trust? The man, who should have been there for his flesh-and-blood son, proved himself more selfish than I thought, demanding I pay back what he gave me?

I feel cheated. Wronged. Used in the weirdest sense of the word.

Lennox is also right about my agent, my publicist, my teammates. Well, apart from Louie. Christ. It's like none of them have any faith in me.

"You're the rebel they expect this from. The man who brawls in pubs and changes women like you do your socks and doesn't give a fuck who sees or knows."

Or maybe I'm just finally seeing it because . . . Lennox has faith in me.

"You don't have to fight this on your own. Let me help you. Let me—" A gasp falls from her lips as my fingers make my way between her thighs.

"No one's ever fought for me before because they thought I was worth it." Another kiss to quiet the doubt. "I stopped hoping for that a long time ago."

Chapter
THIRTY-FOUR

Lennox

WE WERE SILENT THE WHOLE RIDE BACK DUE TO THE WIND AND THE convertible, much like we were on the way up to Montecito, but this time there's an added weight around us.

We had a fight.

I let the thoughts in the back of my head get the best of me, got a little too relaxed, and those thoughts spilled out. Maybe I didn't mean to ask the question how it came out, but my curiosity sure as hell did.

And sure, he woke me up and apologized, but there was so much left unsaid on my part, so much that I feel he silenced with his kiss and then the sex that followed.

But I let him distract me because I was too damn afraid to ruin whatever this is between us. Too scared to rock the boat. But then I realize there is no boat. There's just this small space of time where Rush and I are going to be together. It's perfectly natural to develop some feelings for a man I'm all but living, working, and having sex with. Normal on so many levels. There's no need to overthink it since in the not-so-distant future, we'll be parting ways to go back to our normal lives.

Brexton was right.

Rush is my perfect idea of a relationship. Quick, satisfying, and then over when we both move on.

But if that's the case, why now, as we're crawling through the Hollywood Hills back toward our reality-for-now home, does my head buzz with so many more thoughts and things I want to say? Why now, do I become nervous when Rush pulls the Mustang to a stop in the roundabout in front of Johnny's house?

It's because I'm lying to myself.

I'm lying to myself, and I'm not sure how to convince myself the lies are all true.

"So you got one thing ticked off your 'American things' to-do list, right?" I ask nervously. "What else was there? Tailgating and learning to appreciate why we Americans love our ice cubes? I'm sure there's more. What else can you think of? I mean . . ." I wring my hands in my lap and look out the passenger side window as I try to figure out how to say what I want to say. I turn toward him. "About last night."

"Forget about it."

"No." I reach for his hand to stop him from getting out of the car and wait for him to look at me. "I need to say this. I need to . . . *please?*"

Rush shuts the car door and turns to face me. "It's not a big deal. Really."

"It is because you planned this incredible getaway, and I ruined it."

"You didn't ruin it." He reaches out, cups the side of my face, and runs a thumb over the line of my jaw. "You've gotten to know the real me, Lennox. All I can say is that I hope that's enough for you to believe what I'm saying is true."

I open my mouth and then pause. Just say what really matters, Kincade. "I hope you can hear me when I say this. You're wrong in what you said last night. You can depend on me, Rush, and dammit, you're more than worth fighting for." I hate that my voice wavers on the last few words, but how sad to live a life feeling like you have to face every battle alone.

His eyes never leave mine as he forces a swallow and nods. "Thank you." His voice is barely a whisper but it shouts in my head.

He climbs out of the car without another word said.

The afternoon gets lost with me catching up on work and him training. The evening even more so as Johnny has some friends over who challenge Rush to a game of pool. Their echoes of laughter and trash-talking over winning and losing the ridiculous amounts of money being bet float up the stairs.

I try to read, but every time I get into the page, I hear Rush's voice or laugh and am taken back to the idyllic rendezvous we just left. The rendezvous that at the time was incredible, because it was just the two of us, but now? I'm left feeling like it never happened.

Several times I think to call my oldest sister, Dekker, and talk to her. She'll set me straight with her reasoning. But then that would open a can of worms, because they'll know the man I'm supposed to be recruiting is slowly winning over my heart too.

And until now in my life, my heart has been one hundred percent off limits to anyone other than family.

I'm just about to fall asleep when I hear Rush brushing his teeth in our bathroom. A part of me, the needy part apparently, wants to call out to him and ask him to come and sleep in my bed with me. The sane part of me shuts my mouth and rolls onto my side to face the wall away from the door.

"Hey? Nox?" Rush whispers at my door, and I'm not sure why for the life of me I pretend to be asleep. Maybe it's to quiet the needy part of me. Maybe it's to prove I don't need him, after all.

The last thing I need right now is more sex that confuses how it makes me feel physically with how it makes me feel emotionally.

I hear his feet on the floor and assume he's walking away, but am surprised when I feel the covers lift and the bed dip at my back. Without another word, he slides in behind me, wraps his arms around me to pull my back to his front, and then murmurs, "Good night."

"Hey," I say in mock protest. "My bed."

He presses a kiss to my shoulder as if it's the most natural thing in the world. "You can have the bathroom if I get to keep your bed."

"Are we negotiating again?"

"Nah, this one's already a done deal, love."

And it's the last thing he says before his breathing evens out.

I'm left wide awake, trying to figure out how to deal with an off-limits heart that wants to start playing the game. And why that's with a man with a definite time limit and secrets that guard his heart and soul.

Why is it with someone just like me?

Chapter
THIRTY-FIVE

Rush

7 Weeks Ago

THE CHANGING ROOM IS SILENT SAVE FOR THE GROANS FROM THE guys tired after playing ninety minutes plus stoppage. And while it's quiet, the boos of the crowd echo over and over in my head. The bullshit chants—the word cheater drawn out three times in a row followed by a quick, yes, he is—directed my way every time I was near the sidelines.

It doesn't help that we played like shit. We can make the excuse it was a brutally physical game, seven yellow cards ought to tell anyone that, or that the calls didn't go our way, but it was our fault we didn't advance.

Plain and fucking simple.

We got our arses handed to us and we deserved it, because we played like individuals and not a team.

It doesn't help that it's been less than twenty-four hours since that fucking picture of Esme and Rory hit and owned every social media platform known to man.

Talk about fucking up team chemistry.

I steered clear of Seth as much as possible, but now? Now I fear it's going to come to a head, and I'm so not ready for it.

I lean my head back against the wall, close my eyes, and make a conscious decision to ignore the stares my teammates keep angling my way.

The glares that say I just lost us the place to go to the Champions League.

"Fuck," I groan to no one in particular.

"You sure know about fucking, don't you, McKenzie?" Seth growls, and I open my eyes to find him standing right in front of me. "Since you seem to have no problem fucking my wife."

The atmosphere of the changing room shifts in an instant. It seems like every guy on the team is there in a heartbeat, including Rory, standing a few meters behind Seth, staring bug-eyed at the situation.

"Just like you know about using your hands, right, Seth?" I say thinking of Rory's account of Seth punching Esme. "Good thing you play a sport where you use your feet so you can save your hands for what you really do best."

And from one breath to the next, Seth's fist plows into my face. I return the favor before the two of us are rolling on the floor landing blow after blow.

At first the guys stand there, uncertain what to do, and then their attempts to break us up turn into them throwing punches as if we asked them to pick sides. The entire changing room becomes a brawl of fists and elbows and frustration and anger.

⌒

"That's going to be some shiner," Lloyd says as he crosses his arms over his chest and glares at me.

"You should see the other guy," I say with a chuckle that makes my ribs hurt like a bitch. I'd refuse to admit it if asked.

"You think this is fucking funny, Rush? You think any of this is? I have half a mind to—Fuck!" He barks the word out as he shoves up out of his seat to pace his frustration out. "We lost the fucking game tonight we were hands down favorites to win, and you sit here with a smirk and a smart-arse comeback like it has nothing to do with that picture in the bloody paper."

I stare at him, at a loss for what to say. For what to do. Hell, how do I even keep up the charade? Because I'm fucking pissed off we won't be going to the champions league. We've worked hard for that all year, and now because of a damn photo, LFC is out of the championship. So, yeah, I'm pissed all right. But my hands are fucking tied.

"You do understand that your contract is currently being negotiated and you could be up for a transfer, right? Keep the future star of our club when he's going to ruin it, because he can't keep his fucking dick in his pants? Force management to put Seth up for transfer or go on loan to another club because he's on the tail end of his prime? Or tell both of you to figure your shit out, because this is a business and your fucking team needs you too?"

It hits me. The severity of what I've agreed to do, and the fact that Rory was right: they would have cut him without giving it a single thought.

"I have no problem playing with Seth, mate. None at all." I open my jaw wide and feel the pain in my cheek where his fist landed more than his fair share of punches. "I have a problem with the fact that he likes to plow his fist into more than just my face."

"What the hell is that supposed to mean?"

"Nothing. Never mind." *Not my business.*

"Never mind? You're fucking up my team. Your squad. And fucking over the club and its fans, and you're going to tell me never mind? How about you tell me why the fuck you did this?" he shouts.

How about you tell me why the fuck you assume I did?

I want to scream the words at the top of my lungs. I may fuck things up outside of football, I might be reckless and not care about the consequences, but anyone who really knows me, would know I'd never fuck with my team. With my club. With this game I love more than anything else in the world.

And standing here staring at Lloyd—the man who I bust my arse for every damn day—and realizing he assumes I'm guilty like everyone else does—fucking guts me.

"I can play with Seth without incident," I say in a low growl. "And I will bust my arse and win for this club like I always do. If you've never doubted me or my abilities, then don't start now. I bleed Liverpool red. I have even before I came here."

I stare at him for a long beat before turning on my heels and walking out, not giving my manager any chance to respond.

Chapter
THIRTY-SIX

Lennox

"You didn't have to go to the event tonight?" Johnny asks as he plops down on the couch beside me and turns so he can put his feet in my lap.

"Um, excuse me. I'm not a footrest."

He leans over to make a show of looking at his feet on my lap. "Looks to me like you are." I give him the bird and a roll of my eyes. "So . . . should I be afraid to ask what's going on between the two of you?"

Is it weird I wonder the same thing too? Since we've been back from Montecito, Rush slips into my bed every night to sleep. I feel like so much has been left unspoken.

It has to just be me. It has to be that I need to overthink less and enjoy him more.

"What's going on between Rush and me? A little fun. A lot of sex. I don't know." I shrug.

Johnny chuckles in that *you can't pull this shit over on me* way he has. "You don't know? Woman, the way he looks at you says something altogether different. I'm not buying it. There's more than sex. Nice try."

"Can't a woman and man just want to have some careless and much-needed fun?"

"Easier said than done."

I laugh. "Remember who you're talking to, John."

"I forgot." He snorts. "The queen heartbreaker herself."

"I wouldn't go that far."

"Tell me the last guy you dated—er slept with, because you don't really date—that lasted for more than three months."

"Exactly. That's why this is perfect." If I keep telling myself the lie then maybe I'll start believing it. "We're over halfway into this contract, Rush will go home, and we'll be done. I couldn't have planned it better myself."

"Your words are ringing hollow, Lenn."

I glance over at him and am at a complete and utter loss of words for one of my oldest friends. "I don't know what to say."

"How about you admit you're falling for him?" He immediately holds up his hand to prevent me from rejecting the notion completely. "And what's so wrong with that if you are? He's a good guy. You're an awesome woman. You clicked. You had sex. And now, holy shit, there just might be something more there than just the physical. What's wrong with that?"

I fight the tears burning in my eyes. The tears present because his words are what I've been telling myself but can't seem to accept. "I can't be falling for him." My voice is all but a whisper.

"Why can't you?"

"Because that's not me. *I'm not her.* I don't do hearts and flowers and gushy and—"

"That's not always what love is. There's no mold for it to fit in. It's always give and take, but it's also what each individual person needs it to be. My mom used to tell me everyone has their own love language. Everyone has a way they need to be loved and a way they give love. Whatever the fuck that means."

"Did you actually just say everyone has their own love language?" I snicker.

He lifts a middle finger. "Give me a break here. I'm trying to act mature and give you advice you probably don't want or need," he says but his cheeks turn pink, and it's the most adorable thing in the world.

"Mature? *You?* You should start a relationship blog and call it Dear Johnny."

"And you should stop teasing or find somewhere else to stay," he jokes.

But my sigh is heavy despite the smiles on our lips. "I'm not in love with him, Johnny." I say the words but the knowing look and nod he gives me says he doesn't buy it either. "How can I be? How can I have never had feelings for anyone and now all of a sudden have some? I mean, that's just asinine."

"Sure. Fine. You're not." His tone says everything, contrary to his nonchalance. "But I also know you use the word asinine when you get flustered." He lifts his eyebrows.

"You're frustrating."

"Ditto," he says and then his expression softens. "Don't push him away because you're scared. That's all I'm going to say."

"I'm not scared."

"Just stubborn," he says sarcastically, and I drop my head to the back of the couch and stare at the ceiling.

"He's a loner, Lenn, always has been. The only thing that keeps him tethered is football and right now, he's afraid he's going to lose that."

"He won't lose that," I say with an assertiveness I don't know for certain. "Liverpool would be stupid to let him go."

"Nothing's set in stone. I don't know much, but I do know this whole thing has been hard on him, even though he's doing a good job hiding it." He takes a sip of his drink and points at me. "Maybe you'll be the one to help him get through it."

His words feel like whiplash and I chuckle. "I thought you told me that first night I wasn't what he needed. Remember how I was offended by that?"

"That's because you were a woman on the prowl wanting to get laid."

"Screw you." I roll my eyes and then laugh, because it was so true.

"And now . . . I don't know. You guys are just good together. Maybe . . . who knows?"

I stare at my oldest friend and hear his words. Words that reflect the same thing I feel, that Rush and I are just good together, and then groan in frustration. "He won't talk about it with me."

"Ahh," Johnny hums, knowing I'm talking about Esme without saying her name. "Is that the cause of the sudden chill between you two?"

"It's not a chill, it's a . . . fuck if I know. How can I really "in like" a man who doesn't trust me?"

"The question is, do you trust him?"

How stupid am I that I instinctively want to say yes?

But it's true.

I do trust him. I trust in the things he's said to me and the cryptic things he's not said.

And I think that's part of what's giving me pause. I don't trust freely and yet with Rush . . . I just do.

I tread carefully with my words, so I don't betray what Rush confided in me the other night. But I also know that Johnny doesn't suffer fools nor put up with assholes, so just the fact that he's allowing Rush to stay here tells me he clearly believes Rush is innocent as well. "I think there's more to the story. I think that sometimes it's easier to fall back on a reputation or the image of yourself than to answer truthfully."

"We think alike," he says cryptically. "I know the owner of the magazine that first printed the picture. I offered to Rush to reach out to them and . . . I don't know. Sue them. Get the rest of the pictures the magazine acquired if there were any. Something to defend his name."

"What did he say?"

"He told me to leave well enough alone."

Chapter
THIRTY-SEVEN

Rush

ENOUGH IS ENOUGH.

This quiet game she's playing needs to be done and over with. It's literally driving me mad.

To sleep in the same bed with a woman every night, but then wake up and have her act like you're nonexistent is fucking insane.

Like ten minutes ago. She's talking to some blokes about recruiting for individual teams and when I walk up, she smiles softly, and then introduces me into the conversation before quietly exiting.

What the fuck is up with that?

This is not the right time to do this. Talks are at a standstill between Finn and the club, and I'm in a shitty mood over it. And to make matters worse, the one person I want to turn to, isn't exactly talking to me.

So yes, this has to end. Right here. Right now. She wants to be pissed at me because I can't tell her about Rory and Esme, fine. But that doesn't mean we're going to live like this for the next month as we play out this bloody contract.

"Lennox?" I ask when I see Maggie, one of the assistants who is always wandering around doing a little bit of everything.

"I think she went out to get some air."

I point down the hall to ask if it's the right way and head in that direction when I get a nod. "Thanks."

I push open the doors to the outside and stop. Lennox is standing there with her back to me, her hands braced on the railing, and her face lifted up to the sky. Fairy lights twinkle everywhere in the trees and reflect off her hair and dress.

Much like she was that night before she turned and seduced me in the sauna.

"You're avoiding me."

She turns to look over her shoulder, and I'm sucker-punched in a way that's all new to me. She's been right in front of me all this time, and yet somehow, I've missed her and how we were before we fought.

"Not avoiding," she murmurs and turns to face me with that look in her eye that tells me she's thinking too much. "How can you say I'm avoiding you when we sleep in the same bed every night?"

I take a step toward her. "That's sleeping, Lenn, but when it comes to the talking part, the laughing part, where did you go?" She looks down, and I reach out and lift her chin so she's forced to look me in the eyes. "Talk to me. What's going on?"

She forces a smile. "I'm just trying to figure shit out."

"Like what?"

She chews on her bottom lip. "Let me start by first saying I'm not a needy woman. I don't need affirmations or definitions or someone to stroke my ego to make me feel—"

"Anyone who knows you, already knows that."

"What are we doing here, Rush? What is this?"

She's spoken aloud the words I ask myself every night as I wrap my arms around her and pull her against me. The same question I've yet to answer myself.

"You say that like you want to be mad at me." I chuckle at how adorable she looks right now with that pout on her face.

"I am mad at you."

"Why?"

"Because this is all your fault."

"You're right. It is." I hold my hand up. "It's completely my fault." I lean in closer. "You want to tell me what I did?"

"You made me like you."

My laugh rings out and a smile tugs on the corner of her lips. Fucking adorable. "That's a terrible crime," I say and lean in to press my lips against hers and frame her face with my hands. "Horrible." They soften with my coaxing and open up to me. "How will you ever forgive me?"

"Rush," she murmurs as she rests her forehead against mine. Our breaths feather over each other's lips. "This is . . ."

The unsteady inhale of her breath is exactly how I feel. On shaky ground, uncertain as fuck, but knowing there's nowhere else I'd rather be right now.

"This is us. You. Me. It's just us. And for the record, you made me like you too." I lean back so I can meet her eyes and the emotion that's welling in them. Despite how long I've known her, I've shared more with Lennox than any other person. I do consider her a friend. *I hope she knows that, and doesn't doubt our connection.* "Does there have to be a definition? We both went into this knowing that I'll be leaving to go back home to my life and my team and you'll be leaving to go back home to your life and your family. We're having fun, we're making memories, and"—I press a tender kiss to her lips that feels like so much more than just *having fun*—"and that has to be enough for right now," I say, my lips brushing against hers, not giving a fuck if anyone were to walk out and see us.

"You're right. I'm sorry. It was stupid to—"

I slant my lips over hers to shut her up. I don't want an apology right now. There's nothing to apologize for, I just want her.

I want this time we have left to be memorable.

Later, I can sort through the ache in my chest that burns from the thought of what it will be like when we do part ways.

Chapter
THIRTY-EIGHT

Lennox

"At least I finally found something that you're horrible at," I say as I pull my arms out of my wetsuit and sink down into the sand, its warmth welcome against the cool neoprene.

"Whose idea was it to take surfing lessons anyway?" he says as he collapses beside me, a little less gracefully and with a lot more sand all over him.

"I think my stomach hurts from laughing so hard."

He eyes me as he shoves a lock of hair off his forehead. "Whatever else you have up your Tour-de-America sleeve for me to do before this contract ends, can we make sure it involves something we can enjoy with less water going up my nose?"

I laugh and nod. "Tour-de-America?"

"Yes. We did Disneyland last weekend. The food truck place before that. It feels like you're checking items off a Tour-de-America list for us to complete."

"I thought it was part of my contract to make you happy," I say sweetly and bat my eyelashes innocently.

"I know exactly what would make me happy," he says and gives a slight tug on the tie of my bikini top, "but I think we'd get arrested for it."

I lean forward and press a kiss to his lips. "Pretty please."

"Lennox Kincade," he all but growls, and right before he tugs me down to partially act on the threat, something over my shoulder catches his eye. "Hello there, mate."

"I'm so sorry to interrupt your personal time," a woman with strawberry-blonde-colored hair says, as she races up to her son who is standing staring at Rush as if he's just seen a ghost. "Billy just adores you and—"

"Totally fine," Rush says before turning to address the adorable little boy with curly hair and vibrant blue eyes. "Billy, is it?"

"Yes," he stutters.

"Please tell me you're a Liverpool fan because between you and me, there are not enough of them here in the States."

"I am."

"Whew." Rush holds his hand out and shakes Billy's. "Rush McKenzie, nice to meet you."

They chat for a few minutes, and I watch the interaction, marveling at how very good Rush is at doing this—talking to fans, and kids especially. There's an ease about him that can't be taught. I've seen many athletes stumble or slip and crush a kid's idyllic view of what their sports hero is like.

Not Rush.

Tour-de-America.

Rush's term comes back at me as I watch the two interact and I wonder, is that what I'm doing? Am I trying to check one item off his list of American must-haves so that when he goes home he'll never forget me? Am I trying to forge memories with someone because I know we have a finite amount of time, and I need them for myself to hold on to when my heart is broken?

"Are you staying, Rush?" Billy asks, glancing over to his mom and then back to Rush again. "Are you going to play for the MLS so we can see you all the time?"

"That's a hard one, mate. I'd love to see you all the time too, but I do have a contract to fulfill with Liverpool. It's important to stay true to the word you give."

Billy's face falls and it's heartbreaking. "I understand."

"But we are having an exhibition game next week if you want to come out and see me play in person," Rush says. Billy's eyes widen.

And just like that, Rush is the hero again as he gives Billy's mom instructions before they say their goodbyes on how to make sure Billy sees him prior to the game.

"What?" Rush asks when he turns to find me studying him as they walk away.

"Nothing."

"Why do you keep looking at me like that?" he asks.

"You mean in admiration because of how incredible you are to each and every fan who comes up to you? It is your personal time, you didn't have to—"

"Do you know how many players would kill to be in my shoes? To put on a kit and boots every day and play for a team you love in a game that gave you life? Why wouldn't I be nice?"

And that's the moment I feel Rush take ownership of a piece of my heart . . . forever.

"Don't let the tattoos and rep fool you, folks, because Rush McKenzie is a softie at heart."

He gives me a wink and presses his lips to mine. "Shh, don't tell anyone."

When he sits back on his elbows and holds his face up to the sun, I ask the question he answered to Billy. "So you've made up your mind? You're going back home?"

He slides a glance my way before looking back out at the ocean and at kids in their surfing lessons who are twenty years younger than us and way more coordinated.

"There was never really a decision to be made in my eyes. I'm sure Finn has his ideas but it's my life, my career . . . my say."

"As it should be." I nod several times as I consider his response. It's the right one—hell, yes, it's the right one—but hearing it said out loud means it's real.

It means he's really leaving.

"Why do you sound so disappointed then?"

I can't help my smile. "Because that means I failed at my job, at what I was contracted for."

"That's the only reason?" he asks, fishing for me to tell him I'll miss him.

I will miss him. In fact, I think it's going to sting for some time, but hell if I'm going to admit that to him.

"No, that's not the only reason. Of course not. Something has to put a stop to the horrible sex."

He tackles me onto my back, our laughter ringing out as my shoulders press into the sand before his mouth finds mine again. This time the kiss is longer, a lot less playful, and feels quite different.

I can't put my finger on it, but when it ends and he looks down on me, there's intensity there, a gravity that tethers to the unnamed emotions causing a lump to form in my throat.

"I'm sorry," he says. "I don't mean to hang you out to dry."

"Cannon had to have known it was a long shot to keep you here, and that's why the concept of hiring me rang hollow once I found out you were his target." I reach up and brush some sand off his forehead, the need to touch him becoming stronger with each passing moment. "But I agree with your decision, Rush. What's best for you is back home. Anyone who tells you otherwise is only looking out for their own interests and not yours. You definitely shouldn't leave the Premier League. It's where you belong."

"*Liverpool* is where I belong." I know in his heart of hearts that he believes what he's saying. LFC is his future. It saddens my heart when I see his worried gaze. "Let's hope they keep me." His smile is quick but doesn't reach his eyes, as he pushes off me and moves to sit beside me.

"Hey." My hand moves to his back. "Are negotiations not going well?"

Rush is silent for a beat. "I don't know whether you're asking as a sympathetic friend wanting to lend me support or as an agent extraordinaire."

I smile and shrug. "Can we go with both?"

"At least you're honest." He chuckles. "It does beg the question though: why haven't you suggested I switch over to KSM? You said you were allowed to within your contract with Cannon, and not once have you made a push for it."

My eyes find the ocean as I ask myself the same question. As I wonder the same thing. Rush McKenzie is a straight shooter, and therefore, he deserves an honest answer. I avoided it a few weeks ago, as I wasn't ready to be completely transparent. But now? Now I trust him even more than I did before.

"I took the job with Cannon on a whim. I was pissed at my family for controlling my day-to-day, and angry at some shitty things I overheard fellow agents saying about me at a conference I attended."

"What did your family do to make you mad?"

"They made me feel as if I'd lost their trust. As if they didn't think I could do my job anymore."

"So you took this job vowing to prove them wrong, by what? Succeeding at whatever Cannon wanted?"

"Something like that," I murmur, not wanting to admit that I promised my dad I was going to land Rush as a client.

"Cannon gave you an unsurmountable task considering I never gave an inkling I wanted to stay in America," he says. "What did the agents say that you overheard?"

I take a deep breath, resolved to blow it all off, but then realize that if I tell him, he'll understand why I hesitated to start what is now us.

"They accused me of using sex as a way to lure new clients."

"Did you?" he asks, unfazed and unapologetic.

"Not in the way they accused me of. I dated a player for a while, and he ended up switching over to me for representation. The rumor started there." I draw my initials in the sand with my finger. "I won't apologize for wearing high heels and the way I dress."

"You mean professional?" He laughs. "No woman should ever have to apologize for the way she dresses. A man can think you're sexy because of it, but that doesn't give them the excuse to accuse you of using sex to sign a client."

"Thank you."

"No one should—oh." He stretches the last sound out as it hits him. "And now you're sleeping with me, a player you're supposed to recruit. No wonder you were so adamant that we not—"

"That would be why." I laugh and vacillate on whether or not to tell him that Finn was the miscreant who made the accusations and started the rumors.

But I decide not to.

If Rush ever came to KSM, I want it to be because I earned it, not because he's pissed that his agent was an asshole to the woman he's currently sleeping with.

If Rush were to become my client, I want it to be based on merit and not pity.

"I guess I threw a spanner in the works."

"A what?" I laugh.

"What is it you guys call it?" Deep in thought, he twists his lips for a beat. "Wrench, I think?"

I stare and then chuckle when it hits me. "You mean a wrench in the plans."

"Yes. Sure. A spanner in the works. I threw one in there."

"You sure did, and it was definitely a welcome one." I rest my head on his shoulder and loop my arm through his as we both watch the lessons in front of us.

"But you still haven't answered my question."

"Which was?"

"Why haven't you actively recruited me when we've had all the time in the world?"

"I haven't earned your complete trust yet, so there's no way I can represent you." I feel his body still beside me and know my comment hit home harder than I'd intended. "One of the most important aspects of a client-agent relationship is trust. After all, the decisions I make impact every part of that athlete's life. Without that, it's just empty words, and that's not who I am. Never will be. And honestly, Rush, isn't that what you deserve too?"

Chapter
THIRTY-NINE

Rush

"Any word?" I ask the minute Finn answers the phone.

"Good morning to you too." He laughs as if he's fucking hilarious. He's not.

"Yeah. You too," I say for propriety's sake. "Have you heard anything back from the club?"

"Relax. I'm in constant communication with them."

"And?"

"And nothing. We're going back and forth."

"Why is it that when you've 'gone back and forth' in the past, you've filled me in on every step? This time, I haven't heard shit."

"Because so far I have nothing worthy to report."

"Meaning?"

"Meaning they're still trying to figure shit out."

"Don't bullshit me, Finn."

His sigh is heavy. "Seth's refusing to play with you, and since he has two years left on that long-term hefty contract he signed years ago, some team would have to buy those years out in order to transfer him. You're the easiest candidate to move to remedy the situation since you're up on a contract renewal."

"They know that in any poll taken, I'm the favorite player, right? They've seen the stats, they know I bring more to the club than—"

"You're starting to sound like a little kid begging, Rush. I know how to do my job."

"Sorry. I know. This is just shit."

"Try negotiating without any legs under you, because your own client doesn't give you any to stand on."

I think of Archibald and his call earlier. How he thanked me—again—because it looks like he's going to win the election. The feeling of betrayal is still there. So much so that I felt like telling him that my decision to follow through on my word had nothing to do with him. That I was making this sacrifice for Rory, who is still doing well from what I can gather from his text messages, and for Helen.

But what would have been the point? The deed is done. The seed has been sown. And it looks like everyone seems to be coming out a winner.

Everyone except for me.

"They won't transfer me, Finn."

"The MLS is always another option. I'll have an offer on the table in the next two weeks from them."

"And the answer is no."

Although my answer is immediate, it's Lennox's words that pass through my mind.

What's best for you is back home. Anyone who tells you otherwise is only looking out for their own interests and not yours. You definitely shouldn't leave the Premier League. It's where you belong.

"It's not where I belong."

Chapter
FORTY

Lennox

"That was incredible," Rush says as he grabs the bags from the back of the car and looks at me over its top. "First the tailgating. I mean, this needs to be a thing back home, but then again, we have a lot of shitty weather. But the concept and the food. Perfection."

I give him a look saying he's crazy. "It was the same food we could have had here in the backyard."

"Yeah, but in the car park, with other fans? I can see why you Americans like it."

"Whatever." I laugh. I go to grab a chair from the trunk and am surprised when Rush stops me and pulls me against him.

"Thank you," he says with the simplest of kisses, which heats every part of me from the inside out. He gives the best kisses. "I mean it." His eyes are dark and serious. "You went above and beyond. Between the food and then letting me go into the clubhouse to meet the guys before the game—"

"Only because I have a few clients on the team," I say with a smile.

"It doesn't matter. It was my first baseball game, and I'll never forget it. Thank you."

This time, it's me who leans into him and presses my lips to his. I thread my fingers through his hair and steal one more moment with him. I make one more memory to hold on to, because while this contract felt like forever when we first started, now it feels like it's ending way too soon.

"Well, that was nice," he murmurs against my lips.

"I can make it even nicer upstairs once we get this stuff put away."

"Screw the stuff," he says as he drops it in an unceremonious heap beside the car. "We can get it later." There's a devious look in his eye and a mischievous smile on his lips. "First one upstairs gets oral first!"

"Argh!" I yell and pull on his arm to hold him back. He's much quicker than I am and makes it to the front door first. We both struggle over the handle and when I yank it open first, I'm so preoccupied with gloating at him, I about have a heart attack when I hear "Surprise!"

"Oh shit," I screech.

I look up to find my sisters, Dekker, Dekker's fiancé Hunter, Chase, Brexton, my father, and Johnny, all standing there with party hats on and birthday balloons in their hands. Rush's hand on the back of my shirt loosens, and I stagger back against him in complete and utter surprise.

And then two seconds later, the tears come. Big, sappy tears. The kind that fall so fast I can't catch my breath or say anything coherently. The kind that reflect how very badly I've missed my family.

Within seconds, I'm enveloped in hugs, one after another after another. My sisters are crying too, as they hold on tight and tell me how much they've missed me.

"What in the world are you doing here? My birthday's not until next month—I—" I cover my face with my hands, so utterly overcome with happiness. They're here. They came here to see me.

"Well, you bailed on the surprise birthday party we were throwing you, so we decided to bring it to you," Dekker says as her fiancé, Hunter, waves to me on the outside of the circle.

"Surprise birthday party?" I laugh. "But . . ."

"Yes." It's Chase this time. "That's usually how you throw surprise parties to catch the honoree off guard." She steps up and hangs an arm around my neck. "Chicago? The reason Dad turned down the invite for you to speak at the conference? It wasn't because we didn't think you couldn't hack it, you big dork, but rather because we had a ridiculously over-the-top party planned for you."

"It's not every day that it's your birthday," Brexton chimes in with a gorgeous smile and a blow of a party horn.

"Dad had the rooftop bar at the St. Cloud reserved. All your friends had RSVP'd." Chase shrugs. "And you ran to California because you thought we didn't love you. Such an annoying little sister thing to do."

We all laugh. That might have been a trick she used when she was little. Pretend to run away—like to the sidewalk out in front of the house—so that we'd notice she was gone, and then tell her how much we loved her and never wanted her to leave.

"You're a brat," I say, but look around at all this love and my chest constricts. "I don't even know what to say." I turn to my father, who has been silent until this point. He's been standing back observing as usual. I take a step toward him. "Dad—I—I don't even know—" My words stop as he pulls me into one of his awesome bear hugs, the kind that makes everything bad in the world go away.

The kind that makes me realize I let everything with Finn get to my head, using the hurt against the people I love.

And who love me.

"How's my girl?" he asks before stepping back and framing my face in his hands. "You look good. I think your wandering has paid off." He winks as tears well in my eyes.

How could I doubt his love—this love from my family? The bitter hurt I felt, the unwarranted assumptions I made . . . and here they were just hiding behind a surprise for me. A surprise I went and ruined.

"I'm good, Dad. Really good."

It's then that I look over his shoulder and see Rush with his arms crossed over his chest as he stands beside Hunter. They're talking, but Rush's eyes find mine and his smile lights up my heart.

"You know about this, McKenzie?" I ask looking from him to Johnny, who had to have known.

"Of course, I did. Good thing we had a baseball game today or I would have had to sign us up for more surfing lessons to get us out of the house so they could decorate." He motions to the balloons and decorations all over the place. "God knows, I never want another surfing lesson in my life."

I smile through the tears, overwhelmed by the validation directed my way.

"Rush McKenzie, meet"—I pause and turn to look at everyone. I realize that while they're a pain in my ass, he's never had this. So when I say my next words, they are definitely over a huge lump of emotion in my throat. "Please meet my family."

There's commotion as he's thrown into the Kincade chaos of greet-ings . . . when it hits me.

I'm here.

Rush's here.

Now they know we're staying in the same house. Under the same roof.

Even worse, someone had to have been the lookout for when we came home.

And that lookout would have seen us kiss.

And we kissed-kissed.

Well . . . shit.

I'm sure assumptions are being made and nudges are being nudged.

My face must show it, because Chase walks up and pulls me close. "We'll talk about it later, Lenn. But yeah, I saw. I was the lookout. And damn . . . he's even hotter in person."

Chapter
FORTY-ONE

Rush

LENNOX IS A DIFFERENT PERSON.

Still the same gorgeous smile, but it almost looks as if a weight has been lifted from her shoulders. I can only assume that their presence has healed whatever happened between them before she came to California.

"They're a tight-knit bunch."

I look to my right where Hunter Maddox has just taken a seat. A beer is in his hand, and he's watching the sisters.

"They seem to be," I murmur.

"You'll get used to them clustering around each other and talking in their own language. They do this half-sentence thing and then the other one finishes it for them." He takes a sip and chuckles. "Or doesn't finish it at all, but they all nod because they read each other's minds. If it helps, just nod and smile when they do this and they'll think you understand too."

"Thanks for the heads-up."

"Fights are par for the course too, but you know how siblings are." He shrugs.

"In a sense," I murmur, thinking of the few fights Rory and I've had over the years, and how we'd hate each other one minute and then be fine the next.

"So what other family pointers should I give? Kenyon is fair as fair can be, but he'll protect his girls at any cost. In time, I'm sure he'll have a little sit-down with you like he did me and—"

"What? I don't know what you mean. Why would Kenyon—"

"You're in love with his daughter, so he'll want to have a man-to-man with you."

"You're jumping to conclusions, mate. We're not—I'm not . . ." Why can't I get the words out? "This is just until I head back home."

Hunter eyes me and gives a slow nod before his lips spread in a wide grin. "I said the same thing, and now Dekk has a ring on it. You can hold out hope, brother, but once these Kincade women grab you by the balls, you don't want them to let go."

"Shit," I say and run a hand through my hair. The beers from the game earlier are starting to hit me. And of course, it's right then that Lennox looks across the backyard at me and gives me a soft smile.

Fuck. My heart flips in my chest. *It doesn't need that shit.*

I smile back.

And Hunter laughs so hard as he pats my back, jolting me forward. "You are so fucking screwed, McKenzie." He stands and shakes his head. "Welcome to the club."

Chapter
FORTY-TWO

Lennox

"So . . ." Chase says, as she holds out a fresh glass of wine and pulls my attention from where Rush is talking to Brexton and my dad. "Should we have that talk now while everyone is occupied?"

"What talk would that be?" I feign innocence.

"The one where I tell you it's obvious that you and Rush are a thing. Then you argue back that you're not, and that this is strictly professional. And then I tell you that you're such a lying bitch, because you don't look at someone the way you look at Rush—or the way you kissed him for that matter"—she emits a long, low whistle—"without having something more than an I'm-just-here-for-sex vibe."

"It's complicated," I murmur, my gaze veering right back to him.

"Isn't it always?" She chuckles. "Is it complicated because of the work aspect or is it complicated because of your heart aspect?"

"I haven't once asked him to come to KSM. He knows the truth as to why the MLS hired me, and I've told him I think it was a bad move to leave home with the scandal going on, but I haven't asked him to leave Finn for me," I say hoping that's answer enough.

"So you love him."

I choke on my sip of wine. Gotta leave it to Chase to cut right to the heart of the matter. Tears threaten as I stare at Rush. He's relaxed in a chair, arm resting on the back of the one beside him. He's engrossed in a conversation with my dad, who looks just as interested, and the first thought that comes to my head is, he fits.

What an odd thought, and one I never knew I was looking for the answer to.

"I love you to death, Lenn, but you need some straight-shooting right now. Every time you find someone you really like, you use the lame excuse that you love your freedom and the ability to move as you please as a reason for it not to work. It's just for fun, you say. It's just great sex. But I call bullshit. You're too afraid to let anyone get too close to you so you pick the ones who can't."

"Did you guys all have a group talk on what to say to me, because I swear I've heard this spiel before," I say to try and play off what she's saying, avoiding the uneasiness it brings.

"Mom dying fucked us all up. It's a natural reaction to fear someone getting too close because you're afraid you'll get hurt. But at some point, Lenn, you have to let someone get close to you. But I think Rush already is. I just think you're too scared to admit it."

She's right.

I know she's right, and yet now I've put myself in the exact situation she's talking about. I picked a person to be with who I know is going to leave. Now I've fallen for him, and I'm scared to death because he is *in fact* leaving.

"Like I said, it's complicated," I whisper as Rush's laugh carries over to me.

"And like I said, you love him." She laughs.

But this time when she says it, I don't refute her. This time I look up and watch Rush completely at ease with everyone I care about, and every part of me can see the merit in what my sister is saying.

"How do you know when it's love?" I whisper.

"When he's your beginning, middle, and end. When you think about him for no reason. When you want the world for him even if you're not a part of that world."

"Well, that's depressing," I say sarcastically.

"True, but if it's real and true, he'll find a way to make you a part of that world."

I blow out a breath and twist my lips as everything my little sister says lands a direct hit.

"This can't happen," I murmur.

"You can't tell love that." She puts her arm around me and squeezes me against her.

"Shh."

"What? You think everyone standing here doesn't already know you two are a thing? If you think Hunter and Dekker are the only ones here making heart eyes at each other, you're crazy."

"But I promised you I wouldn't do this, and look what I did."

"No. You promised me you wouldn't sleep with a potential client. Nowhere did you promise you wouldn't fall in love with one."

I eye my little sister over the rim of my glass and sigh. "How did this happen?"

"That's not the question you should be asking yourself. You should be asking yourself what you're going to do about it."

～

"I would like to propose a toast." My dad stands from his seat with his glass of wine in his hand.

Everyone at the party moves toward him, and Johnny reaches down and squeezes my hand. "I hope you don't mind that I let them come," he whispers in my ear. "I didn't think you'd be ready to go home by the date of the party, so I told them they were more than welcome to come here."

"Please, don't apologize."

"I know you were struggling a bit with family stuff and I didn't want to overstep."

"You're my family too, John." I choke up. "I needed this more than you know."

He presses a kiss to the side of my head. "I know. You're simply glowing with happiness."

He puts a hand on my back and pushes me forward to where I walk up and stand beside Rush. It feels like it's been all night that we've walked that tightrope of pretending we're not together. Chase was right. They all know.

Regardless, when I meet his eyes, every part of me warms at the sight of him.

"Lennox, dear. My wild child at heart. The daughter who I wasn't sure would be happy or pissed that we all showed up to crash a few days of her independence to celebrate her birthday."

"Almost birthday," I say amid everyone's laughter.

"Yes, almost birthday. We know you've struggled finding where you fit best lately. Sometimes it's not a matter of fitting best but rather needing to hold on to that moment in time you fit into and living it to the fullest. We know you'll find what you're looking for just as we hope you know how very much we love you. Wander if you need to. Roam to find that fit. Just know wherever it is, you'll always have a home to come back to." My dad's eyes lock on to mine and his are as wet with tears as mine are. "Happy Birthday, Lennox. May you wander where you need to wander and may this be the best one yet."

Everyone says, "Hear, hear," before clinking glasses, as my dad steps forward and embraces me in another one of his bear hugs. The hugs that solved all problems when I was a kid and still fixes things while I'm an adult too. I've felt incomplete without them.

"Your mother would be so proud of you," he says before giving me a kiss on the cheek and stepping back so everyone else can give me love as well.

Rush is last in line. He reaches out and tucks a piece of hair behind my ear before leaning down and brushing his lips over mine and whispering, "Happy Birthday, Nox."

I swear there's a collective hush over the party as they watch their sister—the one who hates public displays of affection and anything that can be considered romantic—not fight it when it comes to this man.

Somehow, it seems so damn natural with Rush, it's ridiculous.

Chapter
FORTY-THREE

Rush

"THAT WAS IMPRESSIVE." DEKKER KINCADE STANDS OUTSIDE THE changing room of the stadium, where I just fulfilled my last contracted MLS exhibition game. There are more events on the calendar, but this was the last big one.

"Thanks, but I'm feeling a bit rusty."

"Oh, please," she says with a roll of her eyes that is so Lennox, it's funny.

I close the distance between us, and she pushes off the wall she was leaning against. Her arms are still crossed over her chest and her eyes are still fixed on mine.

Uh-oh.

It's big-sister protection time.

"It's true. I'm going to be lagging when I get back home to the team."

"So that's the plan? For you to head back when this contract is fulfilled?"

"Despite whatever rumors are out there, yes." She nods, her eyes intense. "What is it you want to ask, Dekker? There's a reason Hunter's not standing beside you, so my best guess is you're going to give me a warning that if I break your sister's heart, I'm going to have to deal with you next. Is that it?"

Her smile is slow to crawl onto her lips but does anyway. "Do I need to worry?"

"We're both adults who went into this knowing where it would end. Will it sting? A lot more than I fucking expected it to, but . . ." I force a smile, but I think both Lennox and I know it's going to hurt like a bitch when we do leave here. I see it in the way she looks at me now. It's in the way she kisses. It's in the way I hold her a little tighter at night when she sleeps, so I can remember everything. "We live in two different worlds. Two different countries. We're two successful people hell-bent on our professional success."

"As are Hunter and I."

"Look"—I laugh—"we're not you and Hunter. We're us and we don't need anyone forcing us into a mold other than one we've created for ourselves."

"Fair enough." She chews on her bottom lip, and I'd kill to know what's going through her mind.

"Have you guys enjoyed your trip?" I ask.

"Who wouldn't with this weather?" she says. "We've all met with some of our West Coast clients, which is always good, but most of all we were able to check in on Lenn and make sure she was okay."

"And is she?" I ask, realizing this might be the point of this whole conversation. "In your eyes, is she doing okay?" I angle my head to the side and stare at her.

"Seems to be," she murmurs. "The bullshit Finn pulled on her really did a number on her self-esteem. It's the first time she's literally dropped everything and flown the proverbial coop, so to speak, taking a job that wasn't the right fit for her."

"What? What did Finn do to her?"

"The Las Vegas conference a few months back?" She stares at my blank look. "Shit, I'm sorry. I figured you—never mind."

"No. I want to know."

"I'm sorry, Rush, but if she wanted you to know she would have told you." She laughs and tightens her ponytail. "And now I see why she didn't. Shit." She takes a few steps away from me, and when she turns around, her expression suggests she's just figured something out. Either Dekker Kincade is really good at playing the game to get me to ask her what she means, or she's being completely sincere right now.

"Would you care to enlighten me?" Sarcasm rings in my tone.

"If Lennox told you, it would look like a dirty tactic to win you over to KSM. A dirty tactic, which was exactly what Finn was accusing her of doing in front of numerous colleagues."

Holy. Shit.

Everything clicks. All of Lennox's comments. "He's the one who accused her of using sex to secure clients?" I ask, already knowing the answer, already able to see the scenario in my head.

A group of men, drinking, shooting the shit, and Finn leading them by the nose to believe exactly what he wanted them to believe. And of course, there's nothing Lennox can do to disprove them since their minds have already been made up.

Hell, I've been in similar situations like that before where guys are talking, everyone is nodding, and the next time you see the woman, your opinion is skewed. It's human fucking nature.

And Finn is a fucking wanker.

I roll my shoulders as the anger hits, and know Lennox was right not to tell me. She was right, because my knee jerk reaction would be to call the arsehole up, fire him on the spot, and then move to KSM.

Problem with that?

It would only serve to strengthen his slander.

She slept with me. Others have seen us kissing, thanks to my own necessity to do so, and of course, conclusions have been drawn about our status.

"Fucking hell," I mutter.

"See the problem?" She lifts her eyebrows.

Fuck. Yes.

"*You might get away with doing whatever you want, whenever you want even if it's trouble, but you still get paid. You still have a public pushing for you because of your incredible talent. Lenn, on the other hand? She'll look like a tart who fucks her way to the top.*"

She'll be considered a trollop, when she is anything but.

Fuck.

༝

Me: Any news with Liverpool?

Finn: I think I'll have two offers for you on the table by the end of next week.

Me: There's only one I want. Make sure that happens. This is the part where the client is always right, so you go after the contract he wants, not the one you want.

Finn: Relax.

Me: This is conditional on you still being my agent. Shitty circumstances or not, make it happen.

I hit send on the text and beg for him to make a comment about Lennox. Something. Anything. All I need is a stepping-off point for me to virtually plow my fist in his face.

Finn: Understood.

I stare at his response for the longest time, wondering how I'll be able to face Lennox and not tell her I know.

But hell, I promised Dekker I wouldn't say a word.

And my word I'll keep.

Chapter
FORTY-FOUR

Lennox

"Excuse me, but I do believe this is my bathroom."

I look at Rush who is standing in the doorway, his shoulder against the jamb, his eyes focused on me as I put my toothbrush in the holder.

"Yours, huh?"

He reaches out and tugs me against him. "Mine."

My breath catches at the look in his eyes and the feel of his hands on my waist. How is that possible? How can desire grow stronger, even though I've already had him before?

"Thank you for helping to surprise me," I murmur, leaning up on my tiptoes to press a kiss to his lips.

"Thank you for taking me to the ballgame," he says and returns the kiss, but this time slips his hand beneath my tank top so his hands are on my bare skin.

"Thank you for putting up with my nosy sisters, who probably asked you way too many questions and assumed way too many things."

Another kiss where my hands roam freely up the plane of his chest.

"Not a problem."

And this time the kiss leads to me jumping so my legs wrap around Rush's waist, before he carries me into my bedroom and lays me on the bed.

It wasn't intentional.

This wasn't supposed to happen.

But day by day and night by night, kiss by kiss and laugh by laugh, this thing between us, which was supposed to be fun and something to fill the time, became something more.

It warmed the parts of me that had grown cold and ignited the parts of me that others had heated but never lit. Not until Rush had I ever really burned, and oh how he made me burn.

I was in love with Rush McKenzie.

But there's no way in hell I could ever tell him.

He has his own crowd to go to, and his own place to be cheered on.

His own life to live.

His own everything to be.

I've always known I'd have to let him go so he could.

"Hey, you okay?" Rush asks as he pushes his way into me. The burn in my chest only serves to heighten the sweet ache of us becoming one.

"Yes," I murmur as I lean up and kiss him again.

"You're crying," he whispers as he kisses each track of my tears away.

"It's okay." I grab his biceps as his hips slowly move against mine.

"You sure?" His eyes find mine in the darkness.

"Yes." Another kiss. "I just need you tonight, Rush."

"You have me, Lennox." Another push in and slow withdraw out. "You have me completely."

Chapter
FORTY-FIVE

Lennox

"It really is gorgeous here."

I startle at the sound of my dad's voice and find him sitting on the chaise lounge, staring at the view of the city. "Dad. You scared the crap out of me. What are you doing here?" I move toward his spot in the shade and take a seat in the chair next to him.

"I know you're sick of us all being here—a couple days of us is a lot— and that we said our goodbyes last night before we headed back to the hotel, but I wanted a moment with you alone if that's okay. Johnny let me in."

"Of course. What's on your mind?"

"I wanted to give you something." He produces a black box with a white ribbon tied around it.

"What's this?"

"A little birthday present for you."

"Dad, you didn't have to," I say as I pull the ribbon off and then gasp when I open the box.

"It was your mother's. She used to wear it, and I thought it was fitting you should have it."

I take the necklace out of the box. It's a plain gold chain, nothing special, but it's the delicate charm dangling from it that makes me catch my breath.

It's a loose version of a compass. Feathered arrows cross over each other, each one depicting a direction. There is a band around the whole of it with the word wanderlust etched in the daintiest of scripts.

I rub my fingers over the pendant and feel more connected to her already. My eyes are full of tears when I look up to meet my dad's.

"Thank you. This is the best present, Dad. It's perfect."

"For you it is, yes." He sniffles away the emotion and then sighs loudly. "I nearly choked when Rush jumped in the pool the other day, and I saw a similar image on his chest in that mess of ink he has."

"You mean his tattoos?"

"Yes, I mean those." He rolls his eyes as only a father can do.

"It's for his mom. She had a medallion with a compass on it. He got the tattoo in her memory."

"Oh." It's a simple sound, but it says so much more coming from my dad. The look in his eyes reinforces it. He's shocked by the coincidence and happy, in a bittersweet way, that I'm seeing someone who understands the kind of loss that's hard to explain to someone who has never experienced it personally.

"Yes. I know. How odd that we both . . ." I blink back tears and then smile. "Nice segue by the way."

"I'm proud of it." He winks at me and then his expression stills.

"If you wanted to talk about him, all you had to do was say so."

"Okay." He nods and chews the inside of his cheek for a moment as he finds the right words. "You really like him, don't you?"

"He's what I need right now, yes. Does that mean he's going to be what I need in a few weeks? I don't know." I try to sell the lie with a soft smile, but I'm not completely sure my dad buys it.

"You're not sixteen, Lenn. You don't have to hide liking a guy because you're afraid you're going to get in trouble." He chuckles. "It's okay that you do. He seems like a nice man."

"I think you're letting me off the hook and not saying what you really want to say."

"And what's that?"

"That I told you I was going to recruit him, and I ended up dating him. It's not exactly putting the most professional foot forward."

"Sometimes life has different plans for you than the ones you made." He lifts his eyebrows and shrugs.

"Not a single one of you has said a word about the Esme situation."

There. It's finally out in the open. The reason I've walked on eggshells around my dad on this. "Why is that, Dad?"

"Because, honey, we trust you." He pats my knee.

"You what?"

"We trust you. It's as simple as that. If you say Rush is who he says he is, then I believe you and trust your judgment over a newspaper article."

"I don't even know what to say."

"There's nothing more to say. I've got a plane to catch," he says as he rises and then leans over and kisses the top of my head like he used to when I was a little girl. "Happy Birthday, Lenn. Everything will work out for the best."

Chapter
FORTY-SIX

Lennox

"WHY WAS I HOPING THAT THIS TIME WHEN YOU SAID GET IN THE CAR, that you were kidnapping me for another retreat to the beach?" I pant. I glance at Rush, who isn't fazed at all by our uphill ascent of Runyan Canyon.

"You're hanging with me just fine." He pats my ass. "Besides, exercise is good to clear the mind, and we need it after that ridiculous thing we had to go to last night."

I laugh. "Mitzy definitely had your number," I say in regards to a little old lady who would not leave Rush's side all night during the MLS benefit for league sponsors.

"I think she drenched herself in ten bottles of perfume." He mock shivers. "Our bet was interrupted the other night by your surprise. C'mon. First one to the top gets—"

"I'm winning this baby," I say as I jog a few steps in front of his long stride. No woman is going to give up the chance of getting a tonguegasm by Rush McKenzie.

The man may have skills on the pitch but when it comes to that tongue of his, it puts everything else he can do to complete shame.

"It's beautiful, isn't it?" Rush asks, as he takes a seat beside me on one of the benches at the top of the hike.

"Not as beautiful as the picture I have when I look down to see the top of your head between my thighs," I whisper into his ear.

"You're filthy, Kincade, and I fucking love it."

"Thank you very much." I glance his way and my smile fades when I see the way he's looking at me. "What's wrong?" I ask immediately.

"It was great meeting your family." He gives a reminiscent smile. "They're a great bunch."

"They'll drive you crazy after too long." I reach out and link my fingers with his.

"I had a small taste of that after the Mathesons took me in."

"The Mathesons?" I ask.

"After I made the academy team, a teammate. Rory Matheson?" he asks and I nod, the name nothing more than a blip in my head. He's definitely not a starter with LFC. "His parents took me in as a part of their family for holidays so I wouldn't be alone. But it was nothing like you guys." He squeezes my hand. "And before that, it was just me and my mum figuring out how to stretch every penny so we had both food and shelter, and preferably both at the same time."

"I'm sorry."

He chuckles. "That's not why I'm telling you this. Again, I don't want your pity, Nox, I . . . shit," he mutters and runs a hand through his hair and sighs.

"Rush?"

He turns to look at me with eyes so clear and focused, surrounded by a host of unfathomable emotion.

"I came from nothing. No dad. My mum was sick for so long, working wasn't an option, and so what little money we had saved, ran out. And when she died, no one asked what would happen to her only child. Distant family members assumed other distant family members had me and vice versa, while I lived in an abandoned shed I found behind a flat."

"Oh my God," I say but it falls on deaf ears, because Rush is on a mission to tell me something. I am here to listen.

"It was dry and I made it livable but it gave me what I needed, an address so that I could train at the academy without them asking questions. My only goal was to play football. At first when she was sick, the dreams were to get her out of where we were so she could be more comfortable, and then after she died, it was the only thing I had to keep me going. I begged, borrowed, and stole, Lennox. Not just kits left in the lost property so I looked like I fit in either. I stole food. I would swipe change left out. I was a fifteen-year-old petty thief who was stealing to put food in my stomach whenever I could."

"I don't even know what to say."

"There's nothing to say. Things got a little better when I received the scholarship to the academy. I had a place to live and regular meals. It was like winning the Lotto. Then the Mathesons became family in a sense, and gave me that taste of normality on the rare days I wasn't playing football."

"Why does no one know this about you?" I murmur.

"My life isn't a feel-good movie, Lennox. It's not something I'm proud of." His voice breaks with shame and it damn near kills me.

"You went from nothing to being arguably one of the best footballers in the world. It's more than a feel-good movie, it's downright inspiring." I throw my hands in the air. I have never met someone as self-made as Rush McKenzie. How did he survive? Thrive? Succeed? "Think of what that little boy at the first exhibition—"

"Scottie," he says, and my heart warms that he remembers his name.

"Think of the hope you'd give Scottie if he knew how you made it."

Rush shoves up off the bench and takes a few steps before coming back and sitting. There's obviously something more here.

"You told me that I didn't trust you. I struggle with trust, Lennox. With letting people get close. Especially after"—he flicks his hand in a show of indifference—"everything that happened recently. But after what you've shared with me this past weekend—your family and your life—I owe you this."

"You don't owe me anything," I say and reach out, needing to reassure him with my touch.

"Let me rephrase," he says, meeting my eyes. "I want to let you in."

My heart swells. I'm not sure whether I should be scared or elated, so I'll settle for somewhere in the middle, because each one of those emotions means different things.

Fear means I know I'm going to hurt him. Elation means I want more with him and from him. And I'm not ready to commit to either yet, because I'm emotionally scared to take the chance.

"Rush." My voice is so heavy with emotion. "I don't know what to say."

"Tell me I'm not making a mistake. Tell me that I'm talking to Lennox the woman and not Lennox the agent. Tell me that what I tell you will stay strictly between us. Tell me that I can trust you."

"You can trust me, Rush." I know the weight those words carry.

And . . . he does. He starts with the stolen cookies and banana, to a police officer who controls his son. He takes me through their history together, including his loyalty to a moment in time Archibald gave him that allowed him the life he now leads. He explains about Helen wrapping him in her motherly love even when she already had a son of her own who struggled often. A mother's love that he so desperately needed. A family to turn to, who supported him, and who helped him bury the past he was so ashamed of.

Then he gets to the pictures of Esme and Rory and my heart sinks.

Not for anything other than how a teenage boy still feels like he owes a debt to others, when he's the one who's made himself the man he is today, not them.

"So that's it. That's everything." His voice is shaky, and the way he stares at me, as if he's waiting for me to look at him differently, nearly undoes me. I itch to pull him against me and hold on tight, but know he'll feel pity instead of the overwhelming compassion I feel for him.

"Thank you for trusting me, Rush."

"No comments? No anything?" he asks.

"If you want me to tell you I think less of you, then you're crazy."

"No, I thought you'd tell me I was crazy because I took the fall for Rory."

"Is that what you're most worried about?"

He refuses to look at me. I squat between his knees so he's forced to look at me.

To anyone else hiking on this hill, we're just a couple having an intense conversation eye to eye, heart to heart.

To me, walls are breaking down. I'm burdened with so much information.

Rush reaches out and toys with the charm on my necklace, the compass that is so similar in meaning to the one he sports over his heart, and a ghost of a smile plays over his lips.

It's fleeting, but it's there.

"It's been a lot harder to keep my promise, but he's my oldest friend. His life is more important than my reputation. As to Archibald . . . fuck, Archibald's career and a successful election isn't something I care about or something that I should bear on my shoulders, but Rory? Rory is. And Helen. How could I let her down? After taking me in, how could I not protect Rory when he was the only one who befriended me? Even after they told me I was a part of *them*, I didn't trust it to be real for the longest time. But Rory never stopped trying. He could have. There were a lot of boys there that were wealthy too. Yet, he knew where I came from and never treated me differently. Archibald wasn't kind to Rory, either, and I often feared Rory would despise me because of his father's constant comparison between us." He takes a deep breath and pauses. "He could have hated me. Yet he doesn't."

My God, this man is amazing. And by the sounds of it, Rory deserves his loyalty.

But I'm not convinced he deserves Rush's enormous sacrifice. So, how do I explain that he doesn't need to repay someone for simply being a decent human being? However, I told Rush I'd listen. It's not my place to judge.

"I understand, but I don't think you're taking enough credit for what's on the line for you right now."

"His life is important. How could I let down the only family I have?" We both look to our left as a couple walk past and wave in greeting. After they pass, Rush speaks. "Esme's in town." He makes the comment like it's an afterthought. He stares at me, waiting to see my reaction. To see if I believe him. "She's in town for a benefit concert."

"Why are you telling me this?"

"Full transparency." He pulls his baseball hat down lower over his eyes as a group of guys come clambering up the hill behind us, one wearing a Manchester United shirt. "If she's here, and I'm here, there's bound to be some rumors. Maybe then you'll see how easy it is for the press to manipulate situations and people to believe whatever they publish."

"I already know about that," I say, trying to digest everything he's said, the fallout he's willing to endure because of it, and the incredulity of the man right before me. "You didn't have to tell me any of this."

"I know."

"Then why did you?" I all but whisper.

"Because there's something here, Nox. Something between us that, for the first time in my adult life, makes me not feel alone. I needed you to know that I trust you."

Placing my hand on the back of his neck, my forehead to his, I press my lips to his. I am in awe of this man. To know he feels there's something between us? Brings me hope, as I am not ready to say goodbye. But I can give him what he needs. *My faith in him.* "You can trust me, Rush. I promise."

Chapter
FORTY-SEVEN

Lennox

I STARE AT THE CEILING WITH RUSH'S SOFT SNORES BESIDE ME. HIS leg draped over mine, I struggle with a serious moral dilemma. Between Lennox the agent and Lennox the woman in love. Between what I know would be best for his career versus what I know would be best for us.

Tell me that I can trust you, Lennox.

My heart swells with a warmth I've never experienced.

Sure there's love for your family, but this . . . this feeling in my chest when it comes to Rush is something altogether different.

My mind reels.

Are there more pictures of the kiss around the world between Esme and Rory? I've stared at image after image of Rory tonight on my Google search and can see exactly how this happened. Hell, my bet is that the photographer knew the man wasn't Rush, but sold the picture that hides the tattoo on Rory's hand.

A pop princess and a Liverpool football star? That's serious money paid out to a paparazzo for a single photo.

I have to turn my agent brain off.

He's not my client.

He's my lover.

He's my love.

Chapter
FORTY-EIGHT

Rush

"I NEED YOU TO TELL ME ALL OF THIS BULLSHIT IS OVER."

"Hello, Finn. Nice to talk to you." I roll my shoulders at the sound of his voice. I've never felt much affinity for Finn Sanderson, but I have zero respect since Dekker's revelation. The prick.

If I'd heard what he'd said before I met Lennox, I might have believed it without question. I would have taken the rumors he gave and assumed they were true.

But I do know her. I've seen how hard she works, I've overheard her fighting for her clients on the phone, and I've watched her worry about their well-being. She's had every chance to ask me to trade agencies and hasn't.

Integrity. Classy. Passionate.

The woman is fucking everything, and the fact that Finn would smear her name only proves that he knows it too. That he's intimidated by her. Because if he was just as talented, he'd meet her on a level playing field rather than drag her through the mud.

My fists clench as I fight not to unload this on Finn and tell him what I really think of him. Currently, he's the one with my future in his hands and I need to heed that.

Besides, if I say something to him, doesn't it prove him right? That she's pulling me over to her side? And, I've slept with her. He'd crucify her.

"I'm serious, Rush. I have two ridiculously large offers for you right now. One comes with strings attached to your public behavior and the other one says the wilder the better."

"I'll take the strings, Finn," I say, already assuming which offer has what restrictions. "I appreciate all that Cannon has offered and can understand the why behind it. You, as my agent, also have to understand why the answer is no."

"It's a once-in-a-lifetime offer, Rush."

"And this is my lifetime." I shift on my feet. "Tell me about the Liverpool offer."

I hear his sigh and can imagine his eye roll too. He truly believes the MLS deal is what I want. Prick. "My ass and credibility are on the line right now. I've given a thousand reasons why they can't win the Premiership without you and why if they traded you, the fans would riot. I've promised up one side and down another that you will be a goddamn choir boy—in the clubhouse, on the field, in your personal life."

"My personal life?"

"Yeah. That means don't fuck any more of your teammate's wives."

My chuckle doesn't hold an ounce of amusement. It's been months, and my own agent still doesn't fucking believe me. Lennox believed me even before I told her the truth.

She's right. There must be trust between an agent and his client and right now, there is none.

It died the minute he looked me in the eye and believed I wasn't a man of integrity. And I'm only realizing that now.

"As I've told you, I never fucked my teammate's wife. But I'll promise. That's an easy one to make. And on the flip side, you figure out how to control the press and their rumors and everyone will be happy."

"I'm fucking serious, Rush."

"So am I," I growl. "You made the promises. I'll make the same to you and to the club. What's the deal?"

"They can't trade Seth and they won't trade you."

"Great. Fine. No skin off my back. Tell the fucker to keep his hands to himself and everything will be just fine."

"But I need less hostility from you too. They demanded it. I promised it. Are we clear?"

"Yes." Anticipation vibrates through me. "What're the terms?"

"I sent you an email spelling everything out. They're looking at you for the long-haul, Rush. They want you to be the face of the club. That's why from here on out, no more bullshit. No more—"

"I already told you," I say, the scare tactic not needed. I already almost lost the one thing I love. There's no way I would ever risk it again. "I understand."

"Don't I at least get a pat on the back?" Finn asks, and I can't tell if he's joking or serious.

"No."

"Jesus, cut me a break, Rush."

"I'll pat you on the back when the ink is dried on the contract."

"Speaking of which, they want to do a big to-do when you sign it."

"It's the digital age, can't we do one of those electronic signatures?" I ask, not wanting to take any chances.

"We're still buttoning up the final details. I'll get it to you as soon as I have it . . . but in the meantime, sit tight for details." Someone says something to him in the background. "I've got to run. Talk soon."

Finn ends the call and when I look at my email, at the staggering numbers on the page and the seven-year contract connected to it, I sag against the wall at my back in relief.

Tears fill my eyes.

I feel stupid, but it's not until right now, this moment, that I realize how fucking scared I was that I was going to be transferred.

That I'd be kicked out of the one and only true place I've ever called home.

I take a minute to soak in the moment. To appreciate that I didn't fuck up my life in the process of saving Rory's.

That this nightmare is finally over.

And then I set off through the house like a madman.

"Nox! Lennox?" God, I need her. "Lennox."

"Rush? What?" She runs into the kitchen and I grab her before she can ask anything else. I press my lips to hers.

Her laughter breaks us apart. "You can't give me a heart attack just to kiss me," she says and then pulls on my shirt to take one more.

"They want me back. Liverpool wants me back. Offer made. Contract in the works."

She freezes momentarily as her eyes find mine, and then a megawatt grin overtakes her face. "Congratulations." She slides her hands around my neck and presses her lips to mine again. "I'm so happy for you," she murmurs.

"Oh, Jesus," Johnny says as he rounds the corner and puts his hands up in an X over his eyes. "I have guests in tow. Can we not put on a live sex show for them? I mean, I'm known as the party boy, but this is a little much."

"No shows will be happening," I say as I pull Lennox against me, my hands digging into her back pockets. "But there will definitely be partying."

Johnny's eyes narrow. "For what?"

"Because I'm going back home soon."

Johnny whoops out and says "Liverpool?"

"Liverpool."

"Fucking A straight, baby," he hollers at the top of his lungs. "Time for alcohol!" And whoever is behind him cheers loudly.

But I'm not so wrapped up in the moment that I don't feel Lennox's jolt.

How could I be when I feel the same way too? How can I be when the woman in my arms feels a lot like home to me now too?

Chapter
FORTY-NINE

Lennox

"Is there a reason you're out here all on your lonesome?" Johnny asks, taking a seat beside me and wrapping his arm around my shoulder.

"No reason," I say and rest my head on his shoulder, welcoming his presence. "Just making decisions."

Rush's laughter floats just above the music playing on the overhead speakers. Inside is a party of sorts, with the friends Johnny brought home and some of the guys from the MLS exhibition team that Rush has been playing with.

I believe there's a drinking game happening over foosball but I don't know for sure.

"Would those decisions have anything to do with the man currently three sheets to the wind inside?"

"Perhaps."

I close my eyes for a beat as the breeze tickles my hair on my cheek, and I allow myself to feel sad.

"Want to talk about it?"

"Not really."

"Yes, you do." He knocks his knee against mine. "Talk to me."

"I'm allowing myself to be sad for tonight only. Pity party of one. And then by the time he wakes up with one helluva hangover tomorrow, it'll be gone."

"Just like that?"

"What he'll see, yes. I'm the queen at hiding emotion, Johnny. You know that." I fall silent, trying to figure out how to articulate what I've concluded since Rush ran into the kitchen with a grin that lit up the room to tell me he was leaving.

It's not like I didn't already know it was going to happen, but it definitely knocked me off balance momentarily.

"So what's your plan then?" Johnny asks.

"My plan is to simply have fun. To have fun and enjoy my time with him. A no-regrets thing."

"Ah, so your goal is to pretend that you're not in love with him by pushing him back to the *we're just going to have fun, wild sex at an arm's length*, right? Do you actually think that's going to protect your heart?"

"No." *Nothing will protect my heart.* "But it's what I need to do for him. This is his time to shine and nothing should hold him back from doing so. I don't need him feeling guilty. I mean, we knew there was a finite time to this. To us."

"It is the digital age, Lenn. You could make the distance work."

"Much easier said than done." I chuckle. "If we had been together for a year, yeah, I could imagine trying to make it work, but this is a drop in the bucket to—"

"Drop in the bucket or not," he says, "that doesn't mean your feelings aren't legitimate."

"Look, I appreciate you trying, but the best thing to do is shove my emotions away, put on a brave face, and—"

"And then I'll hold you when you bawl your eyes out after he leaves."

"Exactly," I say and press a kiss to his cheek. "Thank you for that."

"The MLS gig is up when?"

"Three days."

"At least you'll have some time together after that, and before he leaves, to chill together. I have trips I can take and people I can see to give you guys some space."

"You've done more than enough. The last thing we're going to do is kick you out of your own house."

"There you two are," Rush says, his voice a little slurred as he walks over. "You trying to steal my girl, Johnny-John?"

"Never," Johnny says as we both rise from the chaise. "You done winning all their money at pool?"

"Maybe," Rush says with a sheepish grin as Johnny walks past with a pat on his head and moves inside. "Hey."

"Hey."

Rush reaches out and pulls me against him. I fight the tears that threaten, and I fight the urge to dig my fingers into his back and pull him against me and never let him go.

The music overhead shifts to something softer and Rush presses a kiss to the top of my head. "Dance with me," he murmurs.

"What?" I laugh, but don't let go.

"There's too much beauty where I'm standing right now not to take advantage of it. The night. The moon. You." He lifts my chin so I'm forced to look in his eyes. "Dance with me, Nox."

My heart sighs the softest of sighs as our feet begin to move.

Body to body.

Heart to heart.

Another memory to cling to.

And when I rest my head against his chest, I allow a lone tear to slide down my cheek and go undetected.

Just one.

Because Johnny was right. Tomorrow, I'll begin to keep Rush at arm's length.

~

"Lennox," Rush calls in his slurred voice from where he's sprawled on the couch—legs spread, arms over the back of it, sunglasses on even though it's nighttime. "Leave all of it and come and give me some loving."

"Let me just pick up some of these glasses and bottles," I say as I survey the damage. It was a heavy night of drinking, but not heavy enough for everyone but Rush to want to go out and continue the party elsewhere. "It's the last thing I'm going to want to do in the morning."

"Leave it." Rush's feet clomp across the floor. "Johnny has maids. Hell, I have maids. Do you have maids?" he asks as he grabs me by the waist and playfully pulls me against him. "If you don't, you deserve one. I'll make sure you have one."

"Thanks." I laugh as his hands roam up and over my breasts while I try to keep walking. "But my place is small and I'm rarely there."

"Lennox," he says repeating my name in a chant as I pick up the ice bucket and a few glasses beside it. "You're ignoring me." He pouts like a child as he steps in front of me to block my path.

"Let me pick up, drunk boy."

"You Americans and your ice," he says, plucking an ice cube out of the bucket in my hands before trying to toss it down my top. "You're in love with your ice more than you're in love with me."

And while I hear the words, I take them for what they are: he's drunk and the word love is meant just how he says it. But a tiny part of me dies at the sound of it. The part of me who'd love to hear it for real.

"You all kept saying I'd fall in love with ice, but other than hurting my teeth, I think you're crazy."

A small smile plays over my lips as an idea comes to mind. "I bet I can make you love it right now."

"You're mad."

But when I drop to my knees in front of him, I definitely have his attention.

"Nox?"

"Mmm?" I undo his shorts and pull them down over his hips so his hardening cock springs free.

"What are you doing?" His smile is playful as he reaches down and grabs the base of his shaft.

"Sucking your cock to shut you up."

"In that case, I'll start talking."

But when I place my lips around his cock and apply the warm, wet heat of my mouth and tongue, his words fail him until only a strangled cry fills the room.

"Nox. Yes." His hand finds its way to the back of my head and tightens around my ponytail as I take him as deep as I can before sucking as hard as I can on the way back out.

Moaning as the taste of him hits my tongue, I lick the slit at his crest before starting the whole process all over again.

I work him slowly to the point where his breathing is shallow, his hand is helping guide my head, and he leans against the wall at his back for support.

With one hand sliding over his length, I use my other to dip into the ice bucket and bring a cube of ice to my lips.

Rush's eyes meet mine. A hiss fills the room when I slide him back into my mouth with the ice cube on my tongue.

Fire and ice.

Pleasure and pain.

He opens his mouth to say something, but loses his words to the onslaught of sensations. His head falls back and his hand tenses against my scalp.

He's gorgeous from my position between his thighs. He's sex and desire and temptation and . . . love.

And just when the realization hits me and the tears well—as I understand how devastated I'm going to be when he leaves—he urges me to move faster, to suck harder. Then his whole body tenses, and he empties himself in the back of my throat.

I watch his chest heave and his muscles ease one by one until he looks down at me, seeing his cock still in my hand and a smile on my somewhat swollen lips.

"What are your feelings about ice now?" I ask coyly.

His laugh rings out so that his dick bobs up and down before he helps me to my feet and kisses me soundly on the lips. "Why, Miss Kincade, I do believe I've had a change of heart on the subject."

Chapter
FIFTY

Lennox

"So that's it? You take the contract, you take my money, and you don't deliver on any promises?"

When I look up, I expect to find Cannon standing there with a smile on his lips, but he's dead serious, and it startles me.

"Excuse me?" I partly laugh the words out. "I told you quite candidly that I understood your desire to get Rush, but I didn't think it would work. You told me to try anyway. I tried, Cannon. I truly did, but his heart is elsewhere." *And I can't blame him.* "I'm sorry for that, but I do think we made some positive headway in player advocacy for the league. The plans we created will have some great benefits—"

"So you're not as good as they said you were." There's anger to his voice I never would have expected.

"I'm sorry. I'm not following—"

"I hired you because of the rumors. Finn told me you slept with players and played bullshit games to steal them. What he hates you for, I was depending on. And I guess you weren't that great, because even after Rush had you, he's still not staying."

I stand there, jaw lax, anger firing in every fiber of my body. "You hired me to what?" My voice is barely a whisper.

"Sleep with him. Use that magical whatever you have to keep him here. Make him fall hard enough that he'd take the bait. Hell, I couldn't care less if you broke up with him the minute he signed . . . but isn't that the least you could have done?"

Oh. My. God.

Use that magical whatever you have to keep him here. Make him fall hard enough that he'd take the bait.

What the actual fuck?

Are there any men in sports management that actually have souls that aren't godawful or reprehensible? He was actually fucking banking on Finn's words coming true. He was a tiger lying in wait. Despicable.

My dad was right. My sisters were right. Cannon is a contemptible bastard.

"You son of a bitch."

He shrugs and smiles. "Don't blame a man for playing the game."

"And don't blame a woman for knowing an asshole when she sees one."

I grab my things as quickly but calmly as I can, because I don't want him to think he's gotten to me, and then I walk out of the office without looking back.

It's only when I'm in my car in the parking lot with my windows rolled up that I yell at the top of my lungs to let my anger out. He fucking tried to use me. Does he have any respect for me, or was he always just spewing bullshit?

God, I'm glad Rush is going back to the UK and not involved in the MLS in any way. And I'll be warning him against doing anything with the MLS in the future while Cannon Garner is there. The bastard.

Just thinks of me as a fucking whore that he can—

And then I realize something.

Unknowingly, I just proved them all wrong.

I slept with Rush but didn't achieve anything professionally. I burst out laughing.

And then I realize something else. I'm perfectly okay with being the one to have the last laugh about it.

Asshat Garner just paid me a shitload of money for nothing.

Oh my God, my sisters are going to love this.

Chapter
FIFTY-ONE

Lennox

"WHAT SHOULD WE DO TODAY?" I ask as I lie with my head tucked between Rush's arm and chest staring at where both of our hands are pressed against each other's.

"I don't care," he murmurs as the early morning light filters through the breaks in the blinds. "*This*. Let's do *this* all day."

"What?" I ask, my smile spreading, because this is exactly what I want to do all day—be with him. "There are plenty of things we could do. Like get lost in an art museum."

"Fuck no." He rolls over so he's partially on top of me. "I'd rather get lost in you." He grins and then kisses me tenderly on the lips as if we have all the time in the world.

But we don't.

We're down to days. Ten to be exact. And when I reach out and brush his hair off his forehead, his expression softens, and he rests his forehead against mine.

"Are we ever going to talk about this, Nox?" His lips brush against mine as he speaks, but he does lean back to meet my eyes. "Every time I try to talk to you, you turn it into a joke or kiss me till I'm quiet."

"What's there to talk about?" I whisper. "You have an incredible life to get back to, a crowd to perform for, and I have mine to get back to as well. We knew what we were getting into when we started this, and it's too late to change gears now." I say the words with as much resolve as I can. My heart fractures a bit more in my chest.

"We could meet up on breaks. Take holidays. I don't know, but—"

"And soon it would turn into phone calls where we make them simply so we don't hurt the other's feelings, and trips would be talked about but never planned." I frame his face and push it off my forehead so he can meet my eyes. "I have no regrets, Rush. Maybe this was what we needed, when we needed it, to help us for the next stage in our lives. Maybe this was what we needed to heal and move forward."

"But what if—"

I pull him into me and use my lips to smother his words. To quiet the empty promises and create a temporary salve to the ache in my chest.

His hand runs up the side of my body, pushing my tank top with it.

And then, both of our phones start ringing. And as soon as one stops, the other starts again.

At first we laugh, but then with each sound, we realize something must be going on.

Rush is the first one to reach for his phone.

Chapter
FIFTY-TWO

Rush

THE NAME ON THE SCREEN OF MY PHONE STOPS MY HEART.

"Rory! Are you okay? What's wrong?" And just as I'm yelling, I see Lennox pick up her phone and move to the other side of the room with her finger to her ear.

"Have you seen the news? Social media? Has Finn called you?"

"No. What are you—"

And right then, Lennox holds her phone out in front of me.

Oh God. Esme. There's a picture of Esme with one eye black and blue and all but swollen shut. She's not trying to hide it from the camera either.

The image is shocking to say the least, but it's the caption above it that stops my heart: *Rush McKenzie Gets Physical.*

"No. No. No." I shake my head as the words repeat over and over on my lips.

"Rush? Are you there? Rush?"

"I'm reading." It's all I say. All I can say as I take Lennox's phone and begin to read.

In the latest tale of the torrid affair between pop sensation Esme and football star Rush McKenzie that has rocked the Liverpool organization, comes a new and disturbing revelation. He likes to get physical in more places than just on the field.

The Daily Mail caught up with Esme's husband, Liverpool captain, Seth Haskins, for a statement. "When my wife was in Los Angeles for a benefit concert, she informed McKenzie that they were over. Told him to stop contacting her. His attempts to be with her are becoming quite desperate and constant. He became enraged when she told him that we've decided to work through our differences, and . . . well, you can see what he did to her as a consequence."

The Daily Mail cannot confirm nor deny Haskins's accusations, but pictures emerged of McKenzie and Esme having a private moment together on a balcony in June. A moment that has since sent the Liverpool organization scrambling on how to keep their two stars on the same field without another rumored clubhouse brawl from happening again.

"After what he's done to my wife, I refuse to touch the field with him, and I've made sure the club knows this," Haskins said.

According to inside sources, Liverpool is set to make a comment on this new development by tomorrow morning. Seeing as they have a strict no tolerance of domestic violence, one could assume some changes might be in the mix.

I stare at the article and read it again. When I look at Lennox, she's on her computer typing furiously. Rory's repeating my name over and over, which finally registers.

"I have to call you back."

"No. Wait."

"Rory," I snap.

"Let me—"

"Don't you think you've done fucking enough?" I shout at him. "I have to call you back."

And when I drop the phone and close my eyes, I feel like my world is falling out from underneath me.

I haven't signed the contract yet.

My mobile rings beside me on the bed.

I. Haven't. Signed. The. Contract.

And it rings again.

The world I thought that Lennox had helped me right, just turned upside down again. From elation to despair.

And more ringing.

I know the club's stance on domestic violence. I've seen teammates' contracts voided after convictions.

All I can hear is the thunder of my pulse in my ears. All I can feel is my heart racing in my chest. The room sways around me.

"It's Finn. You need to answer." Lennox shoves my phone back in my hand and pries hers from mine. "Look at me," she says and puts her hands on either side of my face. "We're going to figure this out and get the truth out there. You are not going to lose this contract."

I nod, but when I open my mouth nothing comes out.

"Answer the phone, Rush."

With a stab of my finger, I answer. "Finn."

"What the fuck, man?" Now, I'm just pissed off.

"What the hell do you mean, what the fuck? It's a snow job, Finn. Haskins is pissed that Liverpool is keeping me and is trying to sabotage my contract so—"

"She has a fucking black eye, McKenzie. She was in LA, Rush. How do you circle this square of public perception?" he shouts at the top of his lungs, frustration tinging every single syllable.

"She was here three weeks ago. I didn't see her when she was and if I did, the paparazzi would have been showing photos of that. Besides, do you really think if I'd laid my hands on her three weeks ago the bruises would be that fucking fresh?" I shove up off the bed and pace down the hallway, the anger and disbelief eating me up. "And fuck you for even giving credit to Haskins and this article."

"Well someone had to have done it."

"It was Seth!" I yell.

"And how would you know that?"

"Because I do. Because other players have seen him strike her before. Because . . ." Even if I said because Rory saw it, it would hold no damn weight anyway. "Just fucking trust me."

"Trust you? You need to fucking calm down."

"No. As my fucking agent, you need to believe me. I didn't have an affair with Esme. And I didn't fucking hit her."

"Rush—"

"Fuck this. Get me every interview you can. I'm going to bury the motherfucker."

"No. What you're not doing is going straight to the press. I need you to sit tight while I formulate a plan and figure out what the club is considering. Are you listening, Rush? Don't do a single thing."

"Yeah. I hear you." But when I end the call, I'm not as convinced that sitting tight this time is what needs to be done. Sure, I listened the first time and while everything worked out in the end, my name was never cleared. And now this. This is more than my reputation and career. This calls on who I am as a man.

On my bloody character.

I'm not a coward who hits women.

Anger and disbelief like I've never known before owns and paralyzes every part of me.

I stand on the landing of the third story of Johnny's house and simply stare out the window, hands braced against the railing, and head all over the fucking place.

"Rush." Lennox's voice breaks through to me. I turn to find her walking toward me with a mobile to one ear and her laptop in her other hand. She's still in the shorts set she sleeps in and her hair is a wild mess atop her head, but she's all business.

"I have a flight booked for you to Heathrow. You need to start packing, because it leaves in less than four hours and with LA traffic, it'll be tight. I have people on the ground in London working on what's going on with the Esme deal. Angles we can work to spin this and—"

"Finn told me I needed to sit tight."

"Fuck Finn and his sit tight," she says, pulling me by the arm back toward our wing of the house. "You need to be home right now so people can see you. The longer you're out of sight, the easier it is for them to believe this bullshit. You need to hold a press conference the minute your feet are on the ground there."

"To say what? How do I suddenly acknowledge this when I didn't acknowledge the photo before? How do I—"

"Rory."

I stop and stare at her as she starts opening the closets in my room and pulling suitcases out. "I—"

"Yes, Rush. You have to."

And I know she's right. I know more than anything right now, that he's the only one who can set this straight.

"Lennox." Her name is a resigned sigh and plea combined all into one.

"I promised them," I whisper. How do I betray my friend to save myself? How do I . . .

Lennox walks over and looks me in the eye with a clarity and determination I've never seen before. "You told me once that no one has ever fought for you. Let me fight for you, Rush. Let me believe in you and fight with you."

Her words hit me deep down, somewhere in a place I thought had long ago died. I struggle to find words.

"A starving fifteen-year-old kid doesn't owe anybody, Rush. Especially not at the expense of his integrity nor his career."

"But I am where I am because of that day."

"You're where you are because of you, Rush McKenzie. Your determination. Your grit. Your talent. Your goodness. You are where you are and who you are because of you and no one else." Tears well in her eyes as her voice escalates in urgency. "I beg you. *Let. Me. Fight. For. You.* You are worth fighting for."

She stares at me in a way that owns every part of me and in a way I never expected to feel for someone.

My sigh is as heavy as my heart. I want to tell her thank you. I want to tell her that she's the best thing that's ever come into my life bar football. I want to tell her that I love how she's fighting for me. *With me.* But my throat is hoarse. My soul is crushed. "Do what you have to do."

Chapter
FIFTY-THREE

Lennox

"Do what you have to do."

I spring into action at Rush's words. "You need to pack. I'll deal with the rest."

And then it hits me. Where's the time stamp on the photo taken of Esme? If she was here three weeks ago, the bruises would have faded if Rush hit her. So if the picture was taken this week, there's no way it could be Rush.

Later, Lenn. Get him on that plane and then dig in and find ways to refute this.

The next fifteen minutes are a whirlwind of him packing and me trying to figure out just what else I can do to fix this. I'm well aware that I should patch Finn in on this, that my hatred for him could be set aside for the good of Rush, but fuck Finn. Fuck him and his lack of confidence in Rush. He was talking loud enough on the other end of the call for me to hear.

This is not a wait-and-see operation.

This is a *grab the bull by the horns and throw something red in front of him* moment.

And right now, I'm so livid I'll lead that charge. Hell, I'm furious with Finn, angry at Rory, and infuriated by Esme's silence. Isn't she just as complicit in this as Rory is?

I get why she hasn't spoken up before this, but now? Now she's going to let Rush take the heat for this?

She could have said something when she was away from Haskins in

LA. She could have had a restraining order placed on her husband—who beats her—while she was safely hidden in a country, five thousand miles from home. But no, she stayed silent, allowing an innocent man to be thrown into the fire. An affair is one thing, but abuse? That attack on his character? On his very soul?

That's deplorable.

Fury, rage, and anger course through me—and that's an understatement.

"I'm going to need . . ." My words fade when I walk into Rush's room with instructions and find him sitting on the edge of his bed looking utterly fucking wiped out. "Hey? You okay?"

High on my own adrenaline to fix and solve, I cross the room to him. When I'm within arm's reach he just pulls me toward him, my thighs straddling his, and then he wraps his arms around me and holds on.

At first, I'm at a loss of what to do. Rush is always such a strong, vibrant presence so to see him so . . . vulnerable, it knocks me back.

I thread my fingers through his hair until he tilts his head up so his eyes can look at mine. There's a whole host of emotions swimming in his and every undecipherable one makes my heart race.

"I need you, Nox. Right now. I just need you."

I lower myself to sit on his thighs as my lips find his in a slow, bittersweet kiss. "You have me," I whisper. *Completely.*

We move in silence. My action, his reaction. My exhale, his next inhale. Two strangers who've found each other. Two broken halves who've somehow made a whole.

My shirt over my head and his hands on my breasts. Our clothes shoved to the floor before he lays me down. Our lips meet again and again almost as if they're making up for what will be no more.

Because this is our goodbye.

It doesn't have to be spoken aloud. It's in the soft sigh we both emit when he slips into me. It's in the gentleness of his lips as he kisses the tear tracks from my cheeks. It's in the lacing of our fingers together as if we never want to let go. It's how our bodies fit together in an action as old as time but is intimately special for us.

We make love bathed in the morning sunlight, eyes locked on one another's, with no sense of urgency, even though it feels like the world is burning down around us.

But there's nowhere else I'd rather be right now. There's no one else I'd want to be breaking my heart.

Our bodies move together as our foreheads touch, and our emotions swell to a point where it almost becomes painful to breathe.

I welcome the sudden rise of pleasure in my orgasm only for its ability to drown out the heartache for a moment.

Only for its ability to give me one more memory with Rush. One more sensation to recall. One more moment to cherish.

I look up at him with the sun like a halo around his head. His eyes reflect everything I feel, and I have to hold on to the idea that this is enough for me. *It has to be.* And in owning that notion for all it's worth, I lean forward and press a kiss to the compass tattoo on Rush's chest.

To those who wander.

No matter where I went in life, it would always let me find my way back to what was right. It was her compass so I'd never lose my way.

My only hope is that someday he'll find his way back to me. To what is right.

Because I love him with all my heart.

Chapter

FIFTY-FOUR

Rush

DESIRE IS SOMETHING I KNOW AND UNDERSTAND FIRSTHAND. THE desire to play, to win, to live . . . to have a woman. Simple, basic, masculine wants.

But as I sit on the tarmac waiting to take off, with my hat pulled low over my forehead and my eyes closed, I know there's something about Lennox Kincade that makes me question if I've ever really understood what desire was before.

I don't think I had a clue.

Before she came into the picture, I used the sensations desire induced to help numb me from my past.

But maybe that's where I was wrong.

Perhaps I've always been numb.

And maybe, just maybe, it was Lennox I needed to make me feel again.

To make me live again.

To realize what I thought was living all along was really just existing.

The plane pushes away from the gate and as much as I miss home, as much as I need to get there right now and set shit straight, a part of me will still be here.

Will always be with her.

I need you, Nox.

You have me.

The woman who showed moment after moment that she believed in me.

Had faith in me.

You're where you are because of you, Rush McKenzie. I beg you. Let. Me. Fight. For. You. You are worth fighting for.

Has faith in me. She's the most magnificent woman I'll ever know.

The only woman I've ever let myself love.

Chapter
FIFTY-FIVE

Lennox

"I HAVE A MILLION THINGS I NEED TO DO, JOHNNY," I SAY AS HE STANDS in the living room and stares at me.

"Like?"

"Like find Rory and talk him into confessing to this so Rush can be free and clear of this—"

"Rory?"

"It's a long story. I'll explain later." I stare at my phone and the ten unanswered calls to Rory on my call log.

"What else?"

"I have to find a flight home."

"Home? Already?" He laughs. "Talk about making me feel like chopped liver. The hired sex leaves and you bail on me."

I eye him above the papers I have scattered all over the table. "That's not—"

"You can admit it, you know," he says as he takes a few steps toward me.

"Admit what?"

"That it was Rush who was holding you here. The MLS thing was over and it was time for you to go home, but there was Rush."

Tears burn and I force a swallow down my throat. "Don't do this. I can't do this right now."

"What? Break down and have a good cry? Why the hell not?" He takes a seat beside me and stares at me. "The sooner you do it, the better you'll feel."

"I can't. I have all this work to do. I have—"

"Distractions. All of those things are distractions. Everyone in the UK is asleep right now. No one is going to be responding." He turns me in my chair to face him and when I do, the tears are already there, the sob in my throat not far behind it.

And when Johnny pulls me against him in one of his reassuring hugs, I let myself cry for the first and only time over a man.

I let myself feel.

We were supposed to have two weeks of us. Lazy days where we made love in slow motion. Endless promises to talk or text.

Time.

Just time.

But maybe it is better this way. Maybe the best way is to rip the Band-Aid off instead of the slow pull that devours you with each and every hair it rips out on the way.

Maybe this is all for the better.

If that's the case, then someone needs to tell my heart that too.

Chapter
FIFTY-SIX

Rush

Lennox: If she were in LA three weeks ago, the bruises would be gone by now. I'm trying to get a date stamp for that photo to prove it was taken recently. When she was in the UK and you were here.

Me: It's worth a shot.

Lennox: I can't get hold of Rory. Has he texted you?

Me: No. He's not answering me. I'll try him again.

Lennox: Thanks. Are you okay?

Me: Yes. No. I don't fucking know.

Lennox: Understandable. We'll get this straightened out. Text me once you get home.

Me: Will do.

I look at Lennox's text from a few hours ago and then I scroll past what feels like a hundred other ones—teammates, Finn, journalists who've gotten my mobile number over time—and cringe when I come to the ten I sent Rory to find them unanswered.

At first, I hoped it was shitty phone service on the plane. But considering I just received yet another text from an unknown phone number, I know my service is working.

I know Rory received my texts.

Worry rifles through me over his emotional stability.

Will this push him over the edge? That the woman he loves was beaten— again—*and the fucker who did it is placing the blame on me?*

She's not safe. *His heart must be breaking.*

But there's nothing I can do about it now.

I'm stuck on a plane.

So I just sit and wait.

Chapter
FIFTY-SEVEN

Lennox

MY PHONE STARTLES THE HELL OUT OF ME. WHEN I LOOK AT ITS screen, as I fumble with bringing it to my ear, it says that it's two o'clock in the morning.

"Chase? What in the hell are you doing up right now?"

"Turn on the television. Or computer. I mean computer. Go to ESPN or Sky News online . . . just go."

I jump out of bed. "What am I looking for?"

"A press conference. Rory Matheson. *Holy shit.*"

My fingers miss-hit keys as I search as fast as I can to find a live stream. And when I do, I gasp. Standing in front of a sea of cameras is Rory Matheson, the always-on-the-bubble Liverpool defenseman. He's dressed in what I think is his attempt to look as similar to Rush as possible.

And he does.

I notice it in the first few moments, but it's his words that hold every second of my attention.

"Thank you for coming here today. I'm sure you're wondering what a mediocre player like me is doing holding a press conference about the current situation at Liverpool FC regarding the allegations made about Rush McKenzie by Seth Haskins. I'm here to tell the truth."

There is a shuffling among the reporters as flashes go off, and I'm sure some of them are looking at each other like *what the hell is going on?*

Me, on the other hand? I'm sitting in my bed with my laptop, waiting with bated breath.

"Do you know what this is?" Chase asks in my ear.

"I have an idea." Let's just hope it's what I think it is.

"I once heard someone say that the measure of a man isn't what he'll do for himself, but what he'll do at the expense of himself for others. If that's the case, Rush McKenzie is truly a remarkable man. The kind of man who would let the entire world think it was him caught in an uncompromising position with a married woman instead of destroying a man struggling with depression. That man . . . meaning myself."

There is an audible gasp from the crowd as well as the people standing to the left and right of Rory, who look stunned. I guess he didn't tell anyone what he was going to say.

"Well, shit," Chase murmurs in my ear.

"I'm the one in that photo with Esme that was printed in June. If the photographer would have moved to the left, you would have seen my tattoo," he says, lifting up his hand to show the ink I can't make out, "and this wouldn't even be an issue. But Rush"—he shakes his head—"allowed you to believe it was him. Because at that time I wasn't in a good place. I was depressed and had thoughts of ending my life. I'm a recovering addict . . . so he took the blame. He took the punches. He took the wrath so wrongly aimed at him by you. He left the country to allow the story to die down. He let everyone believe that image was of him and not me, because he knew that you would eat me up and spit me out without a second thought to the damage you'd done to me. He knew I'd break under your pressure. He was worried about my well-being more than his career. And not once did he defend himself. Not once did anyone ask him if the picture was actually him."

Rory shakes his head again and takes a sip from his water bottle before continuing to a rapt audience.

"Oh my God," Chase whispers.

"I know," I whisper back. This is incredible.

"When the picture leaked of Esme and me, I was weak and let him take the blame, but not anymore. I can't in good conscience allow what he was accused of yesterday to stand without speaking up." He clears his throat. "Rush didn't lay a hand on Esme. In fact, I don't think he's even met her. Seth Haskins, her husband, my teammate, and the person who made the accusation in the *Daily Mail* yesterday, is the person responsible for Esme's injuries. How do I know this? Because over the past nine months, I've had to sit by and watch random bruises mar her skin. Seth has a bad game, a new bruise appears. She tells him she wants a divorce like she did four days ago, her eye is bruised so bad it's swollen shut."

"That's a heavy accusation you're making, Rory."

Rory nods and meets the eyes of the reporter. "It is and I'm aware of that, but I have proof." More gasps ring out, mine included. "Esme has provided footage from their in-home security camera of her assault to the police so she can press charges. Charges I've begged her to file for months, but fear and shame and public judgment have prevented her from acting. But not now. Not anymore." More gasps. "A small clip of the "alleged" altercation will be provided to all networks as proof of what I'm saying here today." He glances to the side of the stage and the reporters start murmuring as the camera pans to where Esme stands, sunglasses on, tears streaming down her cheeks.

"Jesus, she's actually there," Chase murmurs, exactly what I'm thinking.

"I'm not standing up here to play the part of the saint. I was in the wrong. I had the affair with Esme. I was in the wrong allowing Rush to be held liable, and I'll willingly take the consequences for my actions. But I will not, *cannot*, stand by and let you"—Rory points to the journalists—"crucify Rush McKenzie for something he didn't do. Something he would never do." He looks to the left to a sports agent I know in appearance before looking back to the press gallery. "I'll make no further statements on the matter. Thank you for your time."

The press erupts in a flurry of questions as I sit watching, open mouth and eyes wide, with Chase talking in my ear.

Rush is finally free.

Chapter
FIFTY-EIGHT

Rush

I'M STANDING IN HEATHROW BAGGAGE CLAIM, HAT PULLED LOW OVER my eyes, staring at Rory on the telly placed high in the corner, completely gobsmacked.

A million things run through my head.

What in the hell is he doing?

Will he be okay after doing this?

What is everyone going to think of me now?

The baggage claim carousel moves in loops at my back and my phone buzzes alerts over and over in my pocket, but I can't tear my eyes away from the screen. From the blurred image the broadcasters keep showing of Esme trying to open a front door with Seth yanking on her from behind, fist cocked back and ready to fly. Even with the blurring of detail—for a modicum of respect perhaps?—you can still see how Haskins could easily overpower his own wife. I cannot fucking believe it. What he's been doing to her. I'm seething in anger now, not only for what that animal is capable of, but knowing that he was willing to have people believe I did that.

And then another thought crosses my mind.

It's over.

It's finally fucking over.

I'm successful in keeping a low profile so I get out of the damn airport without being noticed. The minute I'm in the car park, I suck in a huge gasp of air as if it's the first breath I've been able to take since I left here over four months ago.

I don't have a car or a ride but I don't care, because all I want is a few minutes of privacy. All I need is to hear Lennox's voice.

When I look at my phone and the four missed calls from her, it seems she's on the same page.

I pick up my mobile and dial.

"I guess you didn't need my help after all," Lennox says.

"You didn't put him up to that? You didn't set that—"

"No. I'm as shocked as you are. I'm . . . speechless. See? I'm not the only one who thinks you're worth fighting for." Her words hang on the line as I struggle with the onslaught of emotions the past twenty-four hours have brought.

"Lennox . . . Thank you. God, you're—"

"There's no need to thank me. I didn't do anything."

"You got me to London today. And you were trying to do more. And no one has ever—"

"You're worth it."

"Thank you. Truly." We both fall silent. "It's early there. You must be exhausted. Get some sleep." I say the words, but would sit in her silence all day long if I could.

"Okay. I'll talk to you . . . later."

"Yes. Later."

And when I hang up, it takes everything I have not to call her right back to tell her what's on the tip of my tongue.

I love you.

I sit on the thought before I dial the next person I need to speak with. He picks up on the third ring. "Rush."

"Rory. Mate. You didn't have to do that. You—"

"Yes, I did."

"But what about—"

"I'm a big boy, Rush. They're my cock-ups, and I'll damn well own them. It's time I did the right thing and be the friend to you that you've been to me all these years."

"I don't . . . Fuck, mate."

"I've spoken to Mum, and she cried. And wants to meet Esme sometime. Well. Not yet."

"She loves you, Ror."

"Yeah. It's just . . . But Dad. God. He's livid. I've lived so much of my life desperate for Dad's approval, but I just couldn't. It doesn't fucking matter if I can't live with the man I've become. . . and I couldn't. I couldn't stand by and let you ruin everything out of some skewed loyalty he made you feel." There's shuffling on the other end of the connection. "I was weak in letting him ask you and in going along with it. There's nothing more I can say other than I'm sorry for everything, and I'm the sorriest that I let it get this far."

"Rory. Are you—" I stumble over what to say because his apologies have me fearful they are more of a goodbye than anything. "I mean . . . you're okay, right?"

"Good God, yes. I'm still on the mend, but life is glorious."

"What about the club?"

"Let the team transfer me for what I did. I don't care so long as I still get to play. Besides, Esme will stand beside me regardless."

"I don't even have words." My thoughts are coming too fast to put a voice to them. "All I can say is I'm happy for you."

"Thanks again, mate. You're a saint, and I don't deserve you."

~

"I'm pulling down my street right now, Finn, and after not being home since June, I'm ending the call so I can enjoy the silence of my house without you yakking in my ear."

"Understood. Be ready for the club to want to push you in front of the press sooner rather than later. You look like a goddamn saint right now, so let them use it to erase all of the bad press—"

"I'll do a public signing of the contract, Finn. That's it. No one is going to capitalize off a personal decision I made. No interviews about it. No exclusives. I'm not budging on this."

"Why the fuck not?"

"Because the pitch is where I perform. Nowhere else."

"Fine. Yes," he says, but I can already hear the wheels turning so loud in his head that he hasn't heard a word I've said. "Hey, Rush."

"Hmm?"

"We did it."

I hang up without answering, unsure and unsettled over how I feel about his comment.

We didn't do shit.

It took months.

Back and forth, Rush. Communicating every day, Rush. Utter shit.

I have wondered why I don't feel the same resentment toward the club. And I don't think it's simply about who is employed by whom. But deep down I think that's where it partly sits.

I employ Finn. So, even if out of fiscal loyalty, he should have been shouting from the rooftops, as Lennox said. He was supposed to support me one hundred percent publicly, and shouldn't have doubted me in private.

The club is essentially a business. Yes, it's my career, but I can understand that they had to look at the financial aspects of whether or not to trade me. Their loyalty is a bit trickier to define, and I never suggested that the photo wasn't of me. That loyalty was driven by the pound.

Does it make me feel good knowing they doubted me? Of course not, but . . .

"Welcome back, sir," the driver says with a chuckle as my house comes into view. The gates are just as overloaded with paparazzi as the night I left here but this time, the questions aren't accusations. This time, the shouting of my name isn't with derision but out of desperation to get the first quote. *Bloody vultures.*

And just like last time, I hurry through the lot of them without giving a single comment.

I'll let Rory's press conference speak for itself.

Besides, there's not much more I can say.

But when I sink into my own bed after a quick shower, when I let the silence envelop my thoughts, there's only one thing missing in this balls-up day.

Lennox.

She's not there to hold on to.

There's no hair of hers to tickle my cheek as I rest my chin on her head.

There's no soft snore of hers to fill the room.

There's just the silence and solitude I used to crave that feels fucking rough now.

Chapter
FIFTY-NINE

Lennox

"THINGS GOOD?"

I hate that tears flood my eyes when his face fills the screen. "Yes. And you? Has the media attention died down some?"

"I don't really pay attention," he murmurs.

But I do. I've scoured all websites for any real-time glimpse of him and by the looks of it, he's still being hounded.

"Is it good to be home?"

I miss you.

"There's nothing like your own bed." He chuckles.

Your arms holding me tight.

"I know. All I wanted to do was lie in it for hours the first day I got home."

Your raspy voice when you first wake up in the morning.

"Things are good with your sisters and Dad?"

Knowing I could reach out and touch you to know you're real.

"If you're asking if we're bickering, the answer is of course we are."

Do you miss me?

And so yet another conversation where we talk about nothing, because we're too afraid to address the elephant in the room, and that elephant is us.

Chapter
SIXTY

Rush

Lennox: I saw you called. Sorry I missed you. I'm about to catch a flight to Florida to corral a wild-child athlete. You'll be asleep by the time I land. Have a great team workout today.

I stare at the text and hate this feeling—wanting to talk and knowing I can't.

Wanting to be with her, but she's thousands of miles away.

Needing this ache in my chest to go away instead of steadily getting worse.

Chapter
SIXTY-ONE

Lennox

"DID YOU WATCH?"

I look up at where Brexton is standing in the doorway of my office. "Watch what?"

"Jesus, are we back to you pretending like you're not sitting around this office moping all goddamn day?" she asks with a healthy dose of an eye roll.

"I'm not moping."

"Then you watched."

"Of course, I did," I say, as I think of the twenty times I replayed Rush's big contract signing with Liverpool on YouTube. How I devoured everything about it and him as if I were a stalker desperate for a fix of the person she was obsessed with. "Why would I miss it?"

"Because it was at four in the morning so I thought you might be, you know, sleeping."

"Don't be a bitch."

"I'm not." She shrugs and moves into my office to take a seat. Exactly what I don't want—to be put under the microscope by my sister. "I'm just curious what's going on."

"I'm trying to get a contract reviewed for Johnson, and I have a meeting in two hours with Berringer. That's what's up," I say with a sarcastic smile to reinforce my brattiness.

"When are you going to see him again?" The playfulness is gone from her voice this time, and the compassion in her tone has me looking up from the contract to meet her eyes.

I shrug, because I don't trust my voice at first. "Probably in passing somewhere."

"And why's that?"

"Because that's who we are."

"And who is that? Two people who seem to be perfect together but are too goddamn stubborn to admit it?"

"That sounds about right."

"Then do something about it."

I lean back in my chair and look out at the city below. The hustle and bustle of Manhattan never ceases to amaze me regardless of the time of day or the weather.

"I don't know. I'm feeling a little restless. I might head to Chicago for a few weeks for the draft. See what I can see there. Maybe engage in a little retail therapy."

Her silence remains until I look back toward her. "You just got here, though."

"Three weeks ago."

"Uh-huh."

"Do you talk?"

"Yeah. I guess."

"That sounded enthusiastic."

"You know how it is. When you're together, you share the same world so your conversations make sense. When you're apart it's like you're on an island trying to describe what it's like so the other one understands."

"That made absolutely no fucking sense." She laughs.

"At what point are you just talking and calling and responding simply so you don't hurt the other person's feelings?"

"You've moved on that fast that you're already feeling obligated to respond?" she asks.

And the answer is no, but I don't dare tell her that. The real answer is when will I know that he's doing that to me? At what point do you realize that your feelings are on a way different level than his are?

"I'm just thinking out loud," I finally murmur.

She studies me for a second more before pushing up out of her chair. "I'm going to say one thing and then I'll be out of your hair."

"Thank God," I joke as I look at the mini-globe on my bookshelf behind her and wonder where I should go.

"Sometimes love is hard to hold on to but if he's the one, if he's where you keep wanting to wander to when you look at that globe, then maybe he's the one you're meant to have."

"Did you read that in a fortune cookie somewhere?" I tease.

"You know the minute I walk out of this office that you're going to repeat it in your head and know I'm right."

"Whatever."

"Take the chance, Lenn. You never know until you do."

"How?" I ask, my stoicism finally shattered as the emotion hits me. *I want to say I miss him. I miss him so much every moment of every day. I miss his touch. His smile. His laughs. His gorgeous accent.* But I can't form those words on my tongue. "How am I supposed to do that? His life is there and my life is here. A cross-Atlantic relationship is not exactly the kind that keeps you warm at night. I don't want an Instagram romance where the only time I get to see him is when I check what he's posted."

She stops at the door and turns to face me. "You're a smart woman. You'll figure it out."

Chapter
SIXTY-TWO

Rush

"AFTER ALL THAT FUCKING WORK TO GET YOU BACK HERE AND THAT'S how you play your first match of the season?" Louie asks from where he's leaning against his car parked next to mine. "Did playing with the Americans rob you of your skills? Did they taint you?" He mock shivers, but his grin and our history together tells me he's joking.

"Sod off. I was rusty."

"Rusty?" he says with a snort. "Bush league is more like it."

"What the hell is that supposed to mean?"

"It's an American term. I'm surprised you didn't learn it while you were busy shagging that agent broad." I lift a middle finger in response. "What gives, mate? You sign a big contract and then decide to suck?"

"I'll tell you what you can suck all right." I laugh.

"Is that it? Do we need to hire someone to suck you off before the next game to take the edge off? Whatever you need, I'm at your service." He salutes.

"It's definitely not you I'd be looking for service from." I chuckle. "Besides, I don't think anyone can provide what I need."

"What's that?" he asks, and as I stand inside my open car door and stare at him, I shouldn't be surprised at the answer, but I am.

Knowing the answer, really, but there's nothing anyone can do about it.

But fuck, *I miss her.*

"Nothing. I gotta get home. I have shit to do."

"Hey? You okay? You know I was joking, right?"

I meet the eyes of one of my closest friends and nod. "I'm good. And you're right, I was rusty. Tomorrow's another day to improve."

"Ha. You should tattoo that shit somewhere."

"Maybe I will." I laugh and raise a hand. "Later, Louie."

"See you tomorrow."

When I slide behind the wheel and rev the engine to life, I should be replaying the game in my head like I typically do. What I can do better next time. How I was beat down the line on that one breakaway. Why my headers are veering too far right.

But I don't think a fucking thing, because I'm too busy fucking missing Lennox.

Too busy hating myself for scouring the crowd tonight in the odd hopes that she'd show up for my first game.

Too preoccupied realizing that she's already moved on, while I'm stuck here like a fucking sap.

Could I get laid to help me get over her?

Of course I could.

Do I want to?

No.

I'm still hung up on Lennox.

Scratch that.

I'm in love with Lennox Kincade.

Chapter
SIXTY-THREE

Lennox

"DAD? WHAT ARE YOU DOING HERE?" I ASK WHEN I SEE HIM STANDING on my doorstep.

"Figured I'd come and see if your suitcases were packed," he says as he walks into my place.

"Suitcases?" I ask.

"You're getting restless again," he says with a soft smile. "I figured you'd be itching to go somewhere."

"Suitcases are still stacked empty in the closet." I motion in a sweeping gesture around my family room.

"Why?"

"What's that supposed to mean?" I ask as he takes a seat on my couch.

"You're not happy. You wander when you're not happy."

Out of reflex I reach up and finger the charm on my necklace. "It's not that I'm not happy. It's just that I'm . . ."

"Scared."

"Scared?" I cough the word out. "Scared of what?"

"Of showing up in England with your bags packed, and finding out he's not as in love with you as you and your family thinks he is. Of telling us you're going there and worrying that we'll think you're crazy. Of doing what you need to do out of your loyalty for the company."

I stare at my dad, slowly realizing I'm nodding at everything he's saying.

"It's okay to love him, Lennox. I'd never be mad at you for loving him. What I'd be mad at is if you didn't follow through to see if it's real." He leans forward and picks up a framed picture on my end table of me with my mom before she died. "What I'd hate is for you to look back on this moment in ten, fifteen, twenty years, and wonder what if."

"What are you telling me, Dad?" So many thoughts and hopes are colliding inside of me.

"I'm not telling you anything. I'm sitting here waiting to listen to what you have to tell me."

"Who said I have something to tell you?" I ask, amazed that he knows.

"The way you hang around the conference room a little longer waiting for your sisters to leave but they never do. The way you come in early only to find one of the girls have too." He sets the picture down. "So, what is it that you want to tell me?"

"You're right, I'm restless."

He nods in response.

"And miserable." I twist my fingers together. "I can work from anywhere, really. That's the beauty of this job. And so, what if I head to the UK for a bit to play this out and see if this thing between us is legitimate? Like it's actually real and stronger now that we're back to our everyday lives versus the bubble of Johnny's house."

"Go on."

"And if it is, if things with Rush just keep getting better . . . isn't it time KSM opens a satellite office somewhere? There's a whole market we've yet to tackle over there. I've done some research that I can send over to you. Data on the number of players, the other agents I'd be competing against. Of course, I'd keep my current caseload. It would give me an excuse to come home and see you guys often and . . ." My words fade off and I stop talking, as I suddenly feel shy now that I'm voicing the silly fantasy I've been concocting every night when I go to bed.

That I'd call Rory and he'd tell me where to find Rush. That way I could show up in Liverpool or wherever Rush lives undetected. I'd surprise him and we'd still be so madly in love that we'd vow never to part. I'd open a small office and would work my way into the football industry there until KSM has a foothold in that market.

"You're not responding, Dad."

"What happens if you get there and set up shop and get restless again? You'd be the person in charge there. It's a lot harder to run when you have that level of responsibility, Lenn."

"I won't run."

"And how do you know this?"

"Because I found my home in Rush, Dad. He's the one who quiets my restlessness."

A slow, bittersweet smile slides onto his face. He blinks back tears I pretend not to see. "That's all the answer I need."

Chapter
SIXTY-FOUR

Rush

THE PUB IS SLOW FOR A THURSDAY NIGHT, BUT IT'S EXACTLY WHAT I need to quiet my head and take a step back.

We're three games into the season and the pressure has obviously gotten to me, because I'm not playing up to par like I should be.

I feel off.

Something's fucking off.

And I have half a mind to send Lennox a one-way, first-class ticket to Heathrow so I can lay it all out on the bloody line to her. So I can tell her I fucking love her and I don't care how it works, but that it has to work.

I even considered calling one of her sisters at their office to see if she's as miserable as I am, but nothing reeks of desperation more than calling the family to help you with your game. It's utter tosh.

These feelings aren't one-sided. At least they weren't when we parted ways last month or whenever it fucking was. And if mine haven't gone away, then sure as shit hers haven't either.

"Here, mate," the bartender says as he slides a glass of ice across the bar top to me.

"That's not mine," I say but then immediately sit taller.

Nah. It's not possible.

"Yes. It is. A gift—if you want to call it that—from the lady in the corner over there."

My head whips up in the direction he points, and I'm already on my feet before I see her.

Because it's her.

It has to be her.

Chapter
SIXTY-FIVE

Lennox

My heart stops at the sight of him, and I know every moment of heartache and worry was so worth it when his eyes lock on mine.

When the love and uncertainty and longing that is in my gaze reflects in his.

He's at my table in a second, his arms going around me and pulling me in, and his lips finding mine as if I were the only home they've ever had.

He chuckles against my lips. "You're here. You're really here."

My hands run up his sides, over his cheeks, and into his hair as if they need to make sure he's really here and I'm really touching him. But it's his smile when he leans away to look at me as I do him that tells me the true story.

He wants me here.

I am wanted.

"What are you doing here?" he asks with an incredulous expression on his face, as if he's afraid if he looks away that I'm going to disappear.

"A wise person once told me that I needed to find the roar of the crowd and chase my own happiness. So that's exactly what I'm doing."

"And what exactly would that entail?" he asks, toying with a lock of my hair.

"I'm thinking of opening a KSM branch here in the UK. It'll allow me to be on my own, and yet still be part of a team."

The look of shock on his face is priceless. "Here, here?"

"Yes, here, here." I wait to see his reaction but other than the surprise in his voice, he doesn't show it.

"That's all you came for?"

"Maybe to catch a football match or two."

"I hear the new team captain is incredible."

"You have, have you?"

"Yep." He takes a sip of my water on the table beside him. "And if you're planning on living here, love, you need to order something stronger than this when in a pub." He presses a kiss to my lips that makes me wish we were somewhere a little more private. "What else are you hoping to find in the UK?"

"Some absolutely horrible sex."

His grin lights up his face. "I think I can help you find that as well." His fingers lace with mine.

"Good thing, because I was getting desperate."

"We can't have that now, can we?"

I can't believe the absolute calm I feel sitting here with him. I thought I'd be more worried or nervous, but I feel like I'm right where I belong.

"But that's just all part of finding my crowd, I still need to chase my happiness."

"Are you chasing after me, Kincade?" he asks with a sheepish grin.

"If you'll let me."

Our eyes hold and time feels like it falls still as the pub moves on around us. "There's only one problem."

"What's that?"

"I'll have to be your first client. I mean, it's only fitting."

"I can't steal you away from Finn. He got you this deal. I might hate the fucker but he delivered what you wanted."

"But he did insult my girlfriend and implied that she slept with athletes to win them over to her client roster."

"So wouldn't you being my client prove just that to him?" I ask, wondering which one of my sisters told Rush the backstory.

"Fuck Finn," he murmurs against my lips.

"Fuck Finn." I laugh.

"Besides," he says running a hand up my thigh. "It might look odd for a woman with my last name not representing me."

"What?" I sputter.

Rush shrugs like a mischievous little kid, gives me a slight smile, and humor owns his eyes. "Just a *way off in the future* thought."

"You're talking serious commitment here for someone who hasn't even declared love first," I tease. Rush's smile falls slowly and his eyes grow more intense.

He reaches out to run the back of his hand down the side of my face. "Lennox Kincade, I've been a miserable sod without you. My game is off solely because you turned my life upside down and since then, I don't think I ever want it to be set right again." He gives a half-smile, half laugh that would have stolen my heart if it wasn't stolen already. "I love you. I loved you before I left, but was too damn afraid to tell you. Then I got here and I was too scared to say it because I thought you had moved on . . . but I fucking love you. And now that you're here and in front of me, you better get used to me saying it."

"Oh my," I murmur as I pull him into me and pour my fear and frustration from the past month into one single kiss. "I love you too, Rush McKenzie. And I'm here, ready to start whatever this is together with you. It better start with some of that horrible sex I'm fond of, and it better start real soon."

"Thought you'd never ask," he says and then grabs the glass of ice off the table to bring with us.

Epilogue

Lennox

"So this is where the uber rich go when they want to escape life?" I look at the beauty surrounding us, and it's hard to pick one thing to focus on. The crystal-turquoise water below me where my feet are swinging. The over-the-water bungalow at my back. Or the palm trees on the shore behind us.

Rush looks at me from where he sits in a chaise lounge beside me with the slyest grin on his face. "No, this is where a football star goes after he's won both the Premier League and the Champion's League and wants to escape with his woman."

His woman.

It still gets me when he calls me his. It's been almost a year since my move to England, and the fact that I get to wake up next to him every single day is still exciting.

I hold my face up to the sun to feel its warmth but also to mask the tears that threaten when I realize I almost lost this—I almost lost him—because I was too stubborn to believe love was real.

"Hey?"

I look toward him and smile when I meet his eyes. My heart flips over in my chest. "Hmm?"

"You know I feel that way too, right?" he asks softly.

"What way?"

"The way you're looking at me right now. Like you can't believe you knew how to breathe before you met me. Like you can't believe this is real." He leans down to kiss me, the warmth and familiarity of his kiss is all I need. "Like life didn't have a purpose before this," he murmurs against my lips.

I set my glass of wine down, stand from the edge of the patio, and then sit beside him. His skin is warm from the sun as I snuggle into him and put my hand over his heart.

"To those who wander," he says softly, as his heart beats beneath the tattoo on his chest.

"To those who wander," I repeat, a smile painting the corners of my lips, the good fortune that we've found warming my heart.

"I've been thinking," he says as he twirls his finger in my hair.

"About?"

"About when you chased me to England."

"Mm-hmm."

"I told you that I had to be your first client because it wouldn't be right if you had my last name and I wasn't."

I still momentarily. "You did."

"Well, you've set up your office, you've contracted new clients, I've won everything that can be won . . . and I'm thinking we need to finish what we started."

When I lean back and meet his eyes, every kind of emotion flows through me.

This wild child who's not so wild.

The rebel who rebelled for all the right reasons.

This man, who could have anyone but only has eyes for me.

How did I get so damn lucky?

"You're all I need, Rush. I don't care in what form, last name, plastic ring, marriage certificate or not . . . I don't care. You're it for me. That's all that matters. You."

He gives me the softest of smiles—shy but serious. "McKenzie never meant anything to me, Nox. It was a name given to me by a man I never met. But I made it into something. I made me into something . . . and yes, we don't need any of that shit, but it would mean everything to me if you were proud to be a McKenzie with me."

Tears well in my eyes when I lean up and press a kiss to his lips. It's tender, and has a reverence everyone should get a chance to experience at least once in their life.

But I'm lucky, because I get it every single day. I get the kiss, the man, and the life I never expected but now know I could never live without.

And when the kiss ends, I rest my forehead against his. "I love you, Rush McKenzie, and I'd proudly be a McKenzie with you."

There's a hitch to his breath and then a whisper of a chuckle. "Marry me, Nox. I can't promise you perfection, but I can tell you that my favorite place is beside you." I lean back and look into his eyes. "I can't promise you I won't screw up, but I can promise you that you have my tomorrow and forever after. I can't promise you we won't wander, but I can assure you we'll always roam together." He forces a swallow as his eyes fill with tears. "And I can't promise you things won't get crazy sometimes, but I'll always make it better with some horrible, awful sex."

I laugh. God, I love this man.

"Marry me?" he whispers.

I nod, unable to get the words out at first. "Yes. Of course. Forever. Always."

And this time when our lips meet, the world feels a bit more right.

It feels like I've found my tomorrows, my sunsets, and my forever.

We may have wandered to many places in our lives, but we've finally found our home.

Our place.

Beside each other is the only place we'll ever rush to be.

COMING SOON

Did you enjoy Rush and Lennox story in Hard to Hold? Fall in love with the rest of the Kincade sisters and their love interests in the rest of the Play Hard series:

Hard to Handle—Out Now

Hard to Score—Out February 16, 2021

Hard to Lose—Out March 17, 2021

ACKNOWLEDGMENTS

Just a quick thank you to all the love and support everyone has shown me over the past seven years. When I challenged myself to write my first book, *Driven*, I never could have imagined anyone liking it, let alone this becoming my career.

A million thank yous for letting me take that chance and for helping it to grow in to all of this.

—Kristy

ABOUT THE AUTHOR

New York Times Bestselling author K. Bromberg writes contemporary romance novels that contain a mixture of sweet, emotional, a whole lot of sexy, and a little bit of real. She likes to write strong heroines and damaged heroes who we love to hate but can't help to love.

A mom of three, she plots her novels in between school runs and soccer practices, more often than not with her laptop in tow and her mind scattered in too many different directions.

Since publishing her first book on a whim in 2013, Kristy has sold over one and a half million copies of her books across twenty different countries and has landed on the *New York Times, USA Today,* and *Wall Street Journal* Bestsellers lists over thirty times. Her Driven trilogy (*Driven, Fueled,* and *Crashed*) is currently being adapted for film by the streaming platform, Passionflix.

With her imagination always in overdrive, she is currently scheming, plotting, and swooning over her latest hero. You can find out more about him or chat with Kristy on any of her social media accounts. The easiest way to stay up to date on new releases and upcoming novels is to sign up for her newsletter or follow her on Bookbub.

Made in the USA
Las Vegas, NV
02 December 2020